LOST in the FLAMES

A World War II RAF Bomber Command novel

CHRISTOPHER JORY

MᶜNIDDER | & GRACE

For Jackie

Published by McNidder & Grace
21 Bridge Street
Carmarthen
SA31 3JS
www.mcnidderandgrace.co.uk

Original paperback first published in 2015, reprinted 2016
©Christopher Jory

A catalogue record for this work is available from the British Library.
ISBN: 9780857160782
Designed by Obsidian Design
Printed and bound in the United Kingdom by
Short Run Press Ltd, Exeter, UK

ABOUT THE AUTHOR

Raised on a mixed diet of Enid Blyton and war comics the author has always loved working with words. After studying English Literature at university he taught English living in Italy, Spain, Crete, Brazil and Venezuela. He is married and lives near Oxford though they still have a rather run-down home in Italy.

This book is dedicated to

Flying Officer John Ross
186 Squadron, RAF Bomber Command

And 55,572 others who shared his fate

International Bomber Command Centre

The International Bomber Command Centre is being built to ensure that the personal memories of those involved in or affected by Bomber Command are recorded as a means of educating current and future generations about the Command's fascinating and, at times, difficult history. Contributions from across the world are being collected to add to the archive and inform the exhibition. To find out more please visit: www.internationalbcc.co.uk

HISTORICAL NOTE
RAF BOMBER COMMAND
1939–45

Courage

RAF Bomber Command fought for our freedom from the opening day of the Second World War until the eve of VE Day, the only one of the Services to take the fight to the enemy from the very beginning to the very end. Night after night they went, cramped and frozen in their flying coffins, to strike at Germany's cities and industries. Each time they flew among the searchlights, the night-fighters and the flak, they did so in the knowledge that many of their number would be dead before dawn.

Sacrifice

125,000 men served as Bomber Command aircrew. Their average age was 22. Many were in their late teens. They were all volunteers, most of them civilians before the war intervened. Of every 100 who flew, around half could expect to be killed in the air. On some nights, more men were lost than in the whole of the Battle of Britain. They died in many different ways – from flak wounds and cannon shells, trapped and burning in a spinning plane, hurtling with no parachute from the sky, crushed as their aircraft smashed into the ground, shot or hanged if they reached the ground alive, coming to grief in the fog when landing back at base. At the height of the campaign only one man in six could expect to survive a first tour of thirty operations. One in forty might survive a second. The loss rate was higher than any other Service and the life expectancy of six weeks was on a par with that of infantry officers on the Somme. When it was all over, more than 12,000 Bomber Command aircraft had been destroyed and 55,573 aircrew were dead.

Betrayal

Yet for years the sacrifice and bravery of these young men went largely unrecognised. 2012 finally saw the opening of an official memorial to Bomber Command, but it was nearly 70 years in coming – a long time for the dead to be spinning in their graves – and most of the aircrew who survived the war are no longer alive to see it. Churchill backed the bombing strategy but abruptly disowned it at war's end for reasons of political expediency, snubbing the bomber crews in his 1945 victory speech. The other branches of the Services received their campaign medals but none has ever been awarded to Bomber Command. In the decades after the war, there were increasing attempts, with the benefit of hindsight and the comfortable knowledge of victory, to draw a veil over their contribution, to paint the crews at best as brave but immoral and at worst as war criminals, even drawing comparisons – in A. C. Grayling's *Among the Dead Cities* – with the 9/11 bombers. Whatever the controversies that have swirled around the strategy of the bombing campaign, surely they deserve a better epitaph than that, all those boys who were lost in the flames?

To honour their courage and sacrifice and to regret the death and destruction that the war brought with it need not be mutually exclusive undertakings.

FEBRUARY 1945

The route out took them over the Dutch coast and then suddenly they were on the run-in to the target, the master bomber overhead, guiding them in, Jacob in the nose, fussing over the bomb-sight and the selector switches, the target looming beneath him, edging itself inside him now, eating him away, the way it always did. Then Charlie breathing out adjustments to the course, his voice down the intercom like a ghost, Ralph responding in word and action, adjusting B-Beauty's path, setting his fear aside until the bombing run was over, Roland hurling out bundles of foil strips to scramble the German radar, searchlights lamping up the sky, light flak tracing slow-motion streams of red and green, accelerating as it passed. Then a plane struck away off to starboard, a little lick of flame along the fuselage becoming a stream then a deluge, the flares inside the belly of the pathfinder igniting, dripping bright gobs of light, the plane dipping away, bleeding red and green fluorescence from its guts, spinning down like a Catherine wheel, and Jacob in the front of Beauty, concentrating now, the target coming near, then the aiming point in his sights and he is suddenly cold, and his flares are going down, Christmas trees of cascading light, and the bombs drop away and the plane lifts then settles, freed at last of its bombs. Ralph banks them away as a torrent of flares from other pathfinders goes down, then the intense white light of fighter flares bursting apart the night with their glare, and Beauty is fleeing headlong now, racing towards the darkness, Ralph's hands shaking violently upon the control wheel, flak bursting beneath, then Jacob coming up from the nose and taking the controls as Ralph goes back to the rest-bed, looking back as he goes, guilty and wrong but forgiven all the same, and Jacob is guiding Beauty now, loving her, taking her away from the target, that thing he never wants to see, slipping away beneath him now, another bad glow in the memory and he is leaving it behind.

But then a judder, a ripping sound, like gravel, gravel on a corrugated metal roof, explosive shells raking along the underside, the rear gunner shot to pieces, a leg ripped off at the knee, wind raging around his shattered guns, and Jim silent too in the other turret, slumped in his harness, all but dead, his heart spraying his life away, wasting it all over the ribs of the fuselage, blood hissing on the searing metal of the burning plane as a torrent of flame is sucked down its steel tunnel to where the other gunner sits already burnt black. And then another shrieking pass by the Ju-88, incendiary shells ripping through the mid-section, the wireless set bursting into flames, George bursting apart at the seams as the cannon shells tear through the fuselage, in and out of him, up again into the night through the shattered metal above his head, his blood soaking Charlie's desk, turning the maps and charts blood-black in the light of the flames, the angle-poise lamp throwing its bulb now towards the roof, Charlie on the floor with his oxygen tube around his neck, struggling to throw it off, and Ralph rising from the rest-bed and crawling through slime towards the cockpit where Jacob and Roland struggle to hold Beauty level as she tosses her head and throws her reins and demands to be allowed to let herself fall, tired of the whip, tired of fighting through the fire and the night just to go out again the next day, trailing her mane of fire behind her, shuddering now, shaking again as more shells rip into her guts and another fighter homes in on the blaze and pumps more death inside her, strips of Window cascading up through the cabin in the rush of air that pours in through her wounds as she fills up with smoke.

'We've had it, lads!' shouts Jacob over the intercom. 'Bale out! Bale out! And get out quick!'

Ralph is in the cockpit now, looking up at Jacob from his place on the floor, then standing and staring at him as the foil strips swirl around and glycol from the tank in the nose sprays about and Jacob shouts at him repeatedly.

'Get out!' he shouts. 'Fucking get out!'

Ralph tries to grab the control wheel, tries to haul it back, but Jacob hands him off and Roland pushes him hard towards the hatch at the front and Ralph goes down the step into the nose, kicks the hatch away, sits on the edge, looks back, drops out into the freezing night. Jacob shoves Roland away too and Roland jumps and Jacob is alone now with the dead men. He stares behind him at the blazing interior of the fuselage. He hauls at the wheel, pulls Beauty level, then stands up and steps back towards the navigator's desk and slips on something soft that glistens and seems to be moving still, and he bends down and holds his face close up next to Charlie and hears him whimper, or perhaps it is just the gurgle of the blood that bubbles up in his throat, specking Jacob's face red with spittle as Charlie coughs and tries to say something, then coughs up again and speckles him more. Beauty is pitching forward again now and Jacob lurches back to the wheel and pulls her level and holds her steady then lets her go and returns to Charlie but he will not cough for him now, does not whimper or gurgle, and the blood does not bubble up in his throat but lies flat inside his mouth, flat black ink inside a well from which no more words can come. Jacob looks now to where George is a dark bundle by the main spar and he steps towards him, slipping in a hot slick of blood and slither that is beginning to simmer and burn, and he takes George's gloved wrist and tugs, pulls him towards him, feels him light beneath his grip, realises he is pulling only half a man, the hips separated from the waist by a cannon shell or a ripping piece of fuselage, and Jacob lets go and slips, then stands and moves again towards the main spar to get at the gunners, but he cannot get across it, Beauty's metal burns him, burns him through his flying suit, and the flames really get a grip on him now, force him back, and Beauty is tipping again, tipping away down, and he slithers across to the wheel and hauls it back and Beauty shakes, a great wracking judder as an engine disintegrates and hot shrapnel comes zinging in, and she lurches to one side and bows her head and Jacob is aflame and he takes a last look at the dark shapes that were Charlie and George and he stumbles down the step to the bomb-aimer's dome and he sits beside the hatch, burning he is, burning beside the selector switches and the bomb-sight through which he has seen his war, nights of criss-cross streets of orange, the city's lattice-work kissed by the silent crump of bombs thousands of feet below, and he pushes his flaming feet through the open hatch and the wind wrenches his burning boots away and he thinks again of Rose, his Rose, the reason he had to get through this war ...

DECEMBER 1934

It was nearly Christmas. Jacob Arbuckle was standing on the corner of New Street with his older sister Vera and her best friend Rose, snow sheeting down from a cold December sky, falling for him, he thought, layering him in white. His eyes fell on Norman Miller and he sensed Vera's gaze alight upon him too, observing in that quiet thoughtful way of hers the man who sat stiff and serious on the seat of the trap as the pony tripped up the hill towards Chipping Norton market square, edged by trees and dotted with Model-T Fords and traders' vans.

Norman brought his horse to a halt with a tug of the rein and a click of the tongue, stepped down into the market square, and disappeared out of sight behind the Town Hall as his dogs sidled after him.

'Come on, Jacob,' said Vera, her voice cool but her eyes aflame. 'I've got an errand to run.'

She stepped out into the whitening street as Rose grabbed Jacob's hand and dragged him along.

'What sort of errand?' Jacob called out, griping at the sudden change of plan. They had been on their way to Pool Meadow to skim stones across the pond, an important pursuit for an eleven-year-old boy.

'Mind your own business, Jacob,' said Vera over her shoulder to where Jacob walked hand in hand now with Rose. 'Important errands aren't for little boys like you.'

'I'll remember that next time you ask me to do something!'

'Shush, you cheeky little bugger,' laughed Rose. 'Don't talk to your big sister like that.'

Rose grinned at him but he snatched his hand away and stomped after Vera as Rose swayed along behind in a manner she believed to be indicative of elevated aesthetic preferences.

Jacob caught up with Vera and prodded her.

'I said what sort of errand?'

'Jacob, will you ever stop asking questions?'

'I said what sort of errand?'

'Well if you must know, I need some wool. I have to make some gloves.'

'You've already got some.'

'Shut up, Jacob. Please.'

Jacob saw Norman Miller with an older man on the Town Hall steps, stooping over together as if looking at something small that he was holding in his hands. Vera was looking too, at his hands, big bare reddening things going ruddy in the snow, red with work and cold. Norman glanced up and caught Vera's eye and she spun away and hauled Jacob into the haberdashery. Rose hovered outside momentarily, then swooned in through the door.

'I shall be requiring some wool,' Vera declared to the woman behind the counter.

'Well you've come to the right place, then, haven't you?'

Rose leant down and Jacob felt her breath upon him as she whispered in his ear, just a touch louder than he knew she should, 'Oh Jacob, don't you just hate irony in the uneducated?'

He smiled up at Rose, then smirked at the woman. The woman looked him up and down and readdressed herself to Vera.

'What colour will you be wanting?'

She stumbled over her words slightly now and Rose smiled and Jacob smirked again. Vera peered past the stuttering woman and the rolls of cloth stacked in the bay window and out through the falling snow towards Norman Miller. Jacob followed her gaze onto the stranger outside and felt something inside himself click into place.

'Brown,' said Vera. 'And of the very highest quality. It must be brown like the colour of that man's suit – you see him, over there. Him.'

The woman behind the counter looked at Vera, then at Jacob. Jacob shrugged beneath her gaze.

'It's not my bloody fault,' he said.

'Mind your language, Jacob,' said Vera coolly.

'Yes, Jacob, mind your bloody language,' said Rose.

The woman glared at Jacob again, then pulled out a box and

dropped it on the counter. Up rose a cloud of dust, a small explosion.

'That's Norman Miller, that is,' said the woman, regaining her composure in her natural habitat of gossip. 'Arrived just last month, from up north somewhere. Got a right queer accent, he has. Not unpleasant, mind.' She smiled faintly. 'Hard life, by all accounts.'

'A hard life?' asked Vera, fingering a ball of wool, feigning indifference.

'Yes, poor Norman Miller,' the woman went on. 'Lost his father early on. If he was his father. Not confirmed, apparently, his parentage. Slight ambiguity there. Brought up by his grandmother, so they say.'

'So who says?' said Jacob.

The woman ignored his interruption.

'So who says?' he said again.

'You're a bright little spark, aren't you?' said the woman sharply.

'Oh yes, he's bright, all right,' said Rose. 'Started at the Grammar School in September. They say he has an inquiring mind.'

'Do they really?' The woman studied Jacob down the length of her fulsome nose. 'Well he should save that for when he's a policeman.'

'He's not going to be a policeman,' said Rose.

'No, of course not,' said the woman. 'He'll be on the land all his life. Or the tweed mill if he's lucky. Just like every other poor sod round here.'

'No, he won't,' Rose spat. 'What are you going to be, Jacob? Go on, tell her.'

'A pilot,' he whispered.

'A pilot? Ha! Setting our sights a bit high, are we?'

'It's true. I'm going to be a pilot,' he blurted out now. 'Father always tells us to aim for the sky, so that's what I'll do. I'm going to fly around the world and back again!'

'That's right,' said Rose. 'So leave the little lad alone. Just because you have no hope doesn't mean he should have none too.'

Jacob felt the woman's discomfort, shifting about behind the counter now, her unease washing over him like a balm. He knew they had broken her – him and Rose – they had won again like he knew they would.

Vera was rooting around in the box. She took out several balls of wool of slightly different earthy hues.

'That one,' said Rose. 'The others are far too agricultural.'

'Yes, I like that one too,' said Jacob. 'It's the colour of sparrows.'

The woman would not contradict him now. Rose had quietened her. She had done it for him.

'Right,' said Vera. 'I'll have that one. Sparrows it is.'

She left her coins on the counter and nudged Jacob towards the door. He glanced back at the woman. She was looking at the floor.

Norman Miller was still by the Town Hall, talking to the man, his dogs at his heel. He wore a rough tweed suit with a waistcoat and tie and a pair of solid boots. His physical dimensions were of a magnitude that would disincline the beasts of the field to resist if he whacked them with a clubbing paw of a hand and growled at them to get a move on as his pair of border collies harried them about the ankles. He caught Vera's eye momentarily again as she passed and Jacob sensed Norman's immensity as he hurried by beneath him, this great hulking man, hulking over him but somehow good, reassuring, like a solid piece of timber, a thing you could make something from, a life perhaps. Jacob grinned at Norman and the hulking thing offered an inclination of the head in return.

Jacob and Vera left Rose at the door of the Co-operative store, where she went in search of camphor to exterminate the moths that had been up to no good in her wardrobe and gin for her grandmother's evening pick-me-up.

'Jacob, why were you so horrid to that woman?' said Vera, as they trailed back along West Street. 'You and Rose are always the same. I don't know what gets into you.'

'She deserved it,' said Jacob. 'Rose told me she was rude to her once. And she was rude to me too, didn't believe it, that I'll be a pilot one day.'

'Well maybe she's right. Maybe you won't.'

'Of course I will.'

Norman Miller clipped by again on his pony and trap.

'Hey, mister!' called Jacob. 'My sister thinks you're …'

But Vera cut him short with a swift clip to the head as Norman glanced back and disappeared around the bend. Vera gave Jacob a kick up the backside and chased him down the dirt path that led to the terraced stone cottage next to the orchard where fat porkers belched the day away beneath black-branched apple trees. Alfred Arbuckle was in the back alley that ran along behind the cottages, dragging a knife along a stone step in the snow, keening its edge.

'Hello father,' said Vera as she skipped down the steps past the grating blade.

'Hello father,' echoed Jacob.

'Pork for Sunday dinner,' said Alfred, gesturing his children towards the out-house door opposite the kitchen.

They poked their noses inside and sniffed. A carcass hung from a beam, split from chin to groin, dripping blood from its nose onto the floor.

'You've killed Chamberlain?' whispered Jacob, aghast. 'He was my favourite.'

Alfred Arbuckle was in the habit of naming his pigs after British Prime Ministers before electing which of them would be next for the chop.

'Well,' he said. 'One man, one pig, one vote. And anyway, that's Gladstone. Chamberlain's not nearly fat enough yet. We'll have some of the leg tomorrow and then I'll do some sausages and we'll sell the rest. Vera, there's some potatoes in the kitchen that need peeling.'

He thrust out the knife and she took it and went inside. Jacob was in the out-house now, peering into the cage where he kept Eric and Penelope. He cooed at them and they cooed back, Eric fluffing up his feathers in that way he always did.

'Hello, Eric,' said Jacob. 'Hello, Penelope. Good day to you both, my dears.'

Jacob loved his pigeons. He thought they probably loved him too, in whatever way pigeons do.

'Jacob!' came his father's voice again. 'Go help William dig some more spuds out of the vegetable patch. They've been in the ground far too long already, should have been out weeks ago.'

He handed Jacob a garden fork.

'And make sure you get the big ones, nothing smaller than your fist,' he said, holding his fist up to the boy's face, and the boy held up his own little fist in return.

'See you later, you two,' said Jacob as he drew his face away from the cage.

He went round to the front of the house where the potatoes grew in a patch at the end of the garden, overlooking the valley and the road that led up the hill towards Stow and then on towards Cheltenham and

Worcester and down which he watched the sheep travel to the market on Wednesdays and the cattle on Saturdays.

'Where the bloody hell have you been, Jacob?' a voice called out as Jacob approached down the path to the vegetable patch. William was thirteen, a couple of years older than his brother, and considered this differential in age sufficient justification for superiority of familial rank, despite his silent recognition that Jacob was better endowed in what their mother Elizabeth always referred to as 'the intellectual department'. William knew that at their age brawn would usually overcome brain. Jacob knew it too, but pretended he didn't.

He ignored William's question.

'I said where the bloody hell have you been?' William repeated, a notch louder and half an octave higher.

'Sod off,' said Jacob. 'I've got to dig some spuds.'

'I said where have you been?' said William, grabbing Jacob by the ear and wrenching it, watching his knuckles go white as the ear went red.

'In town, buying wool,' said Jacob. 'You sod.'

William let him go.

'What kind of wool?'

'What do you mean what kind of wool? From a bloody sheep, of course.'

'I meant what colour.'

'Well why didn't you say that, then?'

'Do you want me to break your bloody nose again?'

'Fuck off, William.'

William grabbed a potato, the biggest he could see, and chucked it at Jacob. It caught him on the nose. Jacob chucked it back. When Alfred came round to find out what was causing the commotion, potatoes were strewn around the vegetable patch and Jacob's nose was running with blood.

'Come on William, help me cut up Gladstone. Go round to the out-house. I'll be there shortly.'

Alfred took his handkerchief from his pocket, specked with Gladstone's blood, and passed it to Jacob.

'Wipe your nose, Jacob, there's a good lad. No harm done.'

He patted him on the head and left him to his digging. Jacob heaved up more worms than potatoes, dabbing away the blood as he dug, and he lobbed the wriggling creatures to the robin that hopped around his feet. When he had filled the bucket with spuds, he trailed back round to the kitchen and tipped them into the sink for Vera to wash and peel. Then he went out into the out-house. His heart sank and his blood rose. The cage door was open.

'William!' he screamed, tearing outside again to where his brother sat on the stone steps, humming.

'It was you, wasn't it?' Jacob yelled.

William smiled back.

'You bloody sod! Where are they?'

William glanced upwards and Jacob followed his gaze into the branches of the elm that hung above their heads. Eric and Penelope sat side by side on one of the upper limbs. Eric cooed and Jacob cooed back. Eric puffed up his feathers.

'They're never going to come back now, are they?' said William. 'Up into the blue forever. It's bloody cruel anyway, keeping the poor buggers in a cage all the time.'

'No, it's not. They like it here. I'm like their dad, I am.'

'Course you are. Birdbrain.'

'You're the bloody numbskull, William ...'

But William was gone, leaving Jacob with his nose still running with blood, calling his birds' names up into the tree.

In the house, Vera was hacking at the potatoes with her knife. Her mother Elizabeth was struggling to light the fire. Once the kindling had taken light and started to crack and spark, she placed the fireguard carefully around the grate and went out to see why her sons had been yelling at each other again. Alfred heard the popping sparks and rushed in and touched the fireguard again and again, adjusting its position in the way he had always done since 'the incident'. This unnamed conflagration, too awful even at a distance of several years to be referred to directly among the family, would forever cast its long shadow across Alfred's demeanour and distort the lens through which he had previously seen the world. The family had been living at the time in a larger cottage on the main street in Over Norton, next to a pair of old chestnut trees from which the blackbirds sang away their hearts each morning. Alfred's three older boys, James, John and Ernest, had always slept in the top room in a double bed among the spinning wheels and the wool-pile that Elizabeth turned into rough garments and blankets for the mill. The night of the incident had been freezing cold, thick snow muffling the world outside, a roaring fire warming the front room. The family had sat in the grudging light of oil lamps and orange flames until the dying fire and the creeping cold forced them to their beds. A spark leapt from the near-dead coals downstairs. The conflagration woke Alfred first, smoke and flames climbing the stairs as the edge of the steps glowed orange. Alfred roared the family into wakefulness. Vera snatched Jacob and ran with him under her arm down the stairs through the flames, smacking his head on the banister, breaking his nose and knocking him nearly senseless. Elizabeth hurried down with William while Alfred went panic-stricken and bellowing to the top room where the rising poisonous smoke hung thickest and James, John and Ernest lay utterly still in the big bed beneath the wool-pile. Alfred carried them out and laid them on the ground as the snow slid off the hot roof in sheets and Jacob looked on, his nose streaming with blood, and William buried his head in his mother's folds. The coroner arrived the next morning and within the week James, John and Ernest were gone for good, at rest in the grounds of St Mary's Church a mile down the road in Chipping Norton. Alfred found the family a cottage down the hill off West Street where he now hung his porcine prime ministers from the out-house beam and his two remaining sons flung potatoes at each other in the patch of mud in the garden and his daughter Vera considered just how large she should make her sparrow-brown gloves for Norman Miller.

**

The next day Jacob was in the out-house when he heard William's footsteps and then a pause at the door. His heart beat quicker as he waited for what he knew would come next.

'What the bloody hell are you doing?' William sneered, his usual greeting.

Jacob halted his two-word response as it was forming in his mouth. He was too busy for a violent argument now.

'Nothing,' said Jacob, lifting his head from the sack into which he had been peering.

'Nothing?' said William. 'That sack doesn't look like nothing to me.'

'What sack?'

'That one, knob-head. The one you're holding. And why did you tell Rose I'd let the birds out? She gave me a right doing over. Like she hated me or something.'

'You shouldn't have done it, then, should you?'

'Why the bloody hell not? I told you it's cruel, keeping them in there.'

'No, it's not. They came back, didn't they?'

'Must be bloody stupid, just like you.'

Jacob turned his back and looked at Eric. Eric looked at him and rolled an eye.

'Let's have a look in the sack, then, birdbrain,' said William, tugging at the thing.

'Sod off, William.'

William pushed Jacob away and grabbed the sack and pulled it open, sending a flurry of feathers into the air.

'What are all these doing in here? Planning to make an eiderdown, are you?'

'No.'

'Well what then?'

He grabbed Jacob's ear and twisted, felt something twisting inside of him too.

'Get off me, William.'

'Tell me, or else.'

He twisted the ear some more and Jacob's face went red.

'Some wings.'

'Eh?'

'I'm going to make myself some wings. And then I'm going to jump out of the window.'

'Stupid sod. You'll kill yourself.'

'No, I won't.'

'I'll tell father.'

'Don't you dare.'

'Suit yourself ...'

And William left Jacob to it.

Jacob took the garden canes that he had cut to the right length, and the light cloth he had filched over time from his mother's pile in the top room, and he set about weaving them together with twine, then coated the cloth with cow glue and edged the wings with long pheasant feathers and layered the rest with the ones from the chickens that he had plucked for Alfred. Then he fixed the leather straps that would go round his arms and hid the wings away behind the tool cupboard to dry. The next day he came back and closed the out-house door and winked at Eric and Penelope and took out the wings and slipped his arms into the straps and stood and flapped his arms and pressed his cheek into the feathers and looked up and grinned at his birds.

'What do you think, Eric?' he said. 'Will they work?'

Eric stared at him and cooed. Jacob cooed back.

'Good, then,' said Jacob. 'I'll let you know how I get on.'

He crept out of the out-house and in through the kitchen door and up the stairs to the top room where the dormer window was. He hurried over to the window and pushed it open.

'Jacob, bloody hell, don't jump! I thought you were joking.'

William had been sitting unseen, reading a book about tractors, looking at the pictures mainly.

'Course I wasn't joking,' said Jacob. 'Look at my wings. I'm going to fly.'

And he began to squeeze himself out of the window. William rushed across and grabbed his arm and dragged him back in.

'Get off my wing, you idiot! You'll break it!'

'Don't be a fool, Jacob. Those wings are useless. You'll drop like a stone.'

'Get off me, they're not useless, they're bloody beautiful.'

'Please Jacob,' said William. Jacob had never heard his brother say please before. It caused him to pause. 'Well at least don't jump from the top floor. Try it from the room below. Please ...'

'All right then,' said Jacob.

He hurried off downstairs and heard his brother's footsteps hurrying after him. Jacob perched on the sill and flapped his wings and cooed and cried out, 'Look at me fly!'

He flung himself out into space just as Alfred looked up from the orchard. Jacob felt the wind rush past him as the wings folded beneath his weight and he crashed down into the rose-bed where he lay impaled on the thorns and could see William's little face looking down on him from the window above, a hand held against his brow, and as Jacob felt the pain in his ankle and the blood on his face, he saw Alfred towering over him with a face fluttering somewhere between admiration and rage.

'You bloody little fool,' he said at last as he hauled his son from the thorns and went to call the doctor to cast the broken ankle in plaster.

'How's the ankle, little Icarus?' Rose asked when she saw Jacob later.

'Broken,' he said. 'Almost snapped in two.'

'The shell must break before the bird can fly …'

'Is that Chesterton again?'

'No, that one's anonymous. Does it hurt very much?'

'Course not.'

'Just as I thought,' she said, and she stroked his hair and he smiled at her.

***

Norman Miller lowered himself into the tepid waters of the cast-iron bath and a faint slick of grime slipped across the surface. With just his head and knees above the waterline, the smell of wet sheep seeped up into Norman's nostrils and he ducked his head under the water, then out again, and lathered himself a wig of suds from the block of soap he kept in the drip-tray by the taps. He looked around at the damp brick walls and the single window in the far wall, with its Victorian glass and its bubbles and eddies and sand-speck imperfections. During the day it afforded a transparent view across the fields and at night a clear window onto Norman Miller in his bathroom birthday suit, but no one would be out there at this time, just the sheep, and the fox that visited nightly in search of a chicken dinner until Norman shot it later that winter. And Jacob Arbuckle peering through the glass, spying on the newcomer, hatching a plot.

A single bare bulb hung from the ceiling on a double-twisted wire, illuminating Norman as he rinsed off the soap, towelled down his enormous frame, and retrieved his clothes from the pine rail by the door. He dressed quickly, ordered his hair with a brisk sweep of his hand, called the dogs, and stepped out of the tiny cottage into the farmyard as Jacob melted away into the fields.

Norman could see the bathroom light in Webster's twin cottage next door, so he left him to his ablutions and walked wearily across the yard, past the patch where the strawberries grew in June, and crunched up the gravel path to the porch. In the farmhouse kitchen, Mrs Brailes was preparing the farmhands' evening meal. Norman took his usual seat, nearest the range, a dog each side of his chair.

'Fine weather today, Mrs Brailes,' he said.

'Indeed.'

Mrs Brailes was a woman of few words, rarely wasting three syllables when two would do. Mr Brailes, the farm manager, placed a bottle of Hook Norton ale on the table next to Norman, then held out a raw onion that his wife had just peeled.

'No, thank you,' said Norman. He never accepted anything at the first time of asking and therefore missed out on many of the good things that life had to offer. He did not consider raw onions to be one of them.

'Are you sure, Norman?' said Brailes. 'These little buggers are bloody good for you,' and he took a huge bite out of the onion and chewed on it vigorously. Behind him Norman could hear Mrs Brailes biting enthusiastically into one of her own and when he turned to face her he saw that it had brought tears to her eyes, such were its health-giving properties.

'An apple a day keeps the doctor away,' elaborated Brailes. 'But an onion a day, even better! You'd never need a doctor in your whole life, they'd all be bloody redundant!'

'Never been ill in all my life anyway,' said Norman.

'How was the horse today?' Brailes asked, his voice rebounding off the low ceiling as if he were talking to the hard of hearing.

'The horse is grand,' said Norman. 'It's a good thing we got that nail out when we did or he'd have been lame by now.'

'Excellent!' boomed Brailes.

Norman assumed that this habitual volume went some way to explaining Mrs Brailes' verbal reticence – no word could be got in, edgeways or otherwise, when Brailes was in full flow. Norman and Webster referred to him as The Bellows, their private joke being that if they should find it difficult one night to light their fires, it would be sufficient to have him in the room for a brief conversation and there would be a roaring blaze in no time.

Mrs Brailes placed a steaming bowl in front of each of the men.

'Soup,' she said.

'Swede?' bellowed Brailes.

'Parsnip.'

Norman ladled in a spoonful, then took a swig of beer. The door opened and Webster shuffled in. He sat down next to Norman, yawned elaborately, and only when finished remembered to cover his mouth. He smiled guiltily, then leaned a careless, weary elbow on the table and sent his spoon clattering onto the flagstones and set the dogs off barking.

'Quiet!' said Norman and the dogs cut their noise instantly and settled down again beside his chair.

'Webster, have you always lived your life in a state of such constant bloody confusion?' laughed Brailes, and Webster's other elbow jerked back and sent his fork in the same direction as the spoon and the dogs were off again.

'You're lucky Mr Brailes is of such a naturally charitable disposition,' murmured Norman.

Webster looked distraught.

'Just pulling your leg, Webster,' said Norman.

'Come on, Webster, get that down you,' said Brailes, placing a bottle of ale on the table beside him, then an unwanted onion, and Mrs Brailes ladled out another bowl of soup.

'Parsnip,' she said, then added rather unnecessarily, 'Not swede.'

'Hedging tomorrow, then, lads,' said Brailes, ignoring his wife's sudden verbosity.

'I've sharpened up the bill-hook and the slasher,' said Webster eagerly. He was several years younger than Norman, not quite out of his teens, and having fallen out with his family in Suffolk was eager to please his new boss.

'We'll get plenty of firewood out of those hedges in the bottom fields. They've been left too long,' said Brailes. 'You two can take half a cartload each for your fires. The cottages will be cold now.'

'They certainly are,' said Norman.

'Coalman's coming on Wednesday,' continued Brailes. 'You can have a sack each.'

He was generous like that, Mr Brailes, thought Norman. A good sort, not like some of the people you meet.

'Marvellous soup, Mrs B,' said Webster. 'Is there cabbage in here as well?'

She smiled at him almost maternally. She had no children of her own.

'No, Webster dear. Only parsnip.'

'I have to see someone about a pig in the morning,' said Brailes, breaking a momentary silence. 'Alfred Arbuckle, lives just up the hill there. Norman, come with me. I'd like your opinion. You can have a bit of a lie-in. We'll leave at eight. '

Brailes saw the look on Webster's face.

'Don't worry, Webster, you can come too. We'll only be away an hour – you can clean out the hens and do the hedging when we get back.'

'Pork,' said Mrs Brailes, as she placed a plate in front of each of the men.

They ate, talking occasionally about the ailments of the animals and the difficulties caused by the recent deterioration in the weather, then Norman and Webster left together to return to their cottages.

'Fancy another beer?' asked Webster.

'Yes, but I don't fancy the walk,' said Norman. The pub was half a mile away across frozen fields, or a mile by road. 'I'm dog-tired already. I want my bed.'

Inside his cottage, Norman lit the fire. The logs he had cut from the tree that had come down in the copse behind the house were too long to fit in the grate so he propped one end up on the firedogs to burn and the other end would do for tomorrow. The dogs stretched out on the threadbare rug by the fire and Norman sank himself down into a tatty armchair that Brailes had dredged out of the back of a barn for him. The pigeons had stained the top of it white with their droppings, and its insides had sheltered whole generations of mice, but it was generously proportioned and comfortable and gave off a less powerful smell than most of the people who had ever sat in it. Norman removed his boots and placed them by the fire to dry out so they could get wet again in the morning. They were the ones his father had passed down to him a dozen years before – size 12 Victorian-style ankle boots, tough brown leather that in their early days chaffed the skin off their wearer's heels and bunions, but were now shaped to Norman's feet like well-polished gloves. When Norman left County Durham, his mother had jokingly called him Noah, taking things away with him in pairs – two dogs, two boots, twin memories of two half-brothers lost to the great farms of Canada and Australia, two broad shoulders to carry the weight of the world, and the chips that life had taken out of each of them. Norman's earliest concrete memory, at five years old, was of a brown-clod November field beneath a mizzling sky, lashed to a plough and set on his way with a swipe of a stick across the horse's rump. The horse's tail swished and little Norman craned his head sideways in a vain attempt to see what lay ahead as the plough surfed wildly across the ground, gouging an irregular furrow from one end of the field to the other as his father, whom he only knew as Mr Bainbridge, rushed along beside him in his chaffing leather boots, shouting encouragement and advice to his five-year-old son, then turning the horse at the far end and setting him off again in the opposite direction. Norman and the horse did four lengths of the field before Mr Bainbridge tired of running and pulled the horse to a halt. He was grinning from ear to ear and took his son's head in his hands, shook him tenderly, then untied the ropes and hugged him to his chest.

'Well done, my lad, well done! You're a proper farmer now. I'm proud of you. Dead proud!'

They had gone back to the village and Mr Bainbridge left him at the gate of his grandmother's house, then went back up to Black Hill Farm, the largest in the area and soon to be transferred by inheritance into Mr Bainbridge's tutelage. He had grown up there and learned his trade for years so that he could in turn pass the farm on to Norman one day, despite the complications in his relationship with Norman's mother, Mary Miller. She was younger than Bainbridge, barely into adulthood, when she took the job at Black Hill Farm, but she had heard of the possibilities offered by quiet bedrooms at the end of long corridors and she made it her business to find herself alone with John Bainbridge in one of them one day. The encounter was more extended and pleasurable than she had been led to believe, and it became a regular part of her week until the inevitable happened. She christened the inevitability Norman.

'You can't marry her,' said Bainbridge's mother, 'in circumstances such as these. She'll stay at home and bring the child up there.'

'But I must marry her,' he said. 'For the sake of our child.'

But John Bainbridge wavered and his mother's wishes prevailed.

'Don't worry, Mary, our child will be fine,' he promised, 'and one day we'll all be together.'

But the temporary life they created set too hard in its mould and there was no breaking it. Mary's father passed away within two years from pneumonia and a sense of disgrace, and shortly after they had buried him Mary left for Newcastle.

'Newcastle?' said John Bainbridge. 'You must be mad.'

'Perhaps,' she said, but she was gone and she married a ship-builder and gave Norman two half-brothers he rarely saw. Norman's upbringing was left to his grandmother, John Bainbridge visiting weekly and providing sufficient funds to see to Norman's well-being and training him on his farm for when he would take it on for himself.

'That's my lad over there,' he would say to anyone who would listen. 'Dead proud of him, I am. Dead proud.'

But then, when Norman was thirteen, John Bainbridge was late for an appointment of little consequence and he slipped beneath a bus as he ran to jump on. Gone at thirty-five, too young or too careless to have made a formal will, and with him went Norman's only hope of a comfortable life, Black Hill Farm ending up in the hands of a Bainbridge cousin. Norman worked Black Hill Farm for another dozen years until he woke up one day and declared that he was off down south to make a new life for himself, away from the bastard taunts and the injustice.

He arrived in North Oxfordshire and met Mr Brailes at the Banbury cattle market. Brailes liked the look of the strong young northerner and discerned within minutes that Norman knew his sheep from his goats, his animal husbandry from his labourer's tasks.

'You'll do for me,' bellowed Brailes. 'A fair wage, free food and lodging, and a cracking little farm, out by Chipping Norton.'

'Right, then,' said Norman.

'The contract's dawn till dusk,' added Brailes, a little more quietly. 'Three hundred and sixty-four days a year. Christmas Day's a holiday.'

'You'll have to take my dogs as well.'

'Working dogs?'

'Border collies. I've trained them well.'

'No wife?'

'No.'

'Don't worry. We'll find you one soon enough.'

'Right, then,' said Norman, and he followed Brailes over to a pen to assess the merits of an Aberdeen Angus.

**

From the top-floor dormer window Jacob could see Brailes' van trawling out of the farm gate and up the snow-covered lane past the railway bridge before it passed out of sight along the Churchill Road and then into view again down the hill towards the Arbuckles' house, Mill View Cottage, three storeys of pale Cotswold stone. Brailes pulled the van over by the low stone wall that kept Alfred's pigs penned inside the orchard. Jacob heard Alfred calling the men over and watched him lean over the wall and whack the roof of the sty with a hoe, then the pigs emerging, rooting around beneath the trees. Jacob hurried down the stairs, grabbing Vera's hand and hauling her down after him.

'You can come too, William,' he said. 'If you want.'

The three of them gathered in the porch, three heads poking around the doorframe, listening to the men discussing their business.

'What do you reckon, Norman?' Brailes was saying.

Norman had got into the pen and was sizing up the animals.

'You want a male, right? That looks a good 'un. He'll do the job.'

'Disraeli it is, then,' said Alfred.

Norman cast him a quizzical look.

'Names them all after prime ministers,' said Brailes.

'Bloody healthy set of bollocks on him, that's for sure,' said Norman. 'Disraeli will give you a whole Cabinet of little politicians.'

Then he turned and met the eyes of Vera.

'Apologies,' Norman said, touching his cap, 'for my rudimentary use of language just now. I had no idea a lady was present.'

Jacob and William stood giggling behind their sister.

'Don't worry,' said Vera. 'I've heard far worse than that. Father's always cursing about something or other,' and she took the enamel bowl that she was holding into the garden and began scrubbing furiously with a brush. Norman watched for a moment as her hand sped back and forth in a frozen blur, the skin mottling orange and blue in the cold.

'You'll be needing some gloves,' said Norman.

Vera smiled and took this coincidence as a happy omen.

'Come see my birds, mister?' said Jacob.

'Happy to,' said Norman, and he followed the boy round to the out-house door.

'Eric and Penelope,' Jacob said. 'My lovely birds.'

'Very nice,' said Norman. 'They'd make a lovely pie.'

Jacob glared at him. 'I thought you were a nice man.'

'I am, but you've got to eat.'

'Well you can't eat Eric and Penelope.'

'I was just pulling your leg, son.'

'That's all right, then. I only just got them back, you know. Bloody William set them out of the cage, said they'd gone forever, up into the blue, he said. But they came back. Didn't you, my dears?' He cooed at them. 'They were in the elm and I left the cage door open all night and in the morning they were back home. Isn't that a miracle, mister, a little miracle?'

'I'll say it is,' said Norman, smiling at the boy. 'They must like you.'

'Oh, they do, mister, they do.'

When they got back to the farm, Norman and Brailes and Webster set off to do the hedging, taking the long walk down past the copse to the bottom field where the brook ran beneath the abandoned mill-house, inhabited now by rats and bats and owls. They stopped in mid-morning to drink the sweet milky tea that Mrs Brailes had prepared for them in the thermos, the hot liquid slipping down their gullets as vapour spilled from their mouths in the icy air. Brailes went back to the farm, leaving Norman and Webster to hack at the hawthorn until the sun was setting over Kingham and the first flakes of snow drifted in on an easterly wind. They had cut the hedge back by three feet, opening up the ditch and laying bare the runs in the adjacent bank.

Norman prodded Webster in the ribs and nodded towards the runs.

'We'll be back for those later,' he winked.

'For what?' said Webster.

'Hares, lad. Hares.'

They loaded the branches onto the wagon and Norman slapped the horse and took the reins and led it back up the hill towards the farm as blasts from the Bliss Mill chimney echoed around the valley to signal the end of the tweed-workers' day.

That night Webster persuaded Norman up the hill into town and into the nearest pub. They sat side by side on a pine settle, worn to a grubby patina by centuries of use, and felt the fire warm their feet through the soles of their boots. It was just a week until Christmas and

21

little bursts of seasonal music started up, a violin and an accordion, and Norman recognised Alfred Arbuckle as he ran his bow across the strings. An argument flared up in another room, voices in strident discord about a motor car, but they subsided almost as soon as they had started and peace and music broke out again. Norman went to the bar and positioned himself next to Alfred.

'What can I get you, sir?' Norman asked.

'I've had a skinful already,' said Alfred. 'But if you insist.'

Norman paid for the drinks and Alfred sat down next to Webster on the settle.

'You lads not from round here, then?' he asked.

'No, sir,' said Webster, looking into his pint.

Norman shook his head.

'Family?' asked Alfred.

'Nothing to speak of,' said Norman. 'Him neither.'

He looked at Webster. Webster shook his head in glum confirmation.

'Right, you'd both best come to ours for Christmas lunch, then. I've two sons of my own and I wouldn't want them alone on Christmas Day either. Brailes won't mind. Be at the house at noon.'

Alfred drained his glass, slapped each of them on the back as if banging out a rhythm on a favourite pair of drums, picked up his violin – a gift from a tramp who had called by for soup once a week and left the thing on the doorstep when he took himself off to die – and stumbled out into a street that was thickening again with snow.

CHRISTMAS 1934

At dusk on Christmas Eve, Norman took Webster down to the newly-cut hedge by the brook in the bottom field and showed him how to lay out the hare traps and the valley bottom rang with the piercing shrieks of trapped creatures in the night. Norman rose early to knock on Webster's door and they set off with the dogs across the snowy fields to the brook where the hares had scuffed up the ground as they struggled to be free. Norman snapped their necks and held them up for Webster.

'One for Brailes, one for the Arbuckles,' said Norman. 'We can hardly go empty-handed.'

Back at the cottage, Norman bathed and dressed himself with unusual care, knotting and re-knotting his tie and ordering his hair with a brush instead of his hand, then polishing and re-polishing his boots. He looked at himself in the dark speckled glass of the hall mirror, adjusted his cap, called the dogs, and shut the door behind him. Webster was already waiting outside.

'Bloody hell, Webster, you can't go like that,' said Norman. 'Look at your boots. They're bloody filthy. They'll think we're a couple of tramps.'

They went back into Norman's cottage.

'Here, give those to me. And fill this up with eggs. Brailes won't mind.'

Webster took the pail across to the chicken sheds in his socks while Norman brushed away the mud from his boots and daubed on the polish and brushed them until they shone like his own. Webster came back with the eggs and put on the dry socks that Norman offered him, then his shiny boots, and attempted to knot the tie that Norman gave him.

'No, not like that, lad. Didn't your mother teach you anything?'

Norman knotted Webster's tie, then wrapped a dozen eggs in

newspaper and picked up the gifts he had prepared for Vera and her brothers at dawn. They left half a pail of eggs and a large hare on Brailes' doorstep with a Christmas note, then set off up the lane through the snow with the dogs. Long icicles hung from the gutters of Mill View Cottage as Alfred welcomed Norman and Webster into the house and they all stood around in front of the fire sipping sherry from Edwardian glasses etched with leaves. Webster fidgeted as he spoke. Norman spoke little and of serious things – agricultural matters – while Alfred held forth on developments at the tweed mill, the state of his pigs and chickens, and the relative quality of the beers produced by the Hitchman and Hook Norton breweries, the latter subject accompanied by multiple tastings of several of the local brews. Vera sipped her sherry and listened to the men while Jacob and William sneaked into the kitchen to fill their thimble-sized glasses from various bottles of ale until their mother brought this sport to a sudden end and set them instead upon the vegetables with knives.

At the table in the dining room Vera found herself next to Norman and occasionally their elbows brushed against each other as they ate and she noticed the large protruding knuckles of his giant hands as he cut the food on his plate. She listened to the sound of him chewing like a ruminating goat, then drinking down his beer, then a clearing of his throat and the burr of his voice as he spoke to Jacob sitting opposite about the essentials of tractor maintenance, the correct dosage of worm pills for sheep (four) and lambs (two), and about Roker Park in Sunderland and the derby games against Newcastle United and how the Mackems had stuffed the Magpies 5-0 in 1930. Webster listened mostly in silence, occasionally laughing nervously at a minor joke that someone had made.

'Webster,' said Elizabeth, after she had been studying him for a while. 'Haven't you a given name?'

'Yes, but everyone just calls me Webster, always have. Always will, I expect.'

'Even your family? Your mother and father?'

Webster nodded and turned his attention again to the potato that he had been hacking at ineffectually with his knife before he had been interrupted.

'How odd some people are,' concluded Elizabeth.

Vera cast her mother a reproachful glance.

'I like the name Webster,' said Vera. 'It has a certain dignity about it.'

Webster straightened his back slightly in his chair.

'Go on, Webster,' urged Jacob, struggling to get his words past a mouthful of food that was on its way in as his words were on their way out. 'Tell us your name.'

Webster's pale cheeks flushed pink and he squirmed again in his seat.

'Jacob, don't talk with your mouth full!' said Vera. 'You're not a pig, are you?'

'Go on, Webster, please ...' said William.

'He won't tell you,' said Norman firmly. 'I asked him once. Once is enough. Remember that, lads.'

'Yes, Norman's right. Leave him alone,' said Vera, quietly proud of Norman's decisive intervention and the instant effect it had had on her brothers. 'His name's Webster and that's all there is to it.'

'How old are you, Webster?' asked Elizabeth after a moment's pause.

'Mother!' protested Vera, and she looked across at Norman to indicate to him her disapproval of her mother's continuing inquisition.

'Nineteen,' said Webster. 'And a half.'

'The same as Vera, then,' said Elizabeth.

Vera glared at her mother again.

'Mother, surely you know that a lady's age must never be mentioned in public?'

'And you, Norman?' asked Elizabeth, ignoring her daughter's interjection.

'Old as the hills, I'm afraid.'

Elizabeth's stare indicated that she would not accept such an ambiguous answer.

'Twenty-five,' he confessed.

Satisfied that she had extracted sufficient information for the time-being, Elizabeth served the pudding and then they retired to the sitting room where the family cat sat in a polka-dot chair by the warmth of the fire.

'Thank you for the hare and the eggs, you two,' said Alfred. 'They'll make a cracking dinner!'

'I can bring you more any time you like,' said Norman.

Vera felt a little flutter in her breast and her pulse quickened. 'I'm sure father would like that. He absolutely adores jugged hare, don't you, father?'

'Absolutely,' agreed Alfred quickly, noting the slight urgency of Vera's delivery.

Jacob came hurtling down the staircase with a pair of parcels, tripping over the last step and sprawling across the kitchen floor in his haste. William looked at him with brotherly condescension, accustomed to Jacob's frequent tumbles and secretly wishing he might burst into tears. But Jacob burst into embarrassed laughter instead.

'No wonder you've so many scars on your chin, Jacob,' said Vera, 'rushing around like an absolute lunatic all the time.'

He passed the presents to Vera as she rubbed his chin casually with her thumb, like a billiards player chalking a cue in preparation for the next impact.

'Get off,' he said. 'It doesn't bloody hurt, you know.'

'Mind your language, boy!' said Alfred, and Jacob glared at him and went out into the porch to console himself by petting Norman's dogs and imagining they were his own.

'This is for you, Webster,' said Vera.

Webster opened the present and something welled up in his eyes as he wrapped the bright red scarf around his neck.

'Webster, you look a picture,' said Elizabeth.

Webster was beaming from ear to ear.

'And these are for you,' said Vera to Norman. 'I do hope they fit.'

He pulled off the paper and burst out laughing.

'Don't you like them?' frowned Vera. 'I made them myself. They took ages.'

'They're perfect,' he said, pulling them on. 'Just perfect. And these are for you. But I didn't make them myself, I'm afraid.'

Vera pulled off the wrapping and burst into laughter too.

'Oh, they're lovely,' she said as she admired the black leather gloves, and she held Norman's gaze for longer than could be explained by mere gratitude.

Through January and February the hares in the bottom field learnt additional caution as their numbers diminished week by week, Norman taking them away two by two to the ark he was building for himself up the hill, a vessel to keep himself afloat in now, walking once a week after dinner to Mill View Cottage with his offering of hare. He sat at the kitchen table with Alfred and Elizabeth, and Vera would come and join them and Jacob and William would sneak out of bed and appear on the galley stairs in their pyjamas and listen to the adults and Elizabeth would let them perch there for a while, pretending not to see, and then scold them back up the stairs to bed, Jacob calling out 'Good night, Norman!' as he went, and Jacob would refuse to settle until Norman and Vera had gone upstairs to tuck him into bed and Norman had told him a story about life up north or something that had occurred that day with the animals on the farm. And as Norman told the story, he watched Jacob breathing and the eyelids start to flicker as the boy slipped into dreams, and he wished that when he was young he could have been a boy just like Jacob, not an unwanted parcel that had been lost in life's post and left at an address where they had no use for him.

Then one night Alfred and Elizabeth left the kitchen on a non-specific pretence and Norman and Vera found themselves alone together and conversation came easily as the minutes slipped by and Norman felt the frost inside him thaw a little more. Then they heard a hint-heavy cough from the top of the stairs. Norman looked at his watch.

'Perhaps I should be going. I've got an early start tomorrow. But it's been a very pleasant evening, I've enjoyed our conversations.'

'Yes, Norman, it's been lovely,' said Vera. 'You've been lovely.'

He did not know what to say. She accompanied him to the door and without intending to he suddenly heard himself saying what he had been thinking, his voice soft now beneath the decorative canopy of the porch.

'Vera,' he whispered. 'Will you come out with me sometime?'

She stared at him.

'The cinema, perhaps?' he continued. 'A matinee, I mean, in the afternoon.'

She had replied before he could finish.

'This Saturday, then?' he said.

She touched his gloved hand and felt him squeeze her fingers gently and then he turned and walked up the lane with his dogs either side of him and a single question in his mind. How on earth was he going to persuade Brailes to give him the day off?

***

The following day began and ended in a downpour.

'Norman, there's something I have to tell you,' said Webster as they were fixing the gears of the tractor in the barn. 'I'm thinking of going back home. I wrote a letter, you see, and they said they'd have me back. I think I really should go home, you know.'

Norman patted Webster's shoulder.

'I'll miss you, Webster. You're a good sort.'

'I'll miss you too, Norman. You're like my big brother, you are.'

'When are you planning on going?'

'Whenever Brailes will let me.'

'I'll speak to him for you.'

That night, Norman and Webster walked up to the pub and stayed until closing time. As they staggered home, Norman finally asked the question.

'So then, Webster, what *is* your Christian name? You can tell me now, you're off home soon.'

'I'd rather not.'

'Come on, you're my mate. You can tell me.'

'All right, but don't mock me. It's … Verdun.'

'What?'

'Verdun. Like the battlefield. 1916 and all that.'

'Yes, I know.'

'So what do you think?'

'Well, it's a bloody original name.'

'My dad chose it. He was gassed there in the war. He said it would remind me not to trust too much in human nature.'

'Well, Webster,' laughed Norman, 'Maybe you should just stick to the surname.'

And he gave Webster a bear hug and they staggered on in the dark towards the farm.

Webster left for home on the early bus and when he had gone Brailes and Norman went out to check if the sheep had started to lamb.

'Mr Brailes, there's something I need to ask you,' said Norman. 'I know it's not part of my contract, but I'd like to take Saturday afternoon off. There's something I have to do. Just this once, mind.'

'Whatever can be so important, Norman?' asked Brailes.

'It's Alfred Arbuckle's girl, Vera' said Norman. 'You see, we …

well, I've asked her out, just for the afternoon, like. I can check on the sheep in the evening ...'

'That's fine, the sheep can wait a few hours, a woman can't. And Norman, now Webster has left, we'll be needing more help, so I've been thinking. You do the work of two men, I want to give you more responsibility, a sort of promotion, I mean. There'll be more money in it for you.'

'Thank you, Mr Brailes.'

'And a week's holiday once a year.'

'I'd certainly appreciate that.'

That Saturday, Norman and Vera walked awkwardly into town and sat through a George Formby film barely following the plot, then stopped for steak and kidney pie at the café on the top side of the market square, and as they walked back home Vera slipped her arm through his.

The following week, Vera took Jacob along to Elm Tree Farm as a chaperone, her little brother eager to follow Norman about the farm as he worked. They hiked over the fields with the dogs, from sheep to sheep, and Jacob watched as Norman checked each ewe's nether regions, fumbling about it seemed with his great big ruddy hands. That night Norman was out again in the snow and he was up half the night with the new-born lambs, warming them in front of the fire and feeding them from a baby's bottle.

1935

Winter turned to spring and Vera and Jacob visited Elm Tree Farm regularly, and William just on Sundays when he knew Mrs Brailes would be baking cakes for the week. Jacob found himself alone with Norman in the barn one day.

'Are you going to marry my sister, Mister Norman?' he suddenly asked.

'That's for her to decide,' said Norman.

'Don't you think you should ask her, then? I'll ask her for you if you like.'

'Perhaps I should ask your father.'

'He won't mind. I know he likes you.'

The next time Jacob came down to the farm to follow Norman around the stables and in and out of the barns and across the fields to where the sheep stood strewn about like stones, Norman took him up to the top wood and showed him the trees where the woodpeckers were.

'Can you hear them?' asked Norman, and Jacob nodded at the ra-ta-tat smacking of beak against bark. 'There it is, up there,' said Norman, and the boy saw the flash of green and red.

'Come on,' said Norman. 'I'll show you where the pheasants roost. If your father will let you down at night, I'll take you and we'll bag a few. It's not the season, but nobody need know. And they go down just the same any time of the year.'

His eyes twinkled at the thought of the roasting birds.

'What do you mean he's gone shooting?' said Elizabeth, when Alfred told her later. 'He might get shot, we don't know if it's safe.'

'Of course it's safe,' said Alfred. 'He's with Norman, isn't he?'

Across the valley, Norman and Jacob were in the trees in the dusk and Norman knocked a pheasant down with his first shot and the dogs ran to fetch it and he passed it to the boy and then took it back and stuffed it into one of the deep pockets that lined his coat. They walked on into the wood and out into the glade on the far side of the hill. The moon had risen now and Norman stretched out an arm and stopped the boy.

'Ssh now,' he said quietly. 'Can you see it? There ...'

Jacob followed Norman's pointing hand and saw the hovering thing, an inverse silhouette, a pale silent flutter against the dark.

'What is it, Mister Norman?'

'A barn owl,' he whispered.

'Gosh,' said Jacob. 'I never thought I'd see one of those. Shall we kill it?'

'No, lad. You don't shoot one of those.'

The bird glided silently away and the glade was empty again.

'Thank you, mister. For showing me the owl.'

'You're welcome, lad.'

On the way back down the hill to the farm, Norman took an envelope from the deep pocket where the pheasants were.

'Here you are, Jacob, son. Give this to your sister, will you?' Norman winked. 'Don't go losing it, mind. You're to deliver it straight into her hands as soon as you get home.'

Jacob nodded.

'And give this bird to your father. Tell him it's from me.'

'I think I'd better be going home right now, Mister Norman,' said Jacob, clutching the letter and the pheasant to his chest. 'I told mother I'd be home in good time for bed.'

'Good lad, run along now. And remember,' he called after the fleeing figure, 'straight into her hands, mind, straight into her hands!'

Vera tore the letter open, Jacob at her elbow, craning his neck to read Norman's flowing scrawl.

Dearest Vera, you must know by now my feelings for you, and I have foolishly allowed myself to believe that they are perhaps matched by your own. I hope you do not consider it rash of me, but I should like to ask if you will consider me as your companion, for a life together, I mean. You know I am a humble man of little culture, but I can assure you I am honest and true and I will build a good life for you and will stand by you for as long as you will have me. But if you should turn me down, I will understand, for you could surely find a man more worthy of your hand than I. I await your reply with an impatient heart. Norman

'What is it, Vera? Tell me ...'

'Jacob, did you read this letter?'

He shook his head.

'Oh Jacob, you're not made for lying, are you? Listen, not a word of this to anyone! I have to go and see Rose.'

Vera dashed down the stairs and out of the house and down the path by the orchard, then across the lane to Rose's house, Jacob running after her.

'So what do you think?' she asked her best friend breathlessly. 'Should I? Would you?'

She took a large bite out of the apple that Rose had given her. Rose considered the letter for a moment.

'Vera, my dear, your second question is irrelevant, you know I'm simply not the marrying kind. As to your first, only you can know the answer. You do know the answer, don't you? You must follow your heart, Vera. Your heart must tell you what to do.'

At dawn the next morning Jacob was flying back down the lane to Elm Tree Farm, another envelope clasped in his hand. He tripped half-way down the hill on a rock in his haste and went sprawling in the damp earth and skinned his elbow and grazed his chin on the rough stones, but he leapt up again and wiped the blood away with the back of his hand, laughing with joy as he ran. He hurtled into the farmyard and up the low rise of steps and into the Brailes' kitchen.

'Hello, my dear,' said Mrs Brailes. 'What's all the excitement about? And what have you done to your chin? It's bleeding.'

'Mrs Brailes, Mrs Brailes, where's Norman?'

'In with the cattle. Would you ...'

But Jacob was already out of the door and half-way across towards the cow-sheds. He thrust the envelope into Norman's hands.

'That was quick, Jacob. We'll make a career for you in the post office yet.'

'Sorry I've dirtied it with blood, Mister Norman.'

Norman passed him a handkerchief, took a deep breath and opened the letter. He looked at Jacob, the boy looked back for a moment, and then he flung himself at the man and hugged him tight.

That evening Norman and Vera went together to speak to Alfred and Elizabeth. They sat side by side on the sofa in the front room as

Jacob and William hung silently out of sight on the stairs.

'Mr Arbuckle, I must inform you of a development,' said Norman.

'A development?'

'Yes, Mr Arbuckle. An important development at that.'

'Really?'

'Yes, well, it's like this. You see, we …'

'Go on, Norman, tell him,' Vera said.

'Well, Vera and I, we …' said Norman.

'Father,' Vera interrupted. 'We have developed an affection for each other and we shall be getting married. There now, I've told you.'

Elizabeth raised an eyebrow and smiled at Vera.

'Yes, Mr Arbuckle,' said Norman. 'With your permission, and Mrs Arbuckle's of course, I should like to marry your daughter.'

Alfred looked at Norman sternly, then at Vera. She nodded.

'Are you in trouble, girl?' he said.

'Of course not, father! How could you think such a thing?'

'Look here, Norman,' said Alfred. 'Vera is only nineteen. Come back and ask me again in six months.'

Six months later to the day, Alfred came out at first light to feed the pigs and Norman was waiting by the wall of the orchard.

'Mr Arbuckle, I haven't changed my mind.'

'Very well, Norman, you have my blessing. But you'll have to promise me one thing first.'

Norman nodded.

'You may marry my daughter, but she's only young and must live a little still. She must on no account have a child until she's twenty-one. Do you agree to those terms?'

'Of course.'

'Good.' He shook Norman by the hand. 'Welcome to the family. Now help me feed these pigs.'

***

Norman and Webster sat at the kitchen table as Mrs Brailes poured out their cups of tea from the pot and dropped a plate of toast in front of each of them, a wedge of butter melting into each slice, and went back to the range where she spiked the sausages with a fork and the fat sizzled out. She cracked a pair of eggs and dropped them into the spitting fat, then refilled their cups with tea.

Webster had arrived the previous day, in preparation for the wedding, on the solid-tyre Daimler bus that ran up from Oxford, his face gaunt and his coat hanging around him in loose folds as Norman met him at the set-down point outside the Temperance Hotel. Norman led him across the market square and into the Fox Hotel for a pint.

'Here you go, Webster, lad,' get that down you, said Norman, thrusting the brew into his hand. 'It's bloody great to see you. We've missed you round the farm, you know. Mrs B talks about you all the time, can you believe it? Keeps saying she'll need to feed you up good and proper while you're here.'

Norman gripped Webster round the bicep and squeezed. 'Bloody hell, Webster, haven't your folks been feeding you down there in Suffolk?'

'I know, not what they were, are they?' said Webster, feeling his muscles. 'I haven't been working on the land much. Been down the garage instead, learning to be a mechanic.'

'Well you won't have a chance to work this weekend – you've got best-man duties to attend to.'

Norman slipped his hand into his pocket and pulled out a small square box and flipped open the lid.

'What do you think, Webster? Beautiful, isn't she? I've been saving up six months to buy this.'

He touched the ring with the tip of his finger.

Webster looked at the simple gold band. 'Do I really have to look after it? I don't want to lose the thing.'

'Don't you worry, I'll slip it to you just before the ceremony.'

Norman drained his glass.

'Come on, let's get over to the farm. Mrs B's been baking you cakes all morning.'

Wedding fever had spread like a contagion around the farm, Mrs Brailes – particularly afflicted by this temporary madness – hurling herself into a frenzy of preparation for the possible arrival of unexpected guests, Mr Brailes stocking up on the beer that he kept in crates under the stairs – reasoning that if no one else drank it, he would – and various members of the Arbuckle family wandering down to the farm to wish Norman luck and to avail themselves of the hospitality, returning back up the hill with their bellies full of cake and beer. Jacob arrived first, trailing the kite that Norman had bought him for his birthday that summer.

'Hello Mister Norman, hello Webster. Come on, it's a great day for flying, let's take the kite up the hill.'

'We'll do just that, son, as soon as the others get here.'

Then William barrelled into the yard with his fishing rod.

'What are you looking at?' he said to Jacob.

'Nothing.'

'I'm going to catch a pike from the pond.'

'Bet you don't,' said Jacob. 'There aren't any in there.'

Then Vera came down with Rose and Mrs Brailes ushered them all into the large room at the back overlooking the fields and pushed plates of food into their hands and they talked excitedly as they gulped at their tea, Jacob and William bickering about fish as Vera and Rose discussed the intricacies of the wedding dress and the lace that bordered its sleeves. Then they went outside into the pale sunshine, up the hill behind the farmhouse, and Rose helped Jacob set his kite into the wind and the two of them held onto it together, their hands gripping each other's as the red and blue streamers danced and weaved above them. They laughed and threw back their heads in the sunshine and when Jacob turned to look at the girl she was looking at him already and he saw something in her eyes that he had never seen before and that he did not understand, and then it was gone, as quickly as it had appeared. The kite fell to the ground with a thump and Jacob and Rose gathered up the string together, tying themselves in knots as the wind blew the string about, and then they went to sit by the pond with Webster while Norman showed William where to fish.

Rose hoisted herself up onto the top of the fence that dipped down into the water where the cattle came to drink, and she tucked her dress up beneath the bend of her knees. She was a strange willowy girl, about to blossom abruptly from her teens into the full bloom of womanhood. Her father, a London-based notary, had run off with an exotic dancer from Budapest and her mother had swiftly killed herself with gin as a consequence, so Rose had lived most of her life with her grandmother and developed a youthful fondness for quoting aphorisms plucked from the pages of books on her grandmother's shelves, trying them out on unsuspecting companions to test their effect. Her current favourite was Chesterton's 'The way to love anything is to realise that it might be lost' – and she was, she had to admit, uncommonly afraid of losing things now. She looked at Webster for a moment and then at Jacob for slightly longer. Webster looked away at the pond, then quickly back again.

'It's all right Webster, you can look if you want,' said Rose breezily. 'I don't mind. There is a road from the eye to the heart that does not go through the intellect.'

'You what?' said Webster, and he looked away.

'Who was that one by?' asked Jacob. He was accustomed to Rose dusting her speech with quotation and could spot a cuckoo among the natural nesting of her words as surely as an ornithologist detects the inhabitants of a wood from their voices alone.

'Chesterton,' she said.

'Chesterton again?' said Jacob. 'But you're always doing him.'

Rose reflected for a moment on the urgent need to find a new source of wisdom, then decided to change the subject.

'Have you got a girlfriend, Webster?' she asked.

'Not at the moment.'

'Would you like one?'

He looked away and gulped.

'Have you *ever* had one?'

'Course I have,' he said.

'I'm not sure I believe you. What was her name, then?'

'Er, Harriet.'

'Nice name. Unusual, though. If you ask me, it sounds like you might have imagined her.'

'Good job I'm not asking you, then,' said Webster. 'And you? Got a boyfriend, have you?'

'That depends what you mean by a boyfriend, dear Webster.'

'Course she has,' said Jacob, laughing. 'She's got loads.'

'Who told you that, you naughty little bugger?'

'Vera did.'

'Cow,' she laughed.

Webster took a cigarette from his top pocket and slipped it between his lips.

'Want one?' he said.

'No, thank you,' said Rose. 'It's a disgusting habit. Makes your breath stink too, terrible for kissing.'

She saw Jacob eyeing up Webster's cigarette.

'Want one, Jacob?' Webster said.

'Don't you dare, you little bugger,' Rose said sharply. 'If I ever see you smoking, you're for it! And you Webster, you beast, you shouldn't be trying to corrupt the poor little lad.'

She knocked the cigarette out of Webster's mouth and let out a shriek as the tip of the thing touched her hand as it departed.

'Bloody hell, Webster,' she said. 'Look what you've gone a nd done!'

'It wasn't my fl-flipping fault,' he stammered.

Two hours later the sun was setting behind the hill and William sat alone by the pond at the end of his rod, still fishless, and Jacob and Webster came out and helped him pack up and they walked with him back up the hill.

'Who's that Rose?' Webster asked, as they neared the Arbuckles' house. 'A friend of your sister's?'

'Yes, she's her best friend, lives just opposite us,' said Jacob. 'She's always round at ours.'

'But father doesn't like her,' said William.

'He says she's a bit of a girl, whatever that's supposed to mean,' said Jacob. 'But I like her.'

'She's all right, I suppose,' said William.

'She seems all right to me too,' said Webster, and Jacob felt something tug at him inside. 'Will she be at the wedding tomorrow?'

'Oh yes, she'll definitely be at the wedding,' said Jacob. 'She likes that kind of thing.'

***

The wedding day dawned crisp and golden, a light frost dusting the fields and the late-October sun rising over the back of Chipping Norton as Brailes tied white ribbons upon his beloved Trojan Tourer, lacing up the automobile in the colours of the day. There was no means of transport in the Arbuckle family, so Brailes had offered them a loan of the Trojan to carry the bride in style to the church, and the couple to their honeymoon in Woodstock the following day.

Alfred arrived at the farm in mid-morning and found Norman and Webster gathered around the Trojan.

'Morning, Norman,' he said, shaking him by the hand with excessive vigour. 'I don't know who's more nervous, you or me. I've never done this before, you know.'

'Me neither,' grinned Norman. 'Once in a lifetime.'

'Got the ring?' Alfred winked at Webster.

'Not yet, Mr Arbuckle.'

Norman patted his own breast pocket.

'She'll be safe in here until we get to the church.'

Brailes came stumbling out of the kitchen and down the steps, his voice preceding him by a distance. He marched across to the car and the others gathered around and admired its white ribbons as Brailes settled himself into the front seat and ceremonially turned the key. The engine coughed and died, Brailes tried again, the engine sparked into life, a loud bang ensued, and a puff of black smoke exited the exhaust.

'Well, I'll be buggered!' exclaimed Brailes, even louder than usual, and a pair of sheep in the nearest field hurtled away up the slope. 'I had the bloody thing up the garage just yesterday for a service.'

'Fatal mistake,' said Norman.

'What are we going to do, Mr Brailes?' asked Webster.

'Horse and trap?' said Brailes.

'It's up to Mr Arbuckle,' said Norman.

Alfred looked at the sky and nodded. 'It's a fine day.'

They transferred the white ribbons to the trap and Alfred and Mr and Mrs Brailes disappeared up the lane side by side on the bench-seat behind the horse, Norman and Webster setting off up the hill after them with the dogs. They were half-way along West Street when the horse clipped past again, Vera sitting in something simple and white and edged with lace, Brailes hurrying the horse along with a flick of his wrist and Alfred thrusting back his shoulders with pride. Vera waved at Norman and her gaze stayed upon him until the trap disappeared around the bend.

'You're a lucky man, Norman,' said Webster.

'I know, mate, I know,' said Norman. 'Don't worry, Webster, your time will come.'

'What's that Rose like?'

'Vera's friend? You could do worse.'

'Is she with anyone at the moment?'

'Hard to say with her. Only one way to find out, though.'

As they were passing the almshouses on Church Street, Norman transferred the ring to Webster's hand. They waited outside the church and Alfred sidled up and nudged Norman in the ribs.

'Have a bit of this, Norman. Calms the nerves.'

Norman took a sip from the silver flask and felt the brandy warm his throat. Alfred passed it to Webster, then took several quick swigs for himself. Jacob and William came over and stood by their imminent brother-in-law and attempted to copy his posture, pushing back their childish shoulders in futile imitation of Norman's broadness of beam.

The vicar appeared silently behind them and accepted the flask, ignoring Jacob's repeated requests for a sip.

'No, Jacob,' he said. 'There'll be plenty of time to sin when you're older.' He knocked back a good long swig. 'Good for the constitution, purifies the soul. Right then, Norman, we'd best be going in. Are you ready?'

'Ready as I'll ever be,' said Norman. 'Come on Webster, let's go.'

The dogs waited outside as the ceremony was conducted and when the newly-weds emerged the dogs took their place at their master's heel as the photos were taken, and Vera stood next to Norman and he felt the nudge of her against him, the fit of her hand in his own, and he suddenly realised that for the first time in his life he had someone of his own, someone who would be with him until the end of his days, and he knew that at last everything was going to be all right.

Rose, the maid of honour, took her place next to Webster, and when the photos were done they walked up the hill together to the Fox Hotel for the reception.

'What's your name, Webster?' Rose asked as they stood at the bar.

'Webster.'

'No, Webster. I mean what's your name, Webster? I can't keep calling you Webster, can I?'

'Why not? Everyone else does.'

Several hours later, when the party had passed the stage of politeness and well regimented consumption of food, and moved on to an urgent milling of bodies around the room, Rose cornered Webster in a dark recess where the lights were dim and the fire burned warm beside them. In the orange glow of the flames he saw her lips move and her eyes fix on his.

'Webster, tell me your name. Please.'

She leaned towards him and as he backed away she leaned further in and whispered in his ear.

'Webster, you know what they call me, don't you?'

Webster swallowed and shook his head.

'Wild Rose. Can you guess why?'

Webster shook his head again. 'Because you smell nice and live at the bottom of the garden?'

'No, because I can't be tamed. Do you think that's awful?'

'No.'

'Most people do.'

'Like who?'

'Norman.'

'Norman?'

Webster looked over Rose's shoulder towards the far side of the room where Norman and Vera stood together next to Alfred, his flask long since drained and his feet skipping in time to the music that filtered in from the next room where a violin led a rag-bag medley of sentimental tunes.

'Yes, Norman. He's always telling Vera I'm a bad influence.'

'He told me I could do worse.'

'From him that's almost a compliment. He doesn't understand people, just his cows and his sheep. Just his beasts.'

'I think he understands me,' said Webster.

'That's because you're a bloke,' she smiled. 'And blokes are just one step removed from the animals, and sometimes not even that.'

Rose kissed Webster on the cheek, then brushed her lips against his.

'Tell me your name, Webster. It'll be our secret.'

And as little Jacob Arbuckle looked on from the far side of the room, Rose parted her lips and Webster closed his eyes as the taste of her stilled him, and an aphorism occurred to Jacob that he had heard from Rose the previous day, 'Love is being stupid together', and he thought that if Rose saw him looking she should somehow feel guilty, though he did not understand why. But she did not see him and she carried right on and Jacob turned away and wondered what Eric would have thought if it had been Penelope pecking away at another in the light of the flames.

Rose knew Webster's name by the time dawn lightened the morning mists around Elm Tree Farm. She whispered it to him as he woke, and before the farmyard drifted into life she slipped out of bed and they dressed and walked back up the hill towards Chipping Norton. At the gate of her house they parted. Webster waited until he heard her front door slip quietly shut and as he turned away in the mist she crept up the stairs and past her grandmother's room and was asleep in bed when her breakfast arrived on a tray in mid-morning.

***

'Did you kiss her, Webster?' Jacob asked him later that day.

'Might have done.'

'Liar. I saw you. Did you kiss her much?'

'None of your business.'

'What else did you do? Did you touch her down there?'

'Do you think I'd bl-bloody tell you if I had?' he stammered. The mere thought of her made him quiver.

'Why bl-bloody not?' echoed Jacob.

'Fuck off, Jacob.'

'I'll tell Rose you said that. She'll hate you for it.'

'No, she won't.'

'She will, Webster, she will. Give me a cigarette and I won't tell her.'

'If I did that she really would hate me.'

'Give me one anyway. I won't say that you did.'

Webster took one from the pack and passed it to Jacob. 'Don't you fli-flippin' tell her, though.'

'Don't fli-flippin' worry, Webster, I won't.'

A few miles away in Woodstock, a room in a small guest-house near the gate to Blenheim Palace had been booked for two nights, a short honeymoon fitted in around the needs of the farm. Norman and Vera spent the night in intimate celibacy, only too aware of the promise to Alfred that Norman had made. Norman woke early and turned on his side and watched Vera as she slept, the little twitching around her eyes as she dreamed. She woke later to find him sitting in the chair by the window, looking out over the parkland and the expanse of the lake and the burnished woods beyond, studying the sheep as they grazed up the slopes.

He heard her turn, then her soft voice.

'What are you doing over there, Norman?'

'Thinking about my dogs.'

'Come back to bed for a while.'

They spent the morning in the Blenheim estate grounds and the afternoon in the shops and tea-rooms clustered in the streets either side of the town hall, and by evening they were both longing to get back to Chipping Norton where the rest of their lives awaited them. When they arrived back at the farm the next day, they found a vase of flowers and a loaf of fresh bread on the kitchen table in their cottage.

'That armchair will have to go,' said Vera when she saw the tatty wingback.

'But it's my favourite. And I haven't got another.'

'It's covered in pigeon business,' said Vera firmly. 'I'll ask father to bring one down later.'

They left their overnight bags in the bedroom and Norman showed her the space he had cleared in the bathroom for her bottles and soaps and then they sat in the kitchen and grinned at each other. The dogs saw the open door and hurtled in from the yard, Mr and Mrs Brailes followed, and before long the conversation had turned to the requirements of the day and the jobs that would need attending to before evening, and by the time Brailes was flipping the tops off bottles of beer in the kitchen that evening, Vera's things had been brought down from the house up the hill and she had been absorbed into the life of the farm.

***

A fortnight later a letter arrived for Norman, the address scrawled in a hand unaccustomed to significant use of a pen.

'It's Webster,' he said. 'He wants to come back.'

He passed the letter to Vera.

'Rose!' she said. 'I knew she had her eye on him.'

'Should he come?'

'If he's coming for the job, then yes. If it's for Rose, then I wouldn't advise it.'

'But he doesn't have anywhere else to go. I'll go and speak to Brailes.'

Webster was back within a week and he moved into the cottage again next to Norman and Vera.

'You'll have to share it with Pete the pig-man now, I'm afraid,' said Norman.

'Pete the pig-man?' said Webster.

'We took him on two weeks ago but I've told Brailes to get rid. He's good for nothing, lazy as a toad. You'll meet him soon enough.'

'So this is your room now?' said Pete that evening, standing with Webster in the box-room at the back. 'Looks like you've messed it up already, clothes all over the place.'

'They're my clothes,' said Webster. 'I can put them where I want, can't I?'

'Yes, but I like my cottage to look nice,' said Pete. 'I prefer it that way.'

'Is that right?' said Webster.

'I do hope you'll like it here, Webster.'

'Don't worry, I will, I've been here before.'

'So why did you leave, then? It's a right cushy number, this. That fool Norman does all the work and Brailes doesn't give a sod any more, he's right over the hill and coming down the other side. I reckon the land-owner's going to be after a change of manager soon, someone a bit more youthful. Reckon I could be in there if I play my cards right, know what I mean?'

He winked at Webster, a clumsy movement of the eye.

'Know what I mean?'

Another wink.

'Got something in your eye, Pete?'

A pause.

'Why do they call you Pete the pig-man anyway?'

'Because I look like a bloody pig, don't I? Not my fault.'

'Very true,' said Webster. 'And no, I suppose it's not your fault.'

The following day Norman and Webster left Pete the pig-man to muck out the cow-sheds while they went to set traps for the pheasants in the top wood with Jacob trailing along behind, asking endless questions and hanging on Norman's every word, tipping the small gems of knowledge around in his head as he walked, counting the facts he had learned that day, repeating them internally, silently imitating Norman's verbal mannerisms so that the boy's lips moved as he walked.

'Talking to yourself again, are you, Jacob?' said Webster.

'No, Webster. I'm just thinking,' he said. 'You should try it some time.'

And Norman laughed and Jacob smiled at the man and felt the sunlight on his face and the warm glow of having made Norman happy again and it occurred to him that he probably loved Norman, like a brother, or a father, or something in between. Whatever it was, it did not matter, it was there, that was all.

When they came back at lunchtime they found Vera speechless in tears in Brailes' sitting room. The pig-man and Brailes were in the kitchen, poised on opposite chairs.

'What's going on here, then?' said Norman.

'This bloody bugger's been bothering Vera,' said Brailes in the quiet steady voice of fury. 'Put his foot in the door and wasn't taking no for an answer until she whacked him in the bollocks with a rolling pin.'

'Outside,' said Norman and he felt something lurch up in his chest, then a heavy rush through his arms and a noise in his head, the kind of thing you might hear in a barn.

The pig-man followed Norman out as he marched across the yard. Jacob hurried after them and caught up with Norman and said his name, a tug on the sleeve, a distraction. But Norman could not see the boy who shadowed him now – this would be man's business, no room for boys, no room for kindness now. He stopped by the stone trough in the centre of the yard and turned and looked at the pig-man, this shape that had threatened the only thing that had ever been his own, and he saw the pig-man at the end of a long tunnel now, his mouth somehow moving without making a sound, and Norman realised that the words were consumed by a roaring in his head. He thrust out his massive hands and seized the pig-man by the neck and rammed his head down into the water so hard that the top of the man's skull struck the stone base of the trough and Norman held it there for several seconds as the water tinged red, then he hauled it up and out and down again and the water became redder, then up and out and down again, another smack of red against the stone, and then Norman heard a noise to one side, a bellow from Brailes who was pulling at his arm, and the roar in his head suddenly snapped away into silence and the noise that Norman himself was making hammered around in his skull and he finally let go and the pig-man fell to his knees and flung back his head and coughed up the water and muck that had entered his lungs.

'Are you trying to flippin' kill me?' he screamed as the blood streamed down his face.

'Clear your things out of the cottage and sod off,' said Norman quietly, suddenly tired of the noise. 'If you're still in there in fifteen minutes, I'm coming in after you.'

Then he turned and saw Vera beside him now, tugging at his arm, and the look on her face, something like horror, something like fear, and he whispered an apology and was about to say 'I did it for you,' but he thought better of it and he knew deep down he had done it for someone else, for the lost little boy that he had once been, strapped to a plough, cast out in the fields, the lost little boy that Vera had saved.

Ten minutes later, the pig-man was half-way up the lane, the few things he owned in the bag in his hand, and Norman's lost little boy stepped back inside himself, hid himself away again inside the man he had become.

That night Webster moved back into his old room and Vera stripped the bed in rubber gloves and laid out fresh clean sheets for him to lie on, perhaps Rose too.

***

Rose passed Vera a cup of tea and a cracker topped with a wedge of hard ewe's cheese. The cheese crumbled as she bit into it and the dog snapped up the unintended offering as it touched the ground.

'Oh, Dickie, do learn some manners,' said Rose, toeing away the little terrier with the tip of her shoe. The dog sat on its haunches and quivered. Rose sat on the bench next to Vera and they looked down the slope of the garden and across the valley to the Worcester Road. Across the lane to their right they could hear Alfred sorting out the pigs, considering which of his prime ministers would be next for the outhouse beam.

'So then, Rose, what's the story with Webster?' asked Vera.

'Webster?' said Rose.

'Yes,' said Vera, raising an eyebrow. 'Don't you want to tell me?'

'It sounds like you know already.'

'Not the juicy details.'

'Well, he's quite nice, isn't he?'

'I think so. Norman thinks so too.'

'Yes, very sweet. But …'

'But what? Won't you see him again?' asked Vera.

'Maybe.'

'I think you might.'

'Meaning?'

'He's back at the farm.'

'What?!' Rose bit sharply into her cracker and the dog scavenged about again at her feet. 'Oh Dickie, you little beast!'

'Yes, really. Won't you see him?'

'Yes, but it's complicated. Alan's keen as well.'

'Alan? Who's Alan? I didn't know about him.'

'Recent news. Hadn't had a chance to tell you.'

'Oh dear.'

'What a pickle. What should I do?'

'Come by and see him. Why not this Sunday? I'll make lunch for the four of us.'

'I'll think about it.'

'He wants to see you.'

'I bet he does. He didn't come back just for me, did he?'

'I think you've probably been in his thoughts.'

Sunday lunch was served in the kitchen at Norman and Vera's. Rose talked continually, her back to the fire, warming her up, and Webster watched the orange glow intensify around her darkening silhouette as the autumn dusk crept across the fields and the room slipped into darkness. Norman lit a candle and they finished the meal with an apple apiece, and then it was time for Rose to go home.

'I'd better get out and check the sheep,' said Norman.

'I'll do the dishes,' said Vera.

'I guess you'd better walk me home, then, Webster,' said Rose.

'I can't invite you in,' she said at the top of her road. 'My grandmother's a liberal type, but she has her limits.'

She left him at the gate with a kiss on the cheek.

'See you soon,' she said, and Webster went back home and slept until Norman shook him awake for work at dawn.

'She won't be any good for you,' Norman finally said after ruminating on the thought for most of the morning. 'Rose, that is.'

'What do you mean?'

'She's not the constant type. It won't last, it won't do you any good.'

'Let's wait and see.'

'You can't change her, Webster, no one will. She's set in her ways like that. It won't come to any good, no good at all.'

'She's still better than anything I've had before.'

'She'll take your heart and split it in two, that's all. I've seen her do it before. She's a nice enough lass, but one fella's never enough. You'll go in one end and come out the other, like wheat through a shredder, and someone else will have to put you together again.'

'I'm in pieces already, Norman. I'm starting right down at the bottom anyway.'

'But you've got this place,' said Norman.

He swung his arm around in a panoramic arc before the fields in front of him where the cows stood with their noses to the sweet green grass and a pheasant rang out its staccato call from somewhere down in the copse by the pond and an automobile rumbled along the top road towards Kingham.

'And you've got me,' he said. 'I'll see you right, Webster, don't you worry about that. Old Brailes will be retiring soon and he's got me lined up to take this place over. The landowner's agreed, it's just a matter of time, Vera and me will be in the farmhouse and you can take over cottage number one, no problem at all, you'll be my main man.'

Webster nodded. 'That sounds too good to be true, Norman. I might just take you up on that.'

They ate their lunch out in the fields, cheese sandwiches in wedges so thick they could barely get their lips around them, and when they reached the yard again at the end of the day Rose and Vera were chatting either side of the cottage door.

'Look who it is,' said Rose, smiling at Webster. 'Been out milking the sheep?'

'Don't be daft,' said Webster. 'You can help me milk the cows tomorrow though, if you like.'

The next morning Webster squatted on a three-legged stool, squirting milk in thin streams into the galvanized metal pail between his knees. He sensed Rose behind him before he saw her. She squatted down beside him.

'Let's have a go,' she said.

She pushed and pulled the teat and the milk squirted into the pail and then Webster took over again and Rose followed him from cow to cow and when the last one was done she took Webster's hand in hers and raised it to her face and breathed in the rich scent of warm milk and cows' udders that he wore like an invisible farmer's glove. She kissed his hand and squeezed it in hers and then pulled him towards her and kissed him hard on the mouth, a long lingering kiss as the cattle steamed in the cold air around them.

'Let's go up to the barn, Webster.'

'I can't, Rose. Norman will be looking for me soon. The work's never done and he never stops and I can't leave him to do it on his own.'

'Brailes will help him.'

'Brailes is old. He can't do much heavy work now.'

'Come on Webster. I won't keep you all day ...'

'Really, I can't.'

'Tonight then?'

'I'll come and get you. You can't walk here in the dark.'

'Meet me at the top of my road at seven.'

'Yes, Rose. Yes,' he said, and she was gone, out of sight between the steaming cows.

That night, they walked down to Pool Meadow and the water was still and dark and cold and the coots called to each other in the night, and Rose and Webster talked until the cold drove them back into town and suddenly it was too late to continue on down to Elm Tree Farm and instead they stood and spoke in whispers at her gate until she saw the light in the front room go off and she kissed him goodnight and slipped inside before her grandmother retired for the night.

The next time they met they went straight to Elm Tree Farm and beneath the heavy quilt in Webster's room they reacquainted each other with their bodies, this time without a veil of alcohol to deaden their memories, and when Webster lay alone in bed later that night his thoughts returned to Norman's words and he knew that it was already too late, that he had stepped off the cliff and was falling and the only thing that lay between him and the valley bottom was the very thing that had compelled him to hurl himself off the cliff in the first place, and he no longer knew if she was still up on top or waiting to catch him down below, and he would not find out for sure until he hit the ground or his fall was arrested by gravity turning against itself and holding him in the air forever.

But gravity can only be what gravity is, and Webster's fall could not be slowed and the ground suddenly rushed up to meet him, as the ground rushes up in the end at those falling beneath parachutes spun only of hope, falling from planes struck up high in an exploding sky. And when Webster struck the ground all went black.

'I'm sorry, Webster. That's just the way it is. I told you from the start, that's the way I am. Wild Rose. I told you, remember, I can't be tamed. I told you, didn't I?'

'Yes, you told me.'

'I was honest with you, Webster. You're not the one and you never will be.'

'Yes, Rose. You were honest with me. I know.'

Within a month, Webster was gone.

'What will you do?' Norman had asked him.

'I'm joining the Army.'

'What the bloody hell for?'

'It'll keep me out of trouble, and there'll be plenty to do. There's going to be a war again soon, isn't there? It's obvious, he's not going to stop is he, that Hitler bloke?'

'For God's sake, Webster, you don't have to do that. It's because of Rose, isn't it?'

'That's a part of it.'

'That's all of it.'

'Don't blame her, Norman, it's not her fault. She's a good girl, really. Really she is.'

By Easter, Brailes had gone too, retired to a new semi-detached house along the Burford Road where he spent his days watching the sparrows clustering in the forsythia at the end of his small garden and wondering where the last fifty years had gone.

Norman and Vera moved into the farmhouse and Norman recruited a pair of keen young farmhands to help around the place and they occupied cottages numbers one and two, and Jacob came down regularly to spend time with Norman, and spring turned to summer and summer turned to autumn, life slipping by on rails just like it had before.

SEPTEMBER 1939

The brakes gripped the wheels, the train lurched and stopped, the doors crashed open as dark thunderclouds rumbled overhead, and the hum of several hundred voices floated over the station roof and the up the hill to where Alfred Arbuckle was munching swiftly through an apple he had plucked from a tree in his orchard.

'They've arrived,' he yelled through the open door, and Elizabeth stuck her head out of the dormer window high above.

'Gosh, it's the longest train I've ever seen,' she said. 'There must be a whole army of them.'

'Yes, more than yesterday, more than a thousand they say,' replied Alfred.

'Poor little blighters. I wonder what ours will be like.'

'He'll be fine. He'll love it out here in the countryside, away from that filthy city.' Alfred had been to London only once and had hastened back, swearing never to return. 'I bet he's never even seen a pig before.'

Down at the station, in the shadow of the tweed mill, children squabbled about on the platform, others stood in tight solemn little sibling groups, and the Red Cross nurses moved among them like big-bosomed galleons in a restless sea. The evacuees were led up the hill into town clutching their gas masks in small cardboard boxes, and at the cinema they were passed through the bureaucratic machine that sent them away in little groups behind a nurse with a bar of chocolate in their pocket and a bundle of food under their arm. Billy Bampton hurried along in the wake of his brother and sisters as they were led out of town along West Street.

'Come on Billy, you little tosser!' called his brother Bobby. 'Catch up, will you?'

'Sod off Bobby!' yelled Billy and he thrust his hands in his pockets and scowled at the passersby.

'Yes, sod off Bobby,' said their older sister, Helen. 'You're always picking on him.'

Their other sister, Sarah, hurried back, grabbed Billy by the arm and pulled him along as he glowered at her.

'I'm only trying to help you, you little bleeder,' she muttered under her breath as they caught up with the others.

Alfred and Elizabeth heard the little group of evacuees before they saw them, squabbling and bickering their way down the dirt track towards the house.

'Morning, Mr Arbuckle, Mrs Arbuckle,' said the nurse.

'Morning Mary,' said Elizabeth. 'Which one of these little darlings is ours?'

'Which *one?*' said the nurse.

'Yes, we put ourselves down for one. A boy, we said.'

'I'm sorry,' said the nurse. 'There must have been a misunderstanding. These ones come as a job-lot, four for the price of one.'

She scratched her brow and made a pained sooner-you-than-me expression.

'Well we haven't got room for four,' said Alfred.

The four of them stood clustered around the nurse.

'We're only little, mister,' said Billy. 'We won't take up much room.'

'Shut up, Billy,' said Bobby.

'How old are you, son?' asked Alfred.

'Twelve,' said Billy. He jerked his thumb at Bobby. 'He's fourteen but he acts like a ten-year-old.'

'And you two girls?' said Elizabeth.

'They're sixteen,' said the nurse.

'What, both of them?'

'Twins,' said the nurse. 'Can't you tell?'

'We can't be separated, mister,' said Billy. 'We told our mum and dad we'd look out for each other.'

'I'll go and see Vera and Norman,' said Alfred. 'I'll be back shortly.'

'Please be as quick as you can, Mr Arbuckle,' said the nurse. 'I have to get back to collect another lot.'

Elizabeth sat the four of them down on the settee and brought each of them a glass of barley water and a biscuit.

'I'm flipping starving,' said Bobby.

'Eat some of your chocolate, then,' said Billy.

'Eaten it already.'

'Pig.'

'Did you see those fat pigs outside?' said Sarah.

'Stink like pigs,' said Billy.

'Course they stink like pigs,' said Bobby. 'They're bleedin' pigs, aren't they?'

'Sod off, Bobby!'

Elizabeth stood out of sight in the kitchen and exchanged raised eyebrows with the nurse as they listened to this vaguely familiar form of conversation, reminding Elizabeth of Jacob and William at the Bampton boys' age. She came in and sat opposite the children.

'Now listen,' she said. 'This is my house, and if any of you are going to stay here you'll have to learn to behave a lot better than you're behaving at the moment.'

'Sorry, miss,' said Billy. 'It's Bobby, he's always like this.'

Bobby bit his lip and regarded Billy with unbrotherly eyes while the twins attempted to recover the situation by asking Elizabeth about the town and the neighbours and what she thought would become of them if the war really did progress as expected and the Germans sent airmen to drop their bombs on London.

Then Alfred and Norman walked in, and Jacob too, covered in dirt from the fields where he had been helping Norman with the weekend jobs.

'Let's have a look at you,' said Norman, sizing up the newcomers. 'All right, then,' he said after a moment's thought. 'Vera and I will take the boys. If that's all right with you, nurse?'

'Thank you, Norman,' she said.

'But we promised we'd stay together,' said Helen.

'It's for the best, love,' said the nurse. 'You two boys will be fine with Norman. His farm's just a short walk down the road so you can all see each other every day. And you'll be at the same school during the week anyway.'

'Are these dogs yours, mister?' asked Bobby.

Norman nodded.

'Come on then, Billy,' said Bobby, getting to his feet. 'I like the sound of living on a farm.'

Billy stood up and Norman took their suitcases and the others watched them set off up the lane towards Elm Tree Farm.

Jacob smiled at Helen and Sarah.

'Do you want to come and see my birds?' he said. 'They're just round the back, in the out-house.'

'What kind of birds?' said Helen.

'Pigeons. Half a dozen.'

'Ugh,' said Sarah.

'What's wrong with pigeons?' said Jacob.

'Dirty things,' she said, looking Jacob up and down, her eyes lingering upon the filthy state of his trousers.

'Pigeons aren't dirty,' he said. 'As a matter of fact, they're one of the cleanest of British birds. Haven't you ever seen them preening?'

'Seen them what?'

'Preening,' he said. 'Like this ...' and Helen laughed at his imitation of a cooing, nuzzling bird.

'I think I'd like to see them,' said Helen, smiling at Jacob, and he took her round to the out-house to show her what was inside

Down at Elm Tree Farm, Vera was waiting at the gate, peering up the hill as Norman and the boys came down, two small figures traipsing along in their jackets and their shorts either side of the massive man in whose hands their toy-sized suitcases appeared entirely incapable of transporting the contents of their lives from West Ham to Chipping Norton. Vera held a bundle of her own in her arms, Daphne Miller, born two years earlier, two years after the wedding, just as Norman had promised Alfred. Daphne began to cry, then settled, and as Vera laid her down in her cot in their bedroom overlooking the fields at the back, Norman showed Billy and Bobby up the next flight of stairs to the top room beneath the eaves.

'What do you think?' asked Norman. 'All right?'

'Is this all for us, mister?' asked Bobby. 'The whole room?'

'The whole room.'

'Flipping 'eck, Billy,' said Bobby, looking around the room and then out of the window at the front and across the yard towards the pond and the copse beyond.

'Are there fish in there, mister, in that pond?'

'There are a few, but you'll do well to catch them. They're old and wise, and very, very big.'

'You're fucking joking!'

Billy stared at his brother. 'Watch your mouth, Bobby, we're not at home now.'

'Listen lads,' said Norman. 'There's a rule on this farm about swearing, has been as long as I've been here and for a long time before that too. The old bloke who ran this place before me would only ever permit two swearwords within his earshot. Bloody and bugger. They both begin with B, so they'll be easy enough for you to remember.'

'Bloody and bugger,' said Billy. 'Like Billy and Bobby.'

'Yes,' said Norman, smiling. 'Just like Billy and Bobby.'

'So, mister,' said Billy. 'Bugger me! That's all right then? That's allowed?'

'Yes, that's all right.'

'Bloody hell,' said Bobby, and they both laughed.

'It's not so bad out here in the country,' said Billy.

'Unpack your bags, lads. And keep your voices down, the baby's asleep. You can put your clothes in that chest, and bring your shoes downstairs – they stay in the hall. Be downstairs in ten minutes, I want to show you round the farm.'

As Norman's heavy footsteps descended the stairs, he could hear the boys' voices as they rushed about the room.

'Fuck me, this place is all right,' said one.

'Watch your bloody language, Billy.'

'Bugger off you stupid … bugger.'

'Bugger you too.'

'Look at all those fucking cows.'

'Where?'

'In that field.'

'Oh, yes. They're quite small, aren't they?'

'That's because they're a long way off, you idiot.'

'Bugger off, you bugger.'

Then the sound of them falling about laughing and unpacking their bags, hurling drawers open and bickering over who would have the top one and on which side of the large shared bed each of them would sleep, and all the while trying out in ever louder tones various combinations of the authorised expletives. Down in the hall, Vera looked at Norman and cast her eyebrows towards the sky as the racket the boys were making set Daphne off in her cot, her cries lifting slowly up into a wail like the slow steady rise of an air-raid siren.

'Cut them a bit of slack, Vera,' said Norman. 'They've been through a lot, the poor little lads.'

Norman took them around the farm, first through the yard and the barns and round the pond, then up across the fields and through the woods and down into the shaded valley where the stream ran and the hares scuffed up the grass as they writhed in their traps, then up the far slope and around the main wood and home again along the perimeter fence that ran closest to the Churchill Road. They got back to the farm late for tea and worn out from hours on their feet in the fields.

'Tired, boys?'

'Bloody knackered, miss,' said Billy.

'Shoes off, lads,' said Norman. 'They stay in the hall.'

The next morning, when they came downstairs after a night of wakefulness beneath the creaking beams, they found their shoes in the hall, shone to a mirror shine by Norman during the night.

Up the hill at Mill View Cottage, Jacob and William left together to walk into town to get the newspaper for Alfred.

'What do you think of those two, then?' asked Jacob as they walked. 'Helen and Sarah – all right, aren't they?'

'Not bad. Can't tell them apart, can you?'

'Helen's the prettier one,' said Jacob. 'She's got that little mole on her top lip, just here.'

He poked himself in the approximate position of Helen's distinguishing feature.

'I prefer the other one,' said William unconvincingly.

'That's all right, then.'

'Anyway,' said William. 'Rose is going to be the girl for you, isn't she?'

Jacob felt his cheeks redden. 'Rose?'

'Yes, dear brother, Rose. She's always talking about you. Vera told me. And the way she looks at you, haven't you noticed that, with her mouth nearly hanging open?'

'Shut up, you clot. She's old enough to be my mum.'

'She's only twenty-four.'

'And I'm only sixteen.'

'Don't let that stop you, Jacob, it wouldn't me. And anyway, when you're old and grey, what difference will a few years make?'

When they got home with the paper they were still debating the relative merits of Helen and Sarah, daring each other to attempt increasingly ludicrous means of familiarisation. They pushed noisily in through the door.

'Shut your mouths and shut the door!' said Alfred, slumped in his armchair with a hand to his brow, Elizabeth next to Vera and Helen and Sarah on the sofa, and Norman leaning against the frame of the kitchen door, their faces all hung with silence. As Jacob and William cut their noise they heard the radio in the background, Neville Chamberlain's solemn dry voice already delivering dread words.

'... *speaking to you from the Cabinet Room at 10 Downing Street. This morning the British Ambassador in Berlin handed the German Government a final note stating that unless we heard from them by eleven o'clock that they were prepared at once to withdraw their troops from Poland a state of war would exist between us. I have to tell you now that no such undertaking has been received, and that consequently this country is at war with Germany ...*'

Alfred said something unintelligible and Vera twisted her handkerchief around her fingers and bit her lip and when Jacob looked at Elizabeth he saw her gaze flitting between him and his brother.

'... *what a bitter blow it is to me that all my long struggle to win peace has failed ... to the very last it would have been quite possible to have arranged a peaceful and honourable settlement between Germany and Poland. But Hitler would not have it ...*'

When Jacob looked at Norman, Norman was looking at him too, unnerving him with his stare.

'... *we have a clear conscience. We have done all that any country could do to establish peace, but a situation in which no word given by Germany's ruler could be trusted and no people or country could feel themselves safe had become intolerable. And now that we have resolved to finish it, I know that you will all play your part with calmness and courage.*'

And then silence, followed by a heavy animal sigh as Alfred looked at his sons, eighteen and sixteen, and Elizabeth stood up and hurried out of the room and into the garden with her hand at her mouth, gasping for air.

'Here we go again,' said Alfred. 'Here we bloody go again.'

That afternoon, air raid sirens brought Jacob and William out into the street to see what German planes really looked like and whether they would be dropping high explosive or poison gas or both, but it was a false alarm and the planes did not come and the sirens wailed down into silence and Jacob found himself wondering if this was what modern war would be like.

That autumn, the Durham Light Infantry arrived, billeted near the town prior to their departure for France. Jacob loved hearing them talk as he passed them in the street, like living in a town with a thousand men like Norman, and Norman became accustomed to hearing again the voices of his native north-east, uninvited ghosts from the locked room of his past, brightening the dead embers of a mother who had left him for Newcastle and a father who had left him temporarily at birth and again several years later under the wheels of a bus.

The snow came early and by Christmas the fields were silent and white and a canopy of cloud kept the world at bay. Occasionally a plane passed overhead in the murk, droning away unseen into the distance until the hum of silence overcame the receding burr of the engines. The Bampton children were due in London for Christmas but the snow put paid to that, and instead they woke on Christmas morning still waiting for events in Europe to justify their semi-orphaned status. Norman and Vera set off for the Arbuckles' with Billy and Bobby, and Daphne wrapped up in a bundle in Vera's arms. The weather was too severe for the ageing Trojan, so Norman prepared the pony and trap and the cartwheels cut deep furrows in the snow as the horse pulled them away up the hill. At Mill View Cottage, Alfred fed the pigs and set the fireplace ablaze. The Edwardian glasses etched with leaves were taken down and as they all gathered before lunch a modest collection of presents was passed around in the half-light of the sitting room. By one o'clock the dining room table lay surrounded by the hungry horde, the fat turkey awaiting its fate behind the defensive ranks of potatoes and sprouts and a moat of gravy. Rose had been invited too and she sat opposite Jacob and he saw her peering into him as he looked over the rim of his glass. She looked slowly away, then quickly back again.

Helen was saying something about Jacob's pigeons.

'... always preening themselves, you know,' she was saying. 'Like this ...' and she rubbed her chin against her shoulder and looked at Jacob and giggled and he smiled and then he looked at Rose. She was watching him still, testing his reaction to Helen's display.

'Cleanest of all the birds in England,' Helen was saying now, and she smiled knowingly and Billy turned and made a vomiting gesture at his brother.

'Of course they're not, don't be so ridiculous,' said Rose.

Her sudden interjection caused Helen to let a tower of peas tumble from her fork and they scattered across the tablecloth, leaving embarrassing slicks of gravy in their wake.

'I beg your pardon?' said Helen, looking up suddenly from the little pulses of chaos she had caused.

'I said don't be ridiculous. Pigeons are certainly not the cleanest of birds. Who on earth told you that utter nonsense?'

'Jacob did,' said Helen smugly, sensing the wound.

'Well he was pulling your leg, dear girl. And you fell for it hook, line and sinker. Still, it's hardly your fault, is it? If you were never properly educated, I mean.'

Helen looked away, and saw again the mess she had made around her plate and Jacob looked at her and noticed that she looked as if she might cry. Then he looked at Rose and she smiled at him and winked. She had done it again, he thought, and he knew she always would.

When the hungry horde were done, the turkey sat bare-boned and dismembered on its platter and Norman chucked the scraps outside for the dogs, and everyone turned their attention to the pudding that Elizabeth brought in on a plate lit with flame.

'I guess France will be next,' said Alfred to Norman, as he tipped a generous helping of brandy sauce onto his plate and transferred a towering spoonful of pudding to his mouth. He chewed and swallowed noisily and Elizabeth frowned. 'And then it will be us.'

'There's not a lot to stop them,' said Norman.

'They'll take William, and Jacob too before long,' said Alfred in a low voice. 'Just you wait. They're just the right age for all this carry on, William out of school now and Jacob leaving soon. Jacob's down for university, you know, but they'll have him away too, you'll see. Damn them all.'

After lunch, William and Jacob sat in the window-seat and compared the books they had received that morning, William's a guide to basic tractor maintenance to augment the knowledge he was acquiring in his apprenticeship at the garage in town, and Jacob's a volume on the history of military aviation, including a hastily-written chapter on modern German aircraft and how to identify them – stark black silhouettes drawn to scale, top, bottom and lateral views of the aircraft that everyone feared would soon become all too familiar in the skies over England.

'You'd better get used to those shapes if you're going to be a pilot,' said William.

'I know them all already,' said Jacob.

'Their planes aren't as good as ours, are they?'

'They're better.'

'How are we going to stop them, then?'

'We've got better pilots. And I'm going to be one of them.'

'You'll have to wait a bit, you're not even seventeen. They won't take you yet.'

'We'll see about that. I'm not joining the bloody Army, that's for sure, and that's where I'll end up if I don't volunteer first.'

'I'm going for the tank corps.'

'Tanks? William, are you mad? Riding round in a death-trap?'

'A plane would be worse. At least I'll have my feet on the ground. And they can't shoot you in a tank, can they? Anyway, I always wanted to be a driver. It can't be that different from driving a tractor, can it?'

When the snow had melted and the post-office vans made their way up again from Oxford, a Christmas card arrived from Webster, a soldier now in the Army in France.

'We've been in France since the autumn,' read Jacob, looking up at Rose as he held Webster's card in his hand. 'We don't know when, but we know they will come, it's just a matter of time. I'll write again soon, but if the fighting starts first, remember me when you read of it.'

'Poor Webster,' said Rose. 'What did he go and join the bloody Army for?'

'I think it might have been on account of you.'

'Yes, that's what I feared.'

1940

Early in the New Year, Jacob and Norman and William walked into town to watch as King George VI inspected the Durham Light Infantry in the market square in the snow, a stray dog shadowing the king as he stooped back and forth along the lines of shivering men in their greatcoats. Shortly after, the shivering troops were gone, to wait for Hitler's men in France. The Bamptons soon followed, returned to their family in a London not yet significantly battered by bombs. Norman and Jacob walked them down to the station and the train pulled away and all they could see were four small hands waving from the window and then the train went round the bend and they were gone. That night, the top room of the farm was eerily quiet and just occasionally when they were sitting downstairs in front of the range, Norman and Vera thought they heard the boys' footsteps and their fraternal cursing, but it was just the wind in the chimney and the knocking of the pipes.

In February a recruiting stand appeared at the Town Hall to lure the local youths, and Jacob and William stood in line. William pushed himself to the front, past his eager brother.

'How old are you, son?'

'Eighteen,' said William.

'Right, you'll do. Sign here. And you?'

'Nearly seventeen,' said Jacob.

'Come back when you're older.'

'But I want to join up now.'

'I'm afraid you can't. Come back when you're older.'

Jacob was in the garden later that day when angry voices reached him from the house. The front door slammed and William marched down the path towards him.

'What's wrong, William?'

'It's father. He's bloody furious with me.'

'For signing up?'

William nodded.

'They'll get us all sooner or later anyway,' said Jacob. 'And we've got to do our bit.'

That night at dinner Alfred barely said a word. He passed round the food and exchanged occasional glances with Elizabeth, and every now and then he looked hard at William and shook his head and shovelled another forkful of vegetables into his mouth.

'Elizabeth, these carrots are burnt nearly black.'

'They're still carrots. Eat them up.'

Alfred stood up and went into the living room and sat in the armchair by the hearth and stared at the flames and when he spoke only Elizabeth, who was nearest the door, could make out his words.

'I've already lost three sons to fire,' he said. 'I don't want to lose the only two I have left.'

'What's he saying, mother?' asked Jacob.

'Nothing, dear, eat your dinner. It's been a long day.'

***

William left for basic training and at Easter there were empty places around the table. Little Daphne had sickened with a spring cold, so Norman and Vera stayed with her at the farm and at Mill View Cottage only Alfred and Elizabeth and Jacob sat down to eat. Norman came up later to collect a cut of pork from the carcass Alfred had hung from the out-house beam.

'What's this one called, then?' asked Norman.

'Guderian.'

'Who?'

'General Guderian. Panzer Corps. No point killing off our own any more, is there? Might as well start on the Germans.'

'But not Hitler yet?'

'No, I'm saving him up for Christmas.'

Norman looked at the grizzled snout, the blood still dripping from the dead nose onto the earth floor.

'You'll be eating a lot of pork before this war is over,' Norman said.

'I should say I will. Let's hope it's not like the last one. I only spent six months in the trenches but it was more than enough for a lifetime.'

That evening a man from the Kingham Local Defence Volunteers approached Alfred and Norman and Jacob in the pub.

'Signing up, are we, lads? For the Home Guard, I mean.'

Norman looked him up and down. 'What are you going to kill the storm-troopers with, old man? Cattle prods and spades?'

'That's not the attitude, now is it?' said the man. 'You could be in the real army, a strong young chap your age.'

'Afraid not,' said Norman. 'Reserved occupation, you see, feeding the nation, I am. No time for killing my fellow man. It's all I can manage to keep the farm ticking over, now my labourers have all gone to France.'

'And I did my killing in the Great War,' said Alfred. 'If they come, I'll fight them all right, but I'm not going to waste my bloody time preparing for it.'

'And this young chap here?' asked the man, pointing at Jacob. 'Which of the Forces will you be volunteering for?'

Alfred was suddenly up on his feet and in the man's face.

'None of them if I've got anything to do with it! And he's still too young, so sod off and mind your own business. Bloody do-gooder!'

The man hurried off to talk to a more amenable group.

At home, Jacob helped Alfred hang the black-out curtains and they painted the window panes black around the edges just to be sure, and when he left the house to go and help Norman and Vera to black out the farm, Jacob switched the hall-light off before opening the door and the only light to guide him down the track was the sparking of his match and the glow of the cigarette that he could not allow himself to be seen with at home.

'Been smoking again, Jacob?' said Norman when he leaned over him as they stretched the black tape around the window frame. 'Bad for your health, that, you know.'

'It's hardly going to kill me, is it, the odd puff or two? But don't tell Vera. If father finds out, it really will be bad for me.'

The air-raid sirens wailed infrequently and at Mill View Cottage, without a cellar, Elizabeth tugged at the edges of the black-out curtains and huddled down beneath the kitchen table with Alfred and Jacob as their dinner went cold in the dark, and once, in early May, a lone German bomber did pass overhead and a single bomb fell with a distant crump in a field in the valley.

By day the sky throbbed with the roar of aircraft engines as the Wellington bombers took off on training flights from Moreton-in-Marsh, and at dusk the sky shook as the planes took off again and climbed over Chipping Norton on their way to Germany. Half-way through the night the inbound planes returned in loose gaggles of ones and twos, long intervals between them, their engines whining down across the rooftops as the pilots dropped the airspeed and searched for the gooseneck flares of the airfield, and sometimes on misty nights, when visibility was poor, the planes would pass so low overhead that the windows shook and Jacob would jump from his bed and rush to the window and glimpse a dark shape passing quickly in and out of sight. And once, the voice of an overflying plane was followed by the louder roar of an explosion as it dipped too low and clipped the trees on the brow of a hill and disintegrated in a great eruption of flame and a pall of smoke merged with the mist, nothing left to see, when Jacob went up there the next morning, but a pile of blackened wreckage and a mess in the seats where the crew had been.

***

Towards the end of April, as the Local Defence Volunteers practised their Home Guard drills in the market square outside, Jacob and Vera and Rose sat at a table in the café.

'Webster's still in France, isn't he?' said Jacob, pointing to an article on the front page of the paper. 'Germans mass on border! France and Belgium on guard,' he read.

Rose shifted in her seat and took another sip of her tea.

'That's right,' said Vera. 'Norman got a letter last month. Dug in good and proper, by all accounts.'

In early June, Jacob walked into town to find the pavements strewn with battle-weary remnants of a multitude of regiments, stretched out asleep in the sun as small boys approached them with requests for French chocolate and coins or snatches of what had really befallen them in France. Soon after, Webster arrived for a short spell of leave. With no home to go to, he came to Elm Tree Farm and stayed in the room at the top of the house and divided his days between the fields and the pub, trying to forget about Dunkirk and what he had seen, and the evenings in the kitchen with Norman and Vera, telling them about it all over again, digging up memories he had put in the earth and buried.

Webster went up to see Alfred and Elizabeth, and Jacob took him across the lane to Rose's house.

'Come on, Webster,' said Jacob. 'She'll be pleased to see you.'

'Are you sure?' said Webster.

'Of course.'

Jacob was already across the lane and shouting over the wall towards Rose's window.

'Webster!' she cried, as she stuck her head outside.

She rushed out of the door and opened the gate and the three of them sat on the bench at the front of the house and talked until the swallows were swooping around the telegraph wires in the dusk. Then Jacob and Rose walked Webster back to the farm and when he had gone inside and they were returning back up the hill, Rose slipped her hand into Jacob's and she held it tight for a moment and then she let it go. They paused in the middle of the lane and she coaxed a lock of hair from where it had fallen across his eyes, the tentative easing back of a black-out curtain, and the light behind the curtain blinked at her in the night. She kissed him on the forehead.

'How old are you now, Jacob?'

'Seventeen, you know that. Too young for you.'

'If you're old enough for war, you're old enough for love.'

'I'm not at war yet.'

'But you soon will be, the way you go on. You don't have to go, you know. Not yet.'

'It's too late for that. There was a recruiting stand in town again last week ...'

'Yes, I saw it,' she said. 'The bastards are always here.'

'I've put my name down for the RAF. I'll be going for an assessment before too long.'

'But you're only seventeen. You can't go yet. They won't take you'

'I lied.'

'For God's sake, Jacob, why?'

'The same reason as always – I want to fly. And it's the right thing to do.'

'You're a gem, Jacob, you know that? A real gem.'

And she took his hand again in hers and they walked together up the hill in the warm summer night.

***

The war brought a swelling of the local population and an increase in its variety. The London evacuees had come and gone but the Land Army moved in more permanently, mostly girls from towns further south. Some stayed on the farms, others in the villages and Chipping Norton itself, and a few travelled in on the train, shod in heavy boots suitable for the fields where they helped with the potatoes and the sugar beet. Norman turned the top fields over to crops and took on his quota of help and set them up in Cottages One and Two as these had been vacated when his farmhands went to war.

War Illustrated brought Jacob news from Kent, where German bombers were targeting the airfields and the skies were filled with vapour trails and soaring, falling, spinning planes and the white fungal blooms of parachutes while the invasion barges were prepared on the coast of the Pas de Calais and the country held its breath. One day in mid-September a German Dornier flew low over the farm, blazing flame from its engines as a Spitfire followed it down until it hit the ground in the fields beyond Over Norton, where Jacob and Norman went later that day to see the wreckage.

'It says here that the Germans have lost more planes over Kent than they can bear,' said Jacob the next day, looking up from what he was reading. 'They can't invade us now, without control of the air.'

Alongside the falling German planes had come a steady harvest of German airmen, floating down into the orchards of Kent, frightening livestock and old ladies with the dull clump of their flying boots hitting the ground, to be gathered up by eager volunteers with Home Guard armbands and farmhands with bill-hooks and spades. The land was short of labour and the prisoners were dispersed around the farms of the south and the Midlands and a changing cast was brought to work every day in Norman's fields. They gave no trouble and moved across the beet fields stolid as cattle, heads down and undemonstrative, and like cattle their mood hung between resentment at being fenced off from freedom and relief at no longer being loose in the wild world beyond their invisible prison walls. And the weather was fine and the land girls were pleasant, if not especially friendly, and Norman worked the prisoners hard but treated them with respect and Jacob would come down to the farm at the end of the day when the airmen were coming out of the fields and he watched them as they waited in the yard for the bus to arrive, and one or two of them spoke excellent English and he asked them about their planes and what it was like to fly.

'I'm going to be a pilot myself,' he told them. 'So people like you will be my enemy then.'

'No, we flyers will always be friends,' said one. 'But you're too young to understand that now.'

Jacob looked more closely at the man and saw that he was barely twenty himself.

'Well, good luck,' said the man, as he got on the bus, 'because you'll need it against the likes of us. But if you're a good pilot, flying will keep you young. And if you're a bad one, well, you'll never have the chance to grow old.'

In early September came newspaper reports of the first mass bombing of London, Jacob reading about streams of Heinkels passing above the snaking bends of the Thames around the Docklands and the City, first by day and then by night, the planes silhouetted against orange-tinged clouds above and sheets of flame below. Looking at the photos of those who had been bombed out of their London homes, Jacob's imagination worked up a vision. He saw in his mind's eye the Bampton children in their terraced house on the Isle of Dogs. They were hurrying downstairs into the cellar they had told him about, the one to which he knew they would go when the air-raid sirens wailed.

'Hurry up,' he saw Bobby saying to the scurrying figure of his brother. 'Get a bloody move on.'

'Bugger off!' Billy said. 'I'm going as fast as I can.'

And their cellar stairs shook as a stick of bombs fell in a line all the way up the other side of their street, and the incendiaries that followed, breaking apart with a fluttering sound like a hastily departing flock of birds, set off a chain of fires that merged together into an unbroken conflagration and another plane released its bombs and high-explosive fell through the tiled roof of the Bamptons' house and crashed through to the ground-floor kitchen before it blew away the supporting walls. The roof collapsed and the rubble covered over the cellar stairs and down underground the dim lights went out and the flame of a solitary candle flickered and died in the eruption of dust from the walls. Jacob saw the Bamptons on the trembling floor, listening as more bombs thundered above, tracking away up the street, and then the raid faded away, the diminishing rumble of a passing storm, and there was now only the sound of running water as the firemen trained their hoses on the burning rubble above and broken water pipes leaked their contents around the Bamptons' feet and Mr Bampton went to the top of the stairs, feeling in the darkness for the door, but his hands scraped frantically now across the unfamiliar contours of loose bricks and stone. He called out at half-voice, lifting to a roar, but outside the roar of the flames and the cries of the injured drowned out his shouting as the water crept higher. Mr Bampton roared again, but no one came and the water continued to rise, and finally towards dawn, Jacob decided, a fire crew would hear their cries and they were dug out, shivering in their grimy cloak of fear and exhaustion, and they were led away from where their house had been to a church hall several streets away and they were given hard oat biscuits that stuck in their throats, and they washed them down with weak grey tea in the bleak grey dawn. And as Jacob exhausted his imaginary narrative, he steeled his resolve to join up just as soon as the RAF would have him.

***

Shortly before Christmas, Jacob finally received his letter and took the bus to Oxford. He fidgeted in his chair and bit his lip as he waited to be seen at the RAF recruitment office. They tested him for physical, mental and intellectual preparedness.

'You appear to be an adequate candidate. What role do you envisage for yourself?'

'A pilot. That would be my preference.'

'Of course, everyone says that. How old are you?'

'Eighteen.'

'How old are you really?'

'Eighteen.'

'Very well, then. Bomber crew?'

'Yes, that'll do me fine.'

'You're in. Sign here. We will summon you for training in due course, within a few months at the most.'

Jacob's heart soared. He signed his name on the form and was given his RAF number and went home to count the days. He found

Alfred in the orchard with the pigs.

'Hello, son,' said Alfred glumly. 'How did it go?'

'I'm in.'

Jacob tried to suppress a smile but failed.

'I knew it,' Alfred said.

'It's what I wanted.'

'You're too bloody young. You're still not eighteen.'

Alfred spat at the earth and sighed.

'You've always been a damned fool, Jacob. A damned bloody fool. But at least you'll have some real wings now, not like that time you chucked yourself out of the window playing bloody Icarus.'

'I'll be all right, father. You'll see.'

Alfred prodded a piglet away with his toe.

'That's Churchill, that is. Right feisty little bugger. Look at the way he's chasing Goebbels about.'

'Goebbels?'

'The scrawny little one over there.'

'And that fat one?'

'That's Goering. Go on Churchill, shove the bastard out of the way.'

The fat little piglet squealed and scurried away behind the sty.

'So when are they taking you away?' said Alfred.

'They said they'd write to let me know.'

'Your mother's very upset.'

'Not as upset as you, I bet.'

'She hides it better, Jacob, that's all. She's barely slept all week, knowing you were going back there. Why don't you go up and see her? Go on now, she's in the bedroom.'

Jacob went in the door and up the narrow stairs and he paused on the landing and heard his mother breathing

'Come in, Jacob.'

'How did you know it was me?'

'I know my son's footsteps after all these years.'

Jacob went in and sat on the bed next to his mother.

'Jacob, I want you to know that I understand. I understand why you're going and I'm proud of you. I'll miss you like heaven-knows-what, but I know you're doing what is right.'

'You're not angry with me, then?'

'How could I be angry with you?'

'Father is.'

'He's worried, Jacob, that's the thing. He's afraid he'll lose you, and William too.'

'Is William coming soon?'

'He wrote to say he has some leave after Christmas.'

'Let's hope I see him before I go, then.'

1941

William arrived for three days' leave in early February. The snow had stopped but the ground was white from January's heavy falls and ice placed its chill hand around the countryside and closed its fingers so that by day the fields never lost their hoar frost and the nights set hard and in the morning when Jacob and William collected Rose from the cottage across the lane, and they went together across the field that led down to Pool Meadow, the grass crunched like glass beneath their feet and the tops of the trees were lost in the mist and the calls of the rooks hung ownerless in a void. The shallow pond in the valley had frozen hard and they took off their shoes and laced up the old boots they kept in the loft with the screw-in skates. Rose went first, skimming away across the pond, first on one leg, then the other. She turned half-way across and called back to Jacob and William, indistinct figures now in the mist.

'Come on you two, get a move on!'

Her voice echoed up the valley. She laughed and skated further out across the pond.

'She's lovely, isn't she?' said Jacob to William, as he helped his brother up onto his skates.

'Oh yes,' said William. 'She is that.'

They set off behind Rose towards the far side of the pond where the tips of trees hung trapped in the ice. She smiled as they reached her and she stretched out her hand to steady Jacob as he stopped. William skated past and Rose put her hand on Jacob's shoulder, then pulled him gently towards her and as she hugged him she whispered in his ear.

'I'll miss you, Jacob,' she said in a voice barely audible. 'You must come back to me.'

'I haven't gone away yet,' he said.

She kissed him gently on the cheek, then took his hand and led him off in the direction that William had gone.

***

Jacob spent two more months at home. Then the letter came and he left for an aircrew reception centre in North Yorkshire. He saw the row of Nissen huts adrift in a tide of unrelenting mud and negotiated a path along duckboards that led from the road to the dormitory huts and from there to the gym and the classroom block and the mess. A rat-faced man showed Jacob to his bunk half-way down a row of twenty beds, another twenty opposite.

'Hello,' said a pale young voice two beds further down the row. 'Harry Pollock.'

'Jacob Arbuckle. Nice to meet you.'

'Pleasant here, isn't it? The glamour of the RAF.'

'When did you get here?'

'Lunchtime. I've already sampled the delights of the canteen, I'm afraid. Not exactly the Ritz. A couple of other fellows are here, survived lunch too somehow. They've gone out for a smoke to recover.'

They found the other two by the side of the hut and the four of them stood in the half-light of dusk and their cigarette ends glowed as darkness came and then the rain began to fall and they went inside. A short time later the drill sergeant came across and summoned them to the mess for the evening meal.

'Come on, get a bloody move on,' the sergeant moaned at Harry as he tip-toed along the slippery boards. 'You're not at boarding school now, you're in the RAF.'

Jacob and Harry sat and ate a lukewarm grey meal of non-descript soup, cottage pie heavy with potato, and tasteless bread that was spread with something pale that should have been butter. Throughout the evening more recruits were brought into the dormitory and during the night Jacob heard the doors banging as late arrivals stumbled in the dark and threw themselves down and slept on their beds fully dressed. Jacob spent the next morning bashing his way up and down the parade square as the drill sergeant bellowed at the recruits. More grey food was followed by a ten-mile run through grey-green fields and cloying bogs that sucked at his shoes and sent him slithering about, and all the while the sergeant simmered in his ear as he ran.

'Come on you horrible individual!' he yelled at Jacob, who ignored the splenetic face until it hurried after Harry instead, leaving Jacob muttering oaths under his breath.

'You fat little bugger!' the sergeant screamed at Harry. 'You're not ready for this, are you? What's your name, lad?'

Harry wheezed out a response.

'Harry Pollock? Hairy Bollock, more like! Now run!'

Before the evening meal they went to the classroom block for their first lecture from the Medical Officer. A succession of gruesome slides was projected onto the wall as the medical man offered a swift commentary long on detail and short on doubt.

'This,' he exclaimed grimly, tapping the image on the wall with his long cane, 'is a set of male genitalia, barely recognisable as such due to a rather severe form of infection. And I can assure you this condition cannot be acquired merely by sitting on the seat of a public lavatory. This ...'

He tapped the image again with his cane.

'... is the fate that awaits each of you if you should hazard communion with certain members of the opposite sex. The consequences are serious, and include, but are not necessarily limited to, impotence, infertility, total physical paralysis, insanity, death, and expulsion from the RAF. Though not necessarily in that order. During your service, you will refrain from any activity that places you in danger of such consequences. It takes up to two years to train aircrew, and we will lose enough of you in operations over enemy territory. We cannot afford to lose any of you to ... how shall I put this ... friendly fire.'

Jacob's laughter was cut short by the even more vividly diseased organ on the next slide, and when he went for the evening meal he found his appetite strangely subdued.

'Been having your sexual hygiene lecture, have you?' asked a fat woman as she served dollops of mashed potato onto his plate.

'Can you tell?' asked Jacob.

'Oh yes,' she said. 'They always come in a bit subdued after Doctor Myers has said his bit. But don't worry, lad,' she winked. 'The Germans are far more likely to get you than us girls.'

The next morning, the dormitory door slammed open at half past five.

'Right then, out of bed you lazy blighters! Get your kit on, we're going for a little run!'

Jacob stumbled out of bed and fumbled into his clothes and followed the others as the drill sergeant hared off down the road in the dark and the birds in the bushes tuned up for the dawn chorus.

Four weeks of basic training passed in a blur of sweat and exhaustion, and when the sergeant woke on Jacob's last morning at the camp he found a selection of his underwear drawn up the flagpole and fluttering in the breeze. As the underwear was retrieved, the guilty party laughed his way onto a bus that took him to the railway station, then away on a train to one of the Initial Training Wings that had sprung up around the country in university buildings and conference halls and large hotels. For the next twelve weeks, Jacob worked six days on and one day off, four hours of drill and physical training each day and the rest of his waking hours filled with academic study, hurried intake of food, and beer-fuelled bonding in the nearest pub before he returned to the boarding house in which he had been billeted for the duration of his stay. The classroom instruction took him through a crash course in meteorology, mathematics, and Morse code, armaments, anti-gas procedures, and parachute training. Instruction in aircraft recognition took place in a large lecture room where small models were suspended from the ceiling and the instructors would point at a plane.

'Er ...'

'Too slow, lad. I want an instant answer. Every second counts when Jerry's on your tail. How about you?'

'Messerschmitt?'

'Not good enough. Too vague. You there?'

'Messerschmitt 110.'

'Wrong. It's a Junkers 88. That's you dead.'

Then Jacob was given aptitude and psychiatric tests and was allocated to the pilot group and his training continued with the basics of aerodynamics, airmanship and the principles of flying. At the end of twelve weeks, he was given a uniform and a period of leave.

He caught the train and it ran through fields of wheat ripening to gold in the sun and Alfred and Elizabeth were waiting for him when he stepped down onto the platform in Chipping Norton. As they walked up the hill from the station, Jacob could sense the eyes of curious neighbours upon him and his mother walking slightly more upright than usual at his side, and he walked awkwardly in his new uniform and smiled in embarrassment when two young boys ran up and asked him how many Germans he had killed so far.

William arrived on leave the following day and Vera came for lunch with Daphne while Norman was out in the fields, and it felt strange for the five of them to sit around the kitchen table now, a whole family again. In the evening, Alfred took Jacob and William into town along the blacked-out street, and the occasional car that passed by had headlamps blacked out into slits so as not to be visible from the air. In the pub the landlord gave each of them a free beer and the best seats at the bar and the Local Defence Volunteers no longer bothered Alfred with requests that he join their platoon.

'I'm sorry if I made things difficult for you both,' said Alfred gruffly after he had drunk his fifth pint. 'I just couldn't stand the thought of losing you two. But I understand what you're doing and I'm proud of you.'

Jacob saw Rose again early the next day before he left, but the war was tugging at him now, leaving little time to talk, and shortly after breakfast he was gone.

***

Jacob left England in the early autumn of 1941 aboard the SS Andes, a South American liner built for 600 passengers but in wartime equipped for 6,000. He arrived in Southampton with Harry and several others from the Initial Training Wing on the evening before the ship's departure.

'Where's our hotel, then?' said Harry.

'Lord knows,' someone said.

'Down by the docks,' said another.

They bundled in, six to a room with a bathroom shared by twenty. Jacob slipped himself into a lukewarm bath around midnight, just as the air-raid sirens began to wail. Too tired to move, he slipped his head beneath the surface and the water muffled the frantic banging of the ack-ack guns that blazed away on the roof above his head.

In the morning they found their way up the gang-plank and into their cramped accommodation above the engine room at the back. Hammocks were slung side-by-side between the wooden trestle tables and chairs that served as mealtime furniture. Jacob and Harry dumped their kitbags and went up on deck and the day passed in unceasing bustle down on the quay and a growing sense of anticipation on board. Jacob leant against the handrail as night fell and the ship slipped its moorings and crept out of the harbour under the thickening cover of darkness, the blacked-out town disappearing into the night, and the last signs of England that Jacob saw, as the ship sailed into the Channel, were the wands of the searchlights scraping the sky and the silent flash of bombs that lit up the cloud-base, and all he could hear was the throb of the ship's engine and the rushing past of the waves.

The ship sailed past Land's End and into the Atlantic where the U-boats lurked. In mid-ocean the weather deteriorated and the hammocks swung about below deck and tin mugs and bottles dropped off the tables and rolled about on the steel floor, backwards and forwards, bumping over the rivets and waking him throughout the night. For weeks the ship sailed west, reaching New York on a bright clear November morning, and Jacob watched the Statue of Liberty shining copper-green in the sun as the ship passed by in its shadow.

New York was a blazing blur of light after the grey austerity and blacked-out windows of wartime England. Jacob and Harry ate T-bone steaks washed down with milkshakes and bourbon chasers, then boarded a train at Central Station with dozens of other cadets for the long journey to the main aircrew reception centre in New Brunswick, Canada. From there, the cadets were dispersed to the multitude of flying schools set up across the country as part of the Empire Air Training Scheme. Jacob and Harry arrived at the flying school at Medicine Hat in the vast sweep of prairie near Calgary.

The weather was bright and cold as Jacob sat trembling in the plane for his first flight, sitting in line behind an instructor in a bright yellow Tiger Moth as the earth fell away beneath him and the plane rose up on the prairie winds and his face melted into an enormous smile as the winter sun lit his face with its burning glow and he laughed with joy at being up in the air at last, in a plane, the thing he had always read and dreamed about, soaring above the earth, the gift of flight the war had given him, asking nothing of him in return for now. He looked down at the aerodrome, the criss-crossing runways sketching a rough triangle, and the plane banked away and climbed higher and the buildings became a child's small toys on the carpet of the world and the air turned colder.

Then he took his first solo flight, circuiting the aerodrome at eight hundred feet, bringing the plane back in to land, bumping down onto the runway and coming to an unsteady halt.

'You'll have to do better next time,' said the instructor who was waiting for him when he came in. 'That was a rather ropey landing.'

The next man dropped too fast and his plane tipped over and burst into flames, the war starting to ask for something in return now. The wind howled around the guttering that night and in the morning the aerodrome lay under a blanket of cloud and the snow did not stop for three days. Flying was off, and Jacob and Harry caught a slow bus into town and spent the morning walking around the shops, then headed off on bicycles into the countryside, slipping and sliding along the tyre tracks that trucks had carved in the snow on the unending roads, isolated houses lost in farmland turned white, and the occasional roar of a flat-bed truck sounding its horn as it passed.

On evenings off they went to diners and bars and consumed plates of food as large as a family Sunday dinner in England, then returned to the aerodrome late at night, singing their way back in the brightly-lit bus, a reminder of the other life they had left behind before the war, somewhere beyond the curvature of the earth.

***

At Moreton-in-Marsh near Chipping Norton, the squadron's ageing Wellingtons would head off at dusk, passing over Chipping Norton as they climbed before banking away towards the rendezvous point over Reading. Rose would count them out – nine, ten, eleven, twelve – and stand by the garden wall until the sound of the engines had ceased, and several hours later she would be lying in bed in the dark early hours and she would listen and count the planes back in – twelve, eleven, ten, nine – and on most nights the returning numbers could not match the ones that had departed and the crew room at Moreton would have a number of lockers from which the belongings had to be removed and forwarded to relatives by the Committee of Adjustment. New crews would arrive and go out the following night, and many would fail to return from their first op, and on it went, night after night, the erosive power of darkness dissolving the ranks of aircrew coming off the conveyor belt of the Empire Air Training Scheme, and when Rose heard the planes going out and coming back in, she thought of Jacob, and she wondered when it would be his turn to throw himself off the cliff at dusk and into the long dark valley of night.

1942

Vera looked towards the hall as she heard the postman's footsteps across the yard, then the rattle of the letterbox and the gentle union of envelope and mat. She shivered at the thought of more bad news after the shock of the previous day and she steadied herself in her chair as Daphne dashed out of the kitchen to retrieve the letter.

'From Uncle Jacob!' said Daphne, beaming at the airmail envelope and the now-familiar Canadian stamp as she ran back into the room. 'Open it.'

Vera dredged up a smile.

'Of course, my dear.'

'Mummy, a photo. Look.'

Vera looked at the photo, Jacob in his uniform at the door of a timber building, next to him a taller man in a thick roll-neck sweater and an Irvin jacket.

'Read it to me. Please.'

'Dear Vera,' she began, as Daphne perched on a chair and propped her chin on her hands. 'I hope this letter finds you well, and Norman and little Daphne ...'

Vera paused and inclined her head as Daphne smiled at the mention of her name.

'... and mother and father too. I was very pleased indeed to receive your airgraph. I also recently received a letter from mother, and two airgraphs and a letter with some photos from Rose, so you can guess how pleased I am with all that mail. Thank you for writing, for you don't know the thrill I get receiving letters from home when I am so far away from you all. And have you had news of William recently? I should very much like to know how he is getting along in North Africa. Here things are going well. I spent a very peaceful and enjoyable Christmas with the family of a friend, and I've progressed from Elementary Flying School and am going out nearly every day in the

77

larger twin-engined planes. The training is top-notch, and the class work is extremely detailed, and I know I'll make it to the end of the course and that I'll be well prepared for when I come back to England to get on with the real business. If all goes well here, I'll be home before the end of the summer. I can't wait to see you all. Life is good here, everything is plentiful and the people are most welcoming, but there's still no place like home! Please tell Rose that I'm asking after her, and tell Norman that when I'm back home we can go for that pint he keeps talking about – the beer here isn't nearly as drinkable as good old English ale! Your loving brother, Jacob.'

Norman returned at lunchtime and wolfed down his soup and was out again within half an hour, a thousand jobs to do and too few hours in which to do them. He returned again after dark, soaked to the skin and an early-born lamb in his arms, the little beast shivering and bleating, and he passed it to Vera and went out again into the fields to check on the others. Vera warmed a pan of milk and the lamb sucked away at the teat and soon Norman was back in with another and they sat up through the night nursing the lambs into silence. Vera passed Jacob's letter to Norman. He read it, then looked up.

'Are you going to tell him?'

'I'll have to,' she said.

***

Jacob received Vera's letter several weeks later. Before the evening meal he went to the crew room and sat in the leather chair by the window. He settled down, began to read, then suddenly stopped. He had a shocking vision of William as he looked out of the window to where a Tiger Moth lifted itself up off the runway, silhouetting itself against the fading pink sky and across the setting sun. Jacob stood and walked out of the room, onto the tarmac and across the rough grass that bordered the perimeter fence. He followed the fence the full length of the runway as the wet grass soaked his shoes and a thin mist lifted itself off the ground. He walked past the main gate and out onto the road that disappeared into the mist, across the lip of the world, into the night. He walked through thoughts and memories for hours, past lone farmhouses and picket fences, and finally he saw lights far off in the night and he found himself back at the entrance to the base. He found Harry in the dormitory.

'We spent so much time bickering, you know,' Jacob said. 'Like we hated each other. He bullied me and I bullied him, mentally at least, made him feel stupid, but he wasn't. He just liked different things, tractors and engines, down-to-earth things. And tanks. Can't shoot at me in a tank, safe in all that metal, that's what he always said. It's not fair, is it?' Harry shook his head. 'William in a brewed-up tank in North Africa, whatever's left of him. And all that time we wasted when we were young.'

The instructor called Jacob in the following day.

'I'm taking you off flying for a few days.'

'But sir …'

'Arbuckle, do you want your mother to lose both her sons? Your mind won't be on the job.'

He spent extra time in the classroom while the others were away on cross-country flights. He got into the air again the following week, but the errors crept in.

'You're still not fit to fly. I'm taking you off,' said the instructor.

'But sir, I have to fly. I was born for it.'

'You were born to do what you're told, just like everyone else. Now if you'll please excuse me …'

'Harry,' he said later. 'They've taken me off again. They think I've lost my nerve – I just need more time.'

'They won't give you time, old chap. This place is a conveyor belt, in one end and out the other, back to Blighty as soon as possible. Months more training there too and we won't be on ops for another year – you never know, the war might be over by then, you might not miss a thing.'

When the course ended, Jacob fell to a stroke of the examiner's pen.

'I've been washed out, Harry, right at the last,' he said as they sat in the mess. 'They didn't fail me, as such, but I have to stay in reserve if I want to go the pilot route. Or they'll train me for another role and send me on ops sooner.'

'So what are you going to do?'

'I want to get back home, get on with the job. So I'll take another role, navigation I hope. So I suppose this is where we go our separate ways.'

Harry shook his head glumly.

'Not you as well?'

'Yes, washed out too, I'm afraid. A right pair, we are.'

'Damn it, Harry.'

They were put through further tests and interviews and awaited their fate.

'Arbuckle, there is currently a shortage of all the aircrew trades. Your psychological and written tests show you to be particularly suited to the role of air-bomber. Bombing accuracy is paramount and this is a vital job for which we must take only the most competent candidates – you will be pleased, I am sure, to hear that you are among them. The next course starts in two weeks. Until then you will take leave. You start back here in June. That is all.'

Jacob saw Harry later that day as he was packing to go.

'Hello, Harry. What have the fates decided for you?'

'Bomb-aimer.'

'Snap. Must be a shortage ...'

'Or we're particularly suited to dropping the bombs.'

'Someone has to, I suppose.'

'More important than the pilot, some say.'

'Still, not really what I had in mind.'

'Well, we'll all be in the mire one way or the other.'

'Have they given you leave?'

'Two weeks.'

'Same here. Let's head off for a while?'

They hired a car and pointed its long bonnet to where the highway narrowed into infinity, and the sun-burnt prairie sped away behind. They spent the evenings in dimly-lit taverns and the nights in roadside motels and by the end of the two weeks they had almost forgotten why they were in Canada.

They completed their courses and received their bomber's wings on the same day.

'Beautiful, isn't it?' said Jacob, as he touched the badge that had been sewn onto his jacket, just above his heart. 'They've offered me a training post, you know, as a bombing instructor.'

'You'd be mad not to take it. You'd be safe out here. Let the other bods do the fighting.'

'No, I've been trained for ops – that's my job now, isn't it?

Got to do my bit.'

So Jacob boarded a ship in New York, a cold November rain drumming wet fingers upon the deck, the head of the Statue of Liberty lost in a low squall as the ship slipped by below. The New World fell out of sight beneath the slate-grey waves, the imprecise blur of the horizon at his back. Then the Old World heaved into view and Jacob bounced down the gang-plank above the troubled waters of Southampton docks, boarded his train, and was gone.

***

Rose was sitting with Vera on the bench in front of her grandmother's house when she heard the whistle of the train down in the valley, pulling away again now, and then Jacob was striding up the hill from the station. She could see his face looking up, small and distant, his hand lifting to wave as he walked, and Rose jumped to her feet and hurried to the stone wall that separated the garden from the lane. She saw the blue uniform not yet stained by sweat and fear, a virgin white wing just above his heart and a flight-sergeant's cap pushed back upon his head. She followed Vera out of the gate and down the dusty lane, and as Vera embraced Jacob, Rose paused, not knowing what to do, then suddenly for a moment she was in Jacob's arms, awkward, wanting to cling on but not ready for that, not in front of others, so just a swift hug to hide her feelings, and in that instant the wool of his uniform was harsh against her face, roughing her cheek as she held him, and then his voice in her ear and the sweet smell of him.

Lunch was ready for the table and as Jacob dropped his bag on the bed in the top room he could smell the roast pork as it emerged from the furnace of the oven, and as he came down the stairs he heard the beer tumbling into the glass and the sound of Alfred calling him down. They embraced again where the galley stairs met the back door and the afternoon passed in a haze of news and memories and as the fire was stoked and the flames surged high into the chimney the name of William, which had rested unspoken through the meal, slipped from someone's lips, and a silence fell upon the room and Alfred stared at the fire and the flames continued their rage and the coals glowed hot, and overhead the Wellington bombers wailed a plaintive soaring cry as they carried their crews away to the searchlights and guns of German cities that would hack back in fury as they burned.

Jacob told them about Canada and about Harry and the trip they had made in the old Buick out across the prairies, and Norman, who had come up from the farm when it was too dark to work and now sat exhausted and dozing on the settee, pricked up his ears at the mention of livestock, breeds of cattle he had read about but never seen at the agricultural shows, and it was only when Jacob and Vera were alone in the top room late that night that Jacob told her that what he had really learned to do in Canada was to destroy and to kill as efficiently as modern technology would allow and to avoid being killed himself for the longest possible time while doing so.

The following morning, Rose knocked on the Arbuckles' door and Elizabeth let her in and Jacob and Rose walked into town and ate at the café on the top-side of the market square, then went down to Pool Meadow where they had skated with William two winters before. Jacob picked up a flat stone and sent it skimming across the water into the vegetation on the far bank, a little bouncing bomb that flushed something out of the reeds. They watched as a little ball of black fuzz topped with red, a moorhen chick that had been born too late to survive the winter, scudded around in futile circles, whistling a repetitive plaintive cry, looking for its mother.

'When do you go away again, Jacob?' asked Rose.

'Next month. To an OTU up north. Norman's neck of the woods.'

'An OTU?'

The whistling cry was receding now, the black shape losing itself along the reeds.

'An Operational Training Unit, where we crew up and get the hang of flying in these conditions.'

He glanced up at the low cloud.

'And then to a squadron somewhere. And then Germany.'

'You should have stayed in Canada,' she said. 'You'd have been safe there.'

'I had to come back.'

'I know ...'

They sat together and looked out across the water until dusk came and the wind fell still and the birds stopped singing as they readied themselves for night.

'It's going to be better now, isn't it?' she said at last. 'The war, I mean – it's not so certain we'll lose now, is it?'

'We can't lose. Whatever it takes, we can't lose this war.'

'And the Americans are with us now too – there are some over at Daylesford. I see them at the Army Forces Club here in town. They get through those spam rolls like there really is no tomorrow.'

She paused suddenly at the significance of what she had just said.

'There will be a tomorrow, Rose,' he said, but his voice seemed to fall off a cliff as he uttered the words and he felt compelled to repeat himself. 'There will be a tomorrow, Rose, don't you worry about that.'

As Jacob and Rose walked back up the hill together in the cold, she slipped her hand again into his and they paused as they had on that warm June night three years before, and she kissed him again on the forehead and held him to her, and then, at last, as they stared at each other in the dark, her lips touched his. She was the first girl he had ever kissed.

Jacob spent Christmas at home and then in early January his month was up and he packed his bag and put on his uniform with its silver-white wing and the train took him again and pulled him into the tunnel that led north to the OTU.

EARLY 1943

The hangar was packed with men of the various bomber roles as the Chief Ground Instructor leapt up onto the wooden platform and called them to silence. A Wellington bomber passed overhead, its engines droning into the distance as the instructor raised his voice above the roar.

'OK, gentlemen,' he said. 'I think you know why you're here. It isn't quite a marriage market, but think of it like that. Choose your crew-mates and choose them well. Once you're operational, in fact as soon as you walk out this hangar today, you will depend on them for your lives. And remember, you're in this for the long haul, till death do you part and all that – though that might be only a few weeks. If you think that kind of arrangement might not be for you, then leave now without disgrace or forever hold your peace.'

No one moved a muscle.

'Very good, gentleman. As I expected. Now get on with it, and may yours be a marriage made in heaven. But not one that takes you there ...'

This raised a grim laugh and with that he stood down and left them to it. Jacob looked around the room at the dozens of strangers and saw that they were similarly looking about, as if attempting to discern in their fellows' features some inkling as to what they would be like to fly with and whether they could be depended upon to do their jobs and do them well when fear shoved at their guts over the target. These men were not warriors, he thought, the whole of society was reflected in their faces, their bearing, the air they had about them, the chubby amiable-looking type who might possess some inner strength, the long lean Australian from the outback who had trained in South Africa, or the public schoolboy who had joined the RAF in the hope of flying in Spitfires only to have his reactions deemed too slow for the quicksilver planes of Fighter Command but ideal for the powerful steady bombers. Jacob shifted on his feet as the men began to mingle, approaching each other timidly at first like teenagers at their first ball asking for a dance, then the noise levels gradually rose as the conversations got going and men who had formed themselves into twos found another man or another pair, and in this way the atoms of Bomber Command began to form themselves into little clusters of substance.

'Hello,' said a man next to Jacob. 'Jolly affair this, isn't it? The name's Andrews, Ralph Andrews.'

Jacob noted the man's confident tone, diffident and distant, that presumption of authority a privileged upbringing bestows.

'Jacob Arbuckle,' he said, more quietly than he had intended. 'Bomb-aimer.'

'Ah yes, I'd quite forgotten what this was all about. Pilot Officer Ralph Andrews, I should have said.'

They shook hands and Jacob weighed him up and felt the other man peering into him too, quietly working him out, weighing him up against some vague criteria.

'Right, then,' said Ralph. 'You're in. Now we need some additional members for this fledgling little crew of ours. We can hardly fly on our own, can we? Now let's see, I was talking to a rear gunner last night over   supper.
Oh look, there he is.'

Ralph Andrews strode away across the room, a good three inches taller than anyone else. Jacob followed and by the time he caught up with him, Ralph was already in conversation with a pair of rough-looking types.

'This is my mate Jim,' one was saying. 'He's mid-upper turret, I'm arse-end charlie. We're old mates from Perth, did our initial training together in South Africa. I'm Donald, but call me Don. I don't much care for formality.'

'South Africa? That's where I grew up,' said Ralph. 'Must be serendipity.'

The gunners looked at each other.

'No mate, not Serendipity. Cape Town.'

Ralph ignored their attempt at humour. 'This is Jacob Arbuckle,' he continued. 'He's my bomb-aimer. And a bloody good one too.'

Jacob smiled at the premature compliment and wondered whether Ralph would be proved right in his assessment.

'Good, then,' said Don. 'Four out of seven already. Anyone know a navigator? I've got no sense of bloody direction myself.'

Towards the end of the afternoon, when crewing up was nearly done, they found their navigator, Charlie Appleforth.

'A vicar's son?' said Don, repeating what he had heard.

'That's right. From Kent.'

'Well pray for us, son,' said Don. 'Have a word with the man upstairs.'

'Oh, I will,' said Charlie. 'I will. In fact I already have, several times daily.'

'Glad to hear it,' said Ralph. 'But we won't be needing Him, of course. We'll look out for each other instead, isn't that right boys? Jacob?'

'That's right, skip. That's what we had in mind.'

'Good lad. Now apparently flight engineers won't be allocated until we go to an HCU for training on Lancs, so we only need a wireless op and we've got the full set.'

They found their wireless operator that night in the bar, and they heard him before they saw him. The piano flared up and a voice rose above the hubbub and Jacob and Ralph and the two Australians and Charlie the vicar's son crowded around the piano with their pints of Northumberland ale and sang along. One song followed another and at the end of the evening Ralph approached the pianist with a fresh foaming pint in his hand.

'Here, have this,' said Ralph, pushing the glass towards him. 'I hear you're a wireless man. I expect you're crewed up already? You extrovert types aren't likely to have been left on the shelf this afternoon.'

'No mate, I was bloody late, wasn't I? Train got held up, Jerry bombed the line. I had to get the bus in the end, only arrived when everyone was leaving the do in the hangar. Nearly got crewed up with a spare-bod pilot who was hanging around looking for men by the door on the way out, but I thought better of it. Right fucking basket-case, he looked, a right ruddy weaver, the type who'd kill you first op out. Fuck that, I thought, any pilot worth his salt would have been fully kitted out by then, navigator, radio op, the lot.'

'Well I'm still missing a radio op. Do I look like a basket-case to you? The type who'd get you killed?'

The man looked him up and down. 'Can't say you do. You look all right to me, skipper.'

'Good, then come and meet my boys.'

With the addition of George O'Neill, the swearing singing pianist, the crew was formed. They spent the next three weeks in training and were then given a day's leave. Jacob caught a bus into the Northumberland countryside and on towards Durham in search of Black Hill Farm where Norman had grown up. He got off the bus and walked out of the village, past the church and the pub that Norman had described, past the milestone and the burn that ran gin-clear across mossy stones. Thin white clouds crept across the tops of the hills on the other side of the shallow valley as a freezing wind keened through the hawthorn that grew along the fence. Jacob came to the granite columns of the gate that led up to the house and he walked up the slope and across the yard but the old lady who answered the door would not let him in.

'Yes, I remember Norman Miller,' she said. 'But that was all such a long time ago. I'd rather it stayed that way.'

Jacob looked around at the brown-clod fields and saw upon the crest of the hill a man and a horse and a plough sending crows into the air, and he thought of what Norman had told him about John Bainbridge and the random nature of fate, and he turned and caught the bus back to the airfield and his new life as an air-bomber.

**

Their training flights began the next day. Cross-country daylight runs took them up into Scotland and across the north of England and down into Wales, and then night training began and they found themselves over the Irish Sea with cloud all around suddenly lit by lightning bursts, and the thunder rumbled down their flanks and the plane jumped in and out of giant pot-holes in the sky. Then the cloud broke and they saw in the distance the searchlights of Liverpool clawing around at the sky as the distant flash of bombs blinked through the rain and the city glowed orange beneath the German bombs.

As winter ebbed away, the cold hard frosts of dawn were nudged aside by soft edges of fog that layered the fields through the night and long into the day. Mist thickened around the trucks as the crews awaited the order to board for a dummy raid on Bristol. The station commander tore up in his car and jumped out.

'What are you lot waiting for?' he called out, his irritation doubled by the fact he had tripped up as he leapt from the car. 'Come on, off with you, take off is at 1900 hours in case you hadn't realised!'

'We can't take off in this,' whispered Jacob.

'Too right,' muttered Charlie. 'And far less land in it. They'll be needing the blood wagon tonight.'

'Belt up, lads,' said Ralph. 'Of course we can land in it. We can do anything, this crew.'

'I think old skip's trying to get us killed,' said Don.

Jacob tucked the hare's foot that Norman had given him into the breast pocket of his battledress and closed his Irvin jacket. They boarded the trucks and bumped across the field to the dispersal pans where the planes waited. They climbed into the cramped ribbed interior, the belly of their whale. Don wedged himself in through the tiny door of his tail turret, Jim hoisted himself into the harness from which he would sit suspended beside his mid-upper gun, and the others worked their way to the front of the beast. George sat at the radio adjacent to Charlie's navigator's desk with its angle-poise lamp and maps and logbook and electronic aids, and just beyond them was the pilot's seat, and alongside Ralph the drop-down seat for the stand-in flight engineer. Finally, contrary to regulations for take-off and landing, Jacob crouched down in the nose where the bombsight sat inert and the selector switches were fixed to the fuselage. All around the airfield, engines were starting up and the noise rose to a roar that carried though the night to the nearby villages and farms. The pre-flight checks were concluded and Ralph signed the acceptance form and the flight engineer carried it to the back door and passed it down to one of the ground crew whose mouth moved in silent farewell, his words lost in the well of noise that was erupting from the engines, his cap blown from his head by the wild back-draft of the airscrews. The flight engineer pulled the door shut and worked his way back along the throbbing, straining plane. Ralph edged it forward off the dispersal pan and slipped in behind a Halifax taxiing in front and the Halifax swung onto the runway, its pilot leaned on the throttle, and his plane sped into the fog and lifted and disappeared. Jacob sat and listened to the disembodied voices on the intercom as the engines hurled the airscrews around in accelerating fury and then the brakes hissed and George made a joke and the tension melted a fraction.

'You've got your green, skipper,' said the flight engineer, and the tension came again. Ralph thrust the throttle forward and let the plane off the leash and Jacob felt it pick up speed into the wall of fog and finally it lifted up, rising just above the fence and the trees at the far end of the runway, the flare-path blurring then falling out of sight and he prayed they would not collide with one of the other planes flying blind into the night. The fog had thickened again on their return and as they dropped into it Jacob crouched in the nose and searched for signs of the gooseneck flares and George radioed the tower. The flares rushed up to meet them and the wheels bumped down and Ralph steadied the shaking plane as it slowed along the runway and a voice down the intercom said 'Thank God for that'.

When the fog cleared that afternoon there was a black gash in the trees where a plane had come down in the night, and the smell of burning and fuel was still in the air when the planes took off again that evening to set course above the blackened wood, their engines undulating and melancholy as they left the earth behind.

The next morning the world was white from a late fall of snow and near the mess a small crowd of aircrew were engaged in a snowball fight, their boyish cries rising and falling in the icy air. In the crew room Jacob found 'Humpty' Haynes, prematurely balding, rotund of physique, and with a keen appetite for the eggs that were sometimes available for breakfast.

'I expect they'll scrub training today,' said Humpty, looking out of the window towards the dispersal pans where the aircraft stood beneath their thickening white hoods. 'They can't send us up in this, can they?'

But the ground crew were soon setting about the planes, sweeping the snow off with brooms, and the aircrew were sent out with shovels to clear the runways and the taxiing areas and the dispersals. Jacob watched the ground fall away again at dusk and the plane was lost in low cloud. They touched down several hours later and went to the crew room and sat with those who had made it back earlier. One by one the planes came in and the crews sat and exchanged occasional words as they drank their mugs of tea and smoked their cheap cigarettes and then they drifted off to their quarters to shiver away their night's work beneath thin grey blankets as ice layered the window panes.

'Is Humpty back in?' Jacob had asked as he left, but the following morning he heard as he ate his eggs that Humpty's Halifax had struck a mountain in the Scottish Borders and the blast had scrambled him and his crew across the hillside.

'Poor Humpty, they couldn't put him back together again,' someone said. 'More eggs for the rest of us, though.'

'Sod you,' said Jacob. 'Don't you have a heart?'

'I had one once. Seem to have mislaid it, though, since I came to this place.'

***

Jacob sensed the bond between the crew beginning to harden, a glue to keep them in one piece in the skies over Germany.

'Look at old skip,' he said in the bar late one night when the beer had run out and all the other crews had gone. 'Epitome of the pilot officer, tall and dashing in his Air Force blue ...'

'Let's see how dashing he is when we get out the cricket kit,' said Jim. 'He'll be dashing for the bloody pavilion.'

'Skip played for the Oxbridge side against Middlesex in a pre-season game at Lord's, I'll have you know,' said George. 'Whatever that bloody means.'

'I think it means he's a damned good bat,' said Charlie.

'Damned good bat, my arse,' said Don. 'Just wait till he gets a bit of Aussie leather round his chops.'

They set up a fire extinguisher as a wicket and Don fetched a bat and a ball and they began the inaugural intra-crew Test Match, Australia batting first and reaching twenty-five for no wicket, George providing a musical backdrop to the action with repeated drunken renditions of Waltzing Fucking Matilda, battering away at the piano as his voice filled the room, until a pair of navigation instructors heard the commotion and appeared at the door just as Don launched an elaborate cover drive that sent the ball into the heavy velvet drapes with a satisfying thwack.

'What the bloody hell's going on here, then, boys?' called out one of the instructors in a Yorkshire burr, something wild in his eyes that needed release.

George finished his song with a furious flourish as the cricketers and the instructors all stared at him, and everyone burst out laughing.

'Just whipping these Poms' arses,' said Don, gesturing towards Jacob, who had bowled the previous ball.

'Yeah, that's right, mate,' said Jim, draining his pint.

'We're just getting to know each other better,' said Ralph. 'We're crewed up with these strange marsupial cousins. Nothing wrong with a bit of colonial knockabout, is there?'

The two instructors looked at each other.

'All right, my Aussie mates,' came the Yorkshire growl. 'You want a game of cricket, we'll flippin' give you one.'

He grabbed the ball from Jacob and walked back to the far end of the room and came in off his long run, letting rip at the Australian batsman from twelve yards, bowling the ball hard into the wooden floor. The bouncer reared up towards Don, who rocked back and hooked it away off the far wall.

'Good shot that man!' cried out Ralph. 'I suggest we make you an honorary Englishman.'

'Honorary Englishman, my arse!' said Don, taking guard again and cutting the next ball away past the leather armchair positioned at extra cover.

'And here we are at the WACA,' stated Jim loudly, holding a bottle to his lips in imitation of a radio commentator at his microphone. 'The Fremantle Doctor is howling hot across the ground and here comes Larwood again, bowling to the great Bradman, and the mighty Don swings him away again into the outfield and the Poms know they're bloody beat.'

The game continued until the station commander, passing along the corridor outside, heard the enthusiastic cussing and the heavy smack of ball on bat.

'What the blasted blue blazes are you lot up to?!' he erupted from the doorway. 'What do you think this is, a lunatic asylum?'

He marched up to the two errant instructors.

'Get this lot back to their quarters. And you two, be in my office first thing tomorrow.'

'They were good sports,' said Jacob, as the crew walked back together to the barracks block afterwards. 'I thought we were in for it when they appeared, thought we'd be sent packing to the bloody Army!'

***

'So then, Charlie,' said George in the bar the next night. 'Where does a name like Appleford come from?'

'Not Appleford,' said Charlie. 'Apple*forth*.'

'Yes, sorry, Charles, old chap. Applefart. Born within earshot of the Bow Bells, I'm afraid, lost my hearing when I was just a nipper.'

'I beg your pardon?' mouthed Charlie silently. 'Can you hear me now you big clot?'

'Eh? Eh? Applefart?'

'Go to hell, George,' said Charlie. 'Appleforth is a fine Kentish name.'

'And what do you do in Kent for fun?' asked Jacob. 'Apple bobbing and church fetes, I should guess.'

'I'd guess?' said George. 'You know old Charlie's a vicar's son. That's all they do, those holy types. Cakes at the Sunday stalls and plenty of chat about the impressive size of old Mr Appleforth's marrows and orange pippins.'

'Well, yes,' said Charlie, 'I have to admit I've seen some pretty ferocious scuffling around the cake stand at the church harvest fete, small children and their pocket money, steady flights of angel cakes. You know, that wild Saturday afternoon hunger.'

'Oh, I know it well,' said George. 'I know it well ...'

And he turned his head and made a comment to Don and they both laughed, but Charlie did not notice because he was thinking of old Mr Appleforth, a man of God but also a man of the soil, an academic who revelled in the poetry of prayer and the pleasures of the potato and the plough. On days when he had no parishioners to visit and time on his hands, he would take long walks out to the neighbouring farms and assist the labourers in their humble tasks, returning home in the early evening to flick through the Bible before dinner with hands grubbied by toil and fingernails that sheltered half a field of loam. Charlie was the Appleforths' only child and shared his father's contemplative bent and his mother's owlish stare. He excelled at school and was destined to follow his father into the clergy when the war intervened.

'When the Heinkels were over Kent,' Charlie suddenly found himself declaring, 'I made clear my intentions to volunteer for the RAF.

My father looked up from where he was engaged in a war of attrition with the rows of beans that he sowed like a sapper sowing mines. "Charles," he said to me, "your first duty is to God, but your second is to your country. May the Lord give you wings, may he watch over you when you fly, and may he bring you home to us again when this godforsaken war is over." So I fucked off to Canada and got my wings.'

The others all fell about laughing at Charlie's uncharacteristic use of such a forceful expletive, and Jacob applauded.

'Well done, Charlie, well done. Spoken like one of us.'

'And you, George,' said Charlie, emboldened by the reaction. 'What made you join up?'

'I saw the Blitz, that was enough. Winter 1940, and my gran lit up like a candle on the sofa when an incendiary came through the roof. That made up my mind, all right, an eye for an eye ...'

'Even if it does leave all men blind?' said Jacob.

'Too bloody right. I signed up the next day for bomber crew. Next time it'll be me over a city dropping bombs and incendiaries, and I'll rejoice when that day comes, I can tell you, because I know what it means.'

'I assume that's an apocryphal tale, old chap?' said Ralph.

'A what?' said George. 'Come on, skip, I haven't got your education. Speak to me plain and proper, now.'

'The thing about your granny. Granny and the incendiary. That can't be true.'

'Well they took her away in a fucking bag, skip, if that's what you mean. Like taking away a dog.'

'I'm awfully sorry, George, honestly I am,' said Ralph, as the others nodded. 'But listen, to lighten the mood, I'll tell you another tale of an apocryphal bent. Something I heard from my babysitter when I was a youngster. She'd worked as an assistant at London Zoo, and after she'd been at my father's Beaujolais – as she invariably was – she would always trot out her tale about the South American parrot that learned to quote lines from T.S.Eliot's *The Waste Land* at old ladies. Can you imagine that, not just a talking parrot, but a poetic one too? April is the cruellest month, says this bloody parrot, breeding lilacs out of the dead land ...'

He burst out laughing but stopped abruptly when the others did not follow. 'Well, I guess you had to be there,' he said.

'I don't suppose that was Chesterton, by any chance?' said Jacob.
'Afraid not, old chap. Why?'
'Oh, it's a long story. I'll tell you another time.'
And Jacob thought again of Rose as he drank down his beer.

***

Ralph had not suffered the privations of the Blitz and the wasteland it brought, Jacob could sense that in him, nor any other great hardships in his formative years, unless you count the sting of a scorpion still slumbering in his shoe at dawn, or the primal fear provoked in the heart of a young boy by the roar of the lion in the night as he slept in a tented encampment ringed by thorn-bush. The son of a surgeon, born in South Africa and raised in Rhodesia until the family tired of life half a world away from the mother country, Ralph was ten when they returned to the Surrey countryside, moving into a large Victorian house set in acres of meadowland and woods and with four tall brick chimneys, one for each fireplace, and a lake to one side on which Ralph and his three sisters spent summer afternoons afloat in a flat-bottomed punt as dragonflies alighted on the water and lifted up again, leaving tiny rings where they had been. Ralph's father took the train to London each morning and returned late in the evening as the children were going to bed, and Ralph would lie in bed in his own large room at the top of the stairs and listen to his parents' conversations about the surgical peculiarities of the day, Mrs Andrews' afternoon at the old people's home where once a week she helped with the tea and sandwiches, and the West End theatre tickets that Mr Andrews had brought home for the weekend. Often the tickets were for a matinee, and the trip into London would be an all-day Saturday family affair involving Welsh rarebit beforehand and cake and tea afterwards, but once a month the trips into London were the evening preserve of Mr and Mrs Andrews, and by the time the baby-sitter had arrived Mrs Andrews would be ready to leave, wearing a dark blue cashmere coat and a white silk scarf and surrounded by a small invisible cloud of Eau de Cologne, smelling as Ralph's youngest sister always put it 'of Paris', or as Ralph joked, of northern Germany. As Mr and Mrs Andrews walked to the car and Mr Andrews opened the door with suburban ceremony, Mrs Gibbons, the baby-sitter, would open the larder and start preparing for herself an ample plate of confectionery and buttery goods and a large glass of Mr Andrews' Beaujolais, and she would turn on the radio, sit herself down heavily on the Chesterfield – sending one or other of the adjacent children upwards as if on a see-saw – and munch her way through the first hour of the evening as the children urged her to tell them ever more outlandish stories about her time as a veterinary assistant at London Zoo. By the time the Andrews returned from the theatre, their daughters would be in bed and Mrs Gibbons asleep on the sofa with the radio trilling away on one side and Ralph curled up and muttering in his sleep on the other. This happy state of affairs continued until the evening that Mrs Gibbons failed to arrive and Mr Andrews picked up the phone and received the news that she had succumbed to a massive stroke, and after that it was the Andrews who occasionally went to see Mrs Gibbons at her home, but the stories had stopped and the appetite was gone and she spent the rest of her days immobile and Ralph often wondered if her inability to respond signified too an inability to comprehend and to reason, or whether the stories perhaps still spilled about in her head with no means of expression, a camera clicking away full rolls of film that could never emerge from her darkroom. At thirteen, Ralph was sent away to a Hertfordshire boarding school. He enrolled in the flying club and this fed a growing interest in the machines that one day might bear him up into the air, and this interest endured beyond his schooldays and into his first year at university in Oxford, where the flying club was more practice than theory. Notionally at Oxford to study Mathematics, Ralph spent his days pursuing his four main interests, all of which came to him easily – flying, motorbikes, cricket, and girls. He had spent his summer holidays in his teens around his three older sisters and their female friends, and this had taught him a confident manner and a certain proficiency in the language of charm, and he put this domestic practice to good use once he found himself in the fresh pastures of Oxford. At weekends his motorbike sped him and a companion along the country roads outside Oxford, north through Woodstock and out past Chipping Norton and into the chocolate-box countryside around Burford and the Wychwoods and he got to know the hayfields and the soft riverbanks intimately, and the soft intimacy of his companions too, and they would ride back to Oxford with the setting sun at their backs, the throb of the motorbike below, and the warm glow of physical proximity all around them.

When the war came, Mr Andrews, overly familiar with what sharp metal objects could do to a human body, had forbidden Ralph to put himself forward for the Services until he must, but within a year Ralph had rebelled and was on his way to South Africa under the Empire Air Training Scheme and now, in the early months of 1943, he was Pilot Officer Ralph Andrews, RAF Bomber Command, the captain of a crew comprising a pair of lean plain-speaking Australians, a thoughtful vicar's son, a vengeful survivor of the London Blitz, and a bomb-aimer from an average family in Chipping Norton, the quiet town through which Ralph had roared on his motorbike in the months before the war.

***

They received their posting to a Heavy Conversion Unit in Lincolnshire and were assigned a flight engineer as the final permanent member of their crew.

'Twenty-eight!' said Jacob, when Roland Reynolds told them his age. 'You're an old bloody man. What are doing signing up with a bunch of sprogs like us?'

'Someone's got to look after you, pal,' grinned Roland.

'That's the skip's job, mate,' said Don. 'Ain't it skip?'

Ralph nodded and smiled, then patted Roland on the shoulder. 'Where are you from, Roland? I detect a Highland burr.'

'Yes sir, Aberdeen. I've got a wife and son there now, born just last summer, the wee kid.'

He lapsed into silence as his thoughts turned to home.

'Well, you'll be seeing them again soon, don't you worry about that,' said Ralph. 'And don't worry so much about the sir. We don't bother with that kind of thing in this crew.'

The days were filled with cross-country flights and fighter affiliation training and advanced bombing techniques, and Ralph frequently let Jacob take the controls and fly the plane, just as he had at the OTU, for you never knew if something might happen to the pilot on an op and it was just as well that Jacob, having trained initially as a pilot, should familiarise himself with the controls and the behaviour of the Lancaster.

At the end of their time at the HCU, the crew were given a week's leave and they headed south on the train. The two Australians went with Jacob to Chipping Norton and they spent three days at Mill View Cottage. Jacob took them down to see Vera and Norman at Elm Tree Farm, where Norman quizzed them about Australian livestock and the vast quantities of sheep he had read about in the agricultural journals.

'I saw some of your Australian sheep at the Royal Show in '39,' said Norman, as they stood by the pen in the bottom field. 'Scrawny things, they were. Are they all like that over there, what with the poor pasture and everything?'

'Couldn't tell you mate,' said Jim. 'We're both from Perth. City boys, you see.'

'I see,' said Norman, eyeing them suspiciously.

'Yeah,' said Don, 'I'd hardly seen a sheep in all my life until I came to England.'

'So you don't know much about livestock at all then?'

'No mate, not a sodding thing.'

'Not even cattle?'

'I had a dog once,' offered Don. 'Does that count?'

Vera called them in for tea and Don and Jim entertained Daphne with stories of the duck-billed platypus and the wombat, which Jim sketched for her on a paper napkin and left her giggling at the thought that such odd creatures really existed somewhere in the world.

Meanwhile Jacob went to see Rose and they sat in her grandmother's front room on chairs pulled up close so their elbows touched as they talked.

'So you've been posted, then?' Rose asked. 'Near Bury St Edmunds, Vera tells me.'

'Yes, that's right.'

'I have some news myself,' she said. 'I'm joining the Women's Auxiliary Air Force.'

'You're going to be a WAAF? That's wonderful news.'

'I wanted to tell you myself.'

'I'm very glad you did. Maybe you'll be stationed down my way?'

'Well, I'm not sure I'd like it if I were.'

'What do you mean?'

His voice was strangely hurt, as if he had been stabbed in the throat by something small but wounding.

'It would be very hard,' she said, quickly healing the wound.

'Perhaps too hard, to be close to you, to see you go away and not to know ...'

'... if I'd be coming back?'

'Yes, Jacob, I imagine that would be very hard. I'm not sure I could stand it.'

***

The train reached the village near the airbase in mid-afternoon and the sun beat down on the platform as the new boys stepped out, Jacob's crew and three other little clans fresh from their Heavy Conversion Units, twenty-eight men, each alone with his thoughts. They went outside and waited for the crew bus to arrive and it took them along the road and up a slight incline and as they crested the top of the rise Jacob saw the black planes heave into sight behind the perimeter fence, parked at wide intervals around the vast airfield as the ground crews perched upon their wings or clambered around on platforms beside the engines. Tractors pulled long low trains of trolleys laden with bombs and underneath the planes men scrawled obscene messages on the explosive cargo and then struggled to lift the ordnance into the joists and up into the bomb bay.

The bus dropped the new crews in front of a large brick building with a clock above its door, an incessant consumer of time, whatever time they had left in which to squeeze out their lives. Further away Jacob could see the control tower and dotted here and there, as far as the woods at the far end of the airfield, were clusters of low buildings and Nissen huts laced together by rough intersecting paths. In the middle were the runways, broad tarmac strips sketching out a choice of routes into the air to accommodate the vagaries of wind and weather. Jacob waited in line as the crews were given their medical inspection, the Medical Officer running his cold hands across them in practised little moves he had made a thousand times, going through his well-worn routine of small wry jokes and observations and personal questions in an attempt to gain the confidence of these young men who might not pass through his hands again before they died.

While Ralph went off to his quarters in a permanent brick-built block for the officer class, Jacob and the rest of the crew, sergeants not officers, continued along to the corrugated iron huts further down the path near the woods and they were shown into their long hollow tunnel with its twenty beds on a bare concrete floor and the sound of water dripping somewhere unseen. Around the beds were strewn the belongings of crewmen who had arrived at the station in recent weeks and were now at the briefing for the night's operation. As the two Australians went off for a walk, Jacob and Charlie and Roland dumped their bags on their allocated beds, then went over to the large brick building with the clock above the door, past the crew room and the parachute store and the sergeants' mess and the bar. They lingered outside the briefing room where the doors were shut and the curtains had been drawn. The phone booth too was chained shut.

'In case news of the target slips out,' said Jacob.

'As if we'd bloody tell anyone,' said Roland, and he lapsed into fretful contemplation from which he only emerged when they were back in their hut and he had unpacked his suitcase and placed photos of his wife and son above the bed. Jacob swung his feet onto his mattress and chatted with Charlie. Through the window he could see the men who were on ops that night lighting cigarettes now outside the briefing room, the curtains still drawn to conceal the maps on the walls showing the routes into and out of the target. The ops men smoked incessantly in the hazy afternoon sun, chatting or just staring at the ground until they broke up into little groups and headed off to their rooms. Jacob and Charlie and Roland looked up as a group of them walked in.

'Hello, what's this?' sneered one of the men. 'New boys, eh?'

'Another bloody sprog crew,' said another, and they laughed and sat on adjacent beds and lit up again.

'Want a cigarette?' said one, chucking the pack across the room. It landed next to Jacob and he took a cigarette and passed the pack to Charlie and then on to Roland and they each took one and shared a match and the room filled with bluish smoke as the men puffed away.

'What's the target for tonight?' asked Charlie, looking at the men with his wide quizzical eyes.

'Wuppertal,' said one. He pronounced the first syllable with an exaggerated repeated flourish, as if it were worthy of some kind of celebration. 'Wup-Wup-Wuppertal!'

'Nice jaunt for a summer's night,' said another. 'We should be there and back in four or five hours.'

'It'll burn like flaming hell tonight,' said the first, sucking hard on his cigarette. 'The weather's as hot there as it is here by all accounts. I don't suppose you boys have seen a target all lit up yet, have you? You won't believe it when you do. You won't believe the flames.'

'And don't forget the flak, just a touch of the stuff,' said the other dreamily, as if he were recounting the ingredients of a favourite dish.

'Oh yes, and the flak. How we ever get through I've never understood. Just a bloody great wall of fire and searchlights and you go sailing on through and bomb nice and straight and level and hope you don't shit yourself.'

'How many ops have you lads done?' asked Roland, turning away from his photos.

'This will be our fifteenth. Only fifteen more to go,' the man joked with a wheezing cough followed by a manic little laugh. His face was disfigured by a rash from his oxygen mask, dry scaly skin and red streaks on his cheeks like the painted grin-lines of a clown who has dipped himself in sadness and drowned.

'Only three crews have made it to thirty ops from this squadron in the last year,' said the other, and the clown coughed and laughed again. 'Plenty get shot away on their very first op. Saves them worrying about the other twenty-nine.'

Roland frowned again and sucked hard on his cigarette.

'See those beds over there, chum?' said the clown, jerking his head towards a line of bare mattresses near the door. 'Sprog crew just like you, arrived here four days ago, got the chop on their first trip last night, a real dicey do, Mulheim in the Ruhr – Happy bloody Valley, just one long corridor of searchlights and box barrages and fighters and flak all over the place. And their mates caught a packet too – chop, chop, chop. They had the beds you're in now. They're probably still warm. And that one there,' he said, gesturing towards the bed on which Jacob sat, 'probably stinks still of piss. He wet himself the other night, gushed right out like a garden hose, the noise could have wakened the dead, thought none of us noticed. But we notice everything – heightened perception, you see, got to have it to see the chop coming. And then you weave, you fucking weave, weave right out of its way. Let it chop the others, not you. Choppity chop chop, ha ha ha ...'

Jacob shifted on the mattress and more men came in and the conversation turned away from the newcomers and the men on ops dropped their voices, talking in subdued tones as if sharing a dirty secret until they left for their pre-op meal of bacon and eggs. Later on, Jacob watched the trucks pull up and the ops men got inside and the trucks took them away to the waiting planes and as the sun began to set and the heat of the day turned to a hazy crimson glow, the gunning of engines filled the air. Jacob and the others went out onto the tarmac and watched as the planes trundled to the end of the runway, then one by one the planes paused and shuddered and roared past and lifted off and then banked and climbed high into the darkening dome of a sky just coming to life with the first of the stars.

In the morning, the row of beds opposite Jacob was empty and the men from the Committee of Adjustment drew up in their van and put the ops men's belongings into boxes and took them away.

'Three planes were lost over Wuppertal last night,' said Charlie.

'Including the squadron's senior crew,' added George. 'On their twenty-ninth op, just one away from the end of their tour. What a waste of bloody effort.'

Later that day three new crews arrived and the beds were full again.

***

And then it was their turn, the day when the training stopped and the war began for them. Jacob rose early to check the ops board and Ralph's name was on the list, P/O Andrews, next to his aircraft D-Dog, the take-off slot and an estimated time of arrival back at base to be filled in later after the briefing.

'Ops are on, boys!' said Jacob, when they met outside the mess after breakfast.

'Yes,' said George. 'We're off out dicing tonight at last. Anyone got the gen?'

'Top secret, old chap, didn't you know?'

'We'll find out after lunch, I expect. Main briefing's at four.'

Jacob visited the post room and sat on the bench by the path outside and opened his mail, first a letter from Rose. She had received her posting to a bomber base in Cambridgeshire.

'I think it's for the best,' she wrote. 'This way we're not so very far from each other but neither are we so close that it will cause us pain.

You understand what I mean by that, don't you Jacob, my darling? Your presence here would make our nightly parting unbearable – if it were your plane I had to see off at dusk each night it would simply drive me mad, to think of you hurtling away just yards from me, then suddenly hundreds of yards, then miles, then so many miles that only the passing of many hours of worry could possibly reunite us. I would be paralysed, useless until your plane returned. And I must do my job here too, must bring the boys back down for their landing slots, I must concentrate hard for them, to bring them in, just as I hope your girls will do that for you – perhaps I'm bringing their boys in here too, the very ones, a shared responsibility. So I leave you in their hands, Jacob, I will trust them to get you down in one piece, come fog or rain or hellfire, and I will do the same for the boys here, whoever they belong to, whoever is waiting for them to get home. But please don't think this means I don't wish to see you, I do so much that it hurts, almost a physical pain, not in my heart where I would expect it, but this dull numb thing throughout my being, this awful black ache. I almost dare not see you in case I cannot bear to let you go again. And that just would not do, would it? Stiff upper lip and all that. But when shall we meet, Jacob? Because we must. Because I need you. I expect you'll get leave in six weeks? Let me know the dates and I'll see to it that my leave coincides with yours. Jacob, my love, you are so very dear to me – you do know that, don't you? You always have been and always will.'

Jacob read the letter again. Where had it come from, this thing between him and Rose, who he remembered as a woman when he was still just a boy? She must have seen the thing before he did but she had waited, had let him traipse after her in childhood, had encouraged him in hindsight, always seemed to be around when he was, and now she was declaring the thing that had stood unspoken between them since even before Jacob had understood what that thing was. But now he could see it too, the simplest thing in the world and the most precious.

Then he opened the other letter, from Harry Pollock, stationed with a squadron further north in Lincolnshire, describing his first operation the previous week, how they had got lost on the way back and the plane had nearly run out of fuel before landing at a satellite base in Norfolk, and his relief at having got the first operation out of the way, at knowing now the task that confronted him and that perhaps he was up to it.

***

Jacob and Charlie and George and Roland and the two Australians ate lunch together in the sergeants' mess while Ralph sat in the officers' dining room across the corridor.

'Flying tonight, lads?' asked the waitress as she brought the men their pudding.

'Yes, first op tonight,' said George. 'Just twenty-nine more and we'll be done!'

'Good luck then, lads,' she said. 'Which kite are you in?'

'D-Dog. She looks a lovely crate.'

'Oh yes, the erks all say the Dog's a good one,' she said. 'You'll be just fine, don't you worry about a thing.'

'I bet you say that to all the boys,' said Don.

'Yes, if you're wrong, we're hardly going to come back and correct you,' said Jacob. 'Excuse me, my dear, you do realise of course that your prediction was wildly optimistic ...'

'Very funny,' she laughed. 'Really, you look like a lucky crew to me.'

'Lucky to meet you, anyway,' said Don, smiling at her.

'Are you being saucy with me?'

'I might be, if you give me half a chance,' said Don.

She turned and smiled and walked away and he watched her go as he gulped down his food.

At four o'clock they gathered in the briefing room, sitting together near the back as the other crews filed into the room and filled it with their nervous chatter. Jacob looked around the room as it began to fill, the bearing of the men differing according to the number of operations they had flown. He recognised another sprog crew three rows in front, sitting in a line, six men and their skipper, not saying a word except to offer each other cigarettes and to share a match as it burnt down to nothing. The senior crews had a different air about them, a casual worn-out intimacy with the danger of their lives that they carried in the way they walked and the detached ambivalence of their eyes, the sad eyes of foxhounds who have done it all before and are going to do it again, and again and again, until they exhaust themselves and are put out of their misery. They had seen the briefings and the take-off and the hell of the target and the long exhausted trawl home through skies still punctuated with flak and fighters, the strung-out waiting for a landing slot and the coming down through murk, the debriefing with the hot mugs of tea laced with rum, and the cold-fish eyes of the intelligence officers, and the long wait for comrades who were already dead.

An intelligence officer strode into the room and the doors slammed shut behind him with a noise like a bomb going off, followed by the ack-ack clip of his heels across the wooden floor. He leapt up onto the dais at the front as if he was about to burst into song. He had performed on the stage in his teens, the lead role in a school production of Hamlet, skull in hand, and it occurred to him that he had a room full of them now, pale grey sweating things, so much grey meat, like pork that had been left out too long, smelling already of decay. 'Better that they're consumed when fresh,' he found himself thinking, 'before they start to rot with fear.' He admonished himself inwardly for what his mind had allowed him to think and then he stiffened and the skulls fell quiet as he coughed them into silence.

'The target for tonight, gentlemen,' he announced, 'is Cologne.'

A rustle of noise spread across the room like the whispering of summer rain on broad-leaved trees. Jacob glanced backwards and forwards across the heads in front of him, assessing the reactions of the more experienced crews. He tried to dredge from his memory some notion of what it meant to go to Cologne, the level of defences they could expect, what it was the madmen instructors at the OTU and HCU had told him, but he could recall none of it now, his mind had gone blank when he needed it most, and the tired foxhound eyes of the experienced men gave nothing away.

'Close the blinds, will you?' clipped the intelligence officer.

The blinds clattered across the blue summer sky and the room went black but for seams of light around the edges of the windows. Someone must have cracked a joke at the back because several men laughed briefly and then stopped. The projector started up its humming and a hundred pairs of eyes followed its searchlight glare onto the screen.

'This is your target,' said the intelligence officer. 'And this is your aiming point ...'

He tapped the centre of the photographic image with his cane.

'Cologne Cathedral. Zero hour is 22.30. The marker flares will be green dripping red. We will confirm the enemy colours of the day before you depart. We have good information regarding the nature of the defences from previous raids. The searchlight belts extend from ...'

Jacob found himself listening intently to the details of the briefing, at the same time asking himself questions that so many new crews across the country would be asking themselves now. What on earth am I doing here? Can this be real? And will I survive? Next to Jacob sat George, remembering the bombs over London in 1940 and his granny aflame on the couch and the glimpse he had caught of her little body as they pushed her like a dead dog into a bag and took her away. Next to George, Charlie was fretting over the navigation routes and further along the line Ralph ran a mental list of the pre-flight checks. Jacob thought of home and wondered what it was that had persuaded him to volunteer for aircrew duties, and then he reminded himself it was for them at home that he had made the decision, to do his bit to end the war, to crush the enemy in such a way that they would never be a threat again, in the way that one crushes a wasp beneath the sole of a boot until its venom runs out, but in the next thought he cursed himself again and noticed that he was gritting his teeth. The briefing ended and someone on the far side of the room said 'Let's go kill the bloody Hun,' and someone laughed at the broken voice and the blinds went up and the sunlight streamed in and the men went off for their pre-flight meal.

They gathered later in the crew room and a WAAF helped Jacob into his gear, and he collected his parachute and his operational rations, the flask of coffee and the juice and sandwiches and chocolate that some wolfed down early because of nerves and others for the same reason could not bring themselves to touch until they were home again in the early hours. A truck took them away to the plane and as he waited for the off Jacob watched the world outside from behind his Perspex dome, the Perspex specked with the remains of insects that the Dog had smashed on previous trips, a world in which a summer evening buzzed with life, alive with wasps full of venom and men and women going about their peaceful errands, and Jacob noticed a boy on the other side of the wire returning with his rods and his nets from a day spent fishing as he used to do, and a man riding his bicycle up the lane, then a young couple walking arm in arm on the way to the pub before a night spent making love with the windows open and a veil of warm air streaming in and her hair thrown back upon the pillow, but the woman's hair was blowing about now in the backdraught from the airscrews as wasps hurtled past her in the gale, her world separated from the world of Jacob and his crew – seven helpless wasps in the gale that war had brought on – separated from their world by the wall of noise of four Merlin engines and the grubby claustrophobia of the fuselage and their wasp-specked venom-flecked Perspex prison walls and the prospect of five hours' flight to and from Germany and the impenetrable fiery veil that would shroud the target, and the filthy task that awaited them, and the unknowable nature of whatever it was that must claim them now.

And then Ralph got his green, he opened the throttles, and Jacob watched the tarmac speeding by, a rushing black river beneath his Perspex bomber's dome, and then the tarmac fell away and he was airborne, into battle with his crew, men he barely knew, men of air on their way to bomb a city to destruction and themselves one step closer to the end of their tour or the end of their tether. They joined the rest of the bomber stream nosing across the North Sea towards the Dutch coast as night fell upon them and Jacob lay on his belly in the nose and watched clouds drift across the sky like icebergs across a frozen sea, the sun setting small and distant at his back, starbursts of flak suddenly lighting up the sky, creeping nearer as the ack-ack gunners along the coast found their range, shell fragments pocking the underside of the wings and cordite introducing itself to the infant crew for the first time, and then the flak slowly receded as the bomber flew out of range, but Jacob knew the night-fighters would be taking off now from Heligoland, searching their allocated boxes of sky, guided towards the bombers by the radar operators on the ground and looking for the pale blush of a Lancaster's hot exhausts or the glint of moon on wing, or climbing above the bombers to where the moon pinned their silhouettes against the cloud-base and then down would come the fighters, amok among the flock of lumbering giants. The taste of vomit burnt Jacob's throat from when he had thrown up on the grass before climbing aboard, and the thought of the fighters brought another gurgle back up into his throat and he forced it back down. He strained his eyes at the night and sensed rather than saw the other bombers beside him in the dark, then bright red tracer skating left to right two hundred yards away and a little plume of light far off in the night that quickly stretched itself along the fuselage of a bomber that had been hit, the plane flying on as more tracer angled into it and the fire became a brighter orange glow, then pink and white as the metal alloy combusted and a blinding white flash and the Lancaster was gone, and away on the other side another bomber was in flames as it spiralled down through thin cirrus cloud, then another explosion far below and more tracer exchanges high above. The searchlight belts were set in layers and D-Dog passed through the wands of light and a plane was picked up by a blue-tinged master beam and then coned by a dozen others and it was knocked out of the sky by the flak that poured up through the beams and then night-fighters dropped bright white magnesium flares that turned night into day and Jacob threw up into his oxygen mask.

The knocked-back voices of the crew ghosted back and forth across the suffocation of the intercom.

'Five minutes to target, skipper,' said Charlie.

'Righto, navigator. Bomb-aimer, do you have sight of the target?'

'Straight ahead. Where are the pathfinders? The markers should be going down by now.'

'There they go,' said Ralph. 'Bang on time.'

The flares, green dripping red, fell towards the aiming point in the centre of Cologne.

'Jesus Christ, look at those searchlights,' said Ralph. 'Navigator, come up here and take a look at this.'

'No thanks, skipper, I'm happy here behind my curtain.'

As the flak burst around them, the searchlights sent up a forest of blinding beams, reaching miles into the sky for as far as the eye could see, and more red and green marker flares went down.

'Three minutes to target, skipper,' said Charlie.

'Roger, navigator, I can see it clear as day. OK, boys, here we go, steady now for the bombing run.'

Jacob lay on his belly in the nose of the bomber and his breath came in long rasping draws as he watched the target swallow up the night with its ferocity, the city already burning and the sky aflame with anti-aircraft shells, burning planes, sudden vast explosions, and the cold unforgiving searchlight stare. The Dog rocked as a shell burst beside her, the sound of boulders tumbling alongside, then a sharper crack and the hard rattle of shell fragments against the fuselage. A searchlight swung across Jacob's vision and lit up the dome, blinding him momentarily, but the Dog brushed past the beam and then another plane was lurching this way and that, trying to release itself from the grip of the lights, and it veered off into the path of another bomber and they blew up together and drifted away, a million dying embers, and another was going down now in a precipitous dive into the centre of the burning city.

Jacob was tracking the target indicators towards the bomb-sight and a flak shell burst alongside and the plane jumped and settled. Then it leapt high and dropped and veered off course and there was a great shuddering judder and then Roland's voice indistinct down the intercom, something about an engine on fire.

'Repeat that, please, flight engineer,' said Ralph.

'I said starboard outer alight, skipper.'

'How bad?'

'Gone bloody u/s, I reckon.'

'Damn it. OK, feathering now. Operate extinguisher.'

'OK, done. I think it's out.'

'Bomb-aimer, are we still on course?'

Jacob was choking something back down his throat again.

'I said bomb-aimer, are we still on course?'

'Sorry, skip. Starboard a touch. Starboard again. OK, OK, dead ahead.'

Jacob tracked the aiming point towards the centre of the bomb-sight, flaming streets drifting past thousands of feet below.

'Bomb doors open?'

'Doors open. Left a touch, skipper. Left, left. Steady. Left, left a bit. OK, steady there.'

Jacob's thumb wavered for a moment upon the tit, the paused hand of death, and this moment of reflection almost stopped him from doing the thing he had to do, had to do to himself and the people beneath the bombs, but then his training kicked in and it booted his humanity aside, and he pressed the tit as hard as he could and the plane lifted up as the departing weight of the bombs let it go and a weight lifted from Jacob's shoulders, the weight of uncertainty over whether he could do the job, whether he could hold his nerve and do what was expected of him.

'Bombs gone,' he said as the lumps fell away and another one formed in his throat. 'Hold her steady, skip, photoflash coming. OK, we've got our photo. Bomb doors closed.'

And he breathed out hard and felt something damp upon his cheeks and the salt edged around the sides of his oxygen mask and lifted red lines upon his face and he knew he was one of the clowns now, dipped in sadness, drowning in an endless ocean of war that had filled up the space where his future had been.

'Well done, bomb-aimer,' said Ralph. 'Top job. Now let's go home. Navigator, get me a course.'

Ralph took the plane into a shallow dive, out and away from the sea of flame below, the burning grid of streets with their roofless houses, empty boxes in which people had previously kept their lives. Then Jacob saw a black shape flashing past below, turning up in a hurtling arc.

'Fighter, skip! Four o'clock.'

'Gunners, can you see him?' shouted Ralph.

'Coming in now!' yelled a voice.

Then a smacking sound down the intercom, high-explosive shells ripping holes somewhere back along the fuselage, and a smell of smoke that smothered up the vomit.

Then Ralph down the intercom, 'Where's that bloody fighter gone?' and heavy breathing as someone flicked on their intercom switch, and then Don's voice, 'He's gone down beneath us. We've got a fire back here, by the way.'

'Do a banking search, skipper,' said Jim. 'We'll take a look underneath.'

Ralph rocked the plane to one side, then the other, then back again.

'He's below us. Corkscrew starboard, go!' yelled Don, and cannon shells burst in again and something else began to burn and Jacob felt the world fall away as Ralph rammed the Dog into a steepling dive, Jacob pinned to the roof of his dome by the speed of the descent, then a sickening lurch as Ralph and Roland were hauling them level and seven pairs of eyes stared out on stalks in search of the fighter.

'It's getting awfully smoky back here,' Don was saying suddenly.

Then Ralph, 'Wireless op, go see what's happening back there.'

Then nothing for minutes, just the roar of the engines and the ringing in Jacob's ears and the sound of his own breathing, panting like a dog, thinking of Rose all of a sudden, then pushing her away, this was no place for her, not here, not now, not this world. And then George's voice again.

'Done it, skip. Not such a big blaze after all, three squirts and out.'

'You sure?'

'Affirmative. Positively definitely out. It's burnt the parachute stowage all to hell, though.'

'How's that engine now, flight engineer?'

'Could be better.'

'Gravy levels?'

'Good enough. Go steady and we should be OK.'

'Navigator, get me a new course.'

'Yes, give me a sec, skip.'

'And gunners,' said Ralph. 'All OK with you? Keeping wakey-wakey, are we?'

'Yes, skip.'

'And you, Jimmy boy? Eyes peeled?'

'Sure, skip. I've swallowed so much Benzedrine I won't sleep for a year.'

'I could do with some myself,' said Charlie. 'Feeling a touch tired now.'

'You always were a dozy sod,' someone said.

'Have you got that course for me yet, navigator?'

'With you shortly.'

'Good lad, make it snappy. What about you, Jacob? Are you still with us?'

'Of course, skip. Just maintaining operational silence, like I was taught.'

'Good point boys, cut the chat, will you? We're not home yet.'

They flew on in silence until Charlie got a fix and Jacob watched the dark line of the Dutch coast pass beneath him, drifting away behind them now as the flak ships sent up their shells but the puffs of black smoke, grey in the moonlight, never came close and they flew on across a shimmering sea towards England. Then finally the magic words from their home tower, 'Pancake! Pancake!' and the plane wallowed around in line with the runway and the flare-path grew broad and welcoming and then they were down and George was humming them along the runway, then the engines winding down and the crew scrambling together across the massive main spar and down the length of the fuselage, squeezing along the cramped ribbed interior to where one of the gunners had flung the rear door open and was sorting out the ladder. They waited for the crew truck on the grass beside the plane, the dew soaking their boots, and then the truck hurtled up, Hairy Mary at the wheel, a WAAF with a shock of red hair that she failed to restrain in an orderly fashion, and Jacob saw her red mane blowing in the pre-dawn breeze as she jumped from the cab.

'Hello Mary,' Don was saying. 'Boy, am I glad to see you again!'

'Hello Hairy, how are things?' said Jim casually.

'How are you, more to the point?' said Mary.

'Oh, you know. Pleasant little jaunt.'

'Yes, wizard prang,' concurred Ralph. 'She's a lovely bus, this one.'

Jacob and Roland were examining the holes in her fuselage now.

'Blimey!' said Roland. 'You could fit your bloody head through that one.'

'Well done, Dog,' said Jacob, patting the scarred metal. 'You got us home in the end.'

Then he threw up again on the grass.

'You all right there, Jacob?' said Roland.

'Blasted pre-op beans, that's all.'

'I know, they're murder, aren't they? Was feeling sick myself when that fighter came in.'

'Come on, let's get you boys back for your breakfast,' said Mary, and she got into the truck and revved the engine and tore away across the airfield as the men bumped about under the tarpaulin in the back. They gathered in a huddle around a trestle table outside the kit room and took their mugs of hot milky tea. The Wing Commander came across and patted Ralph on the back.

'Well done, Andrews, the first one's always the hardest,' he lied.

Three other sprog crews had returned before them and they stood together in their clannish little groups discussing the night's events with weary voices and tired eyes, foxhound puppies now, wet behind the ears but the blood of their first fox wet upon their lips as they awaited their turn with an intelligence officer eager to glean information regarding the accuracy of the bombing, the searchlight belts and fighter activity they had encountered, and any clues they could provide regarding bombers they had seen lost over the target. Jacob sat through the meticulous questioning, staring over the man's shoulder at the pretty curve of a WAAF's gentle face, then into his mug of tea, as if the night's events could still be seen in these suddenly mundane but all-too-gentle precious things, and when the questioning was over the crew picked up their things and went to the mess and ate their bacon and eggs in silence punctuated with wry observations and speculation as to what tomorrow might bring. In the operations room they checked the estimated landing times of other planes and watched as several more came in and the blank spaces on the blackboard were chalked with the hour of each crew's return, but one of the empty spaces refused to yield a landing time.

'He can't have any fuel in his tanks now,' someone said.

'Been gone too bloody long.'

'Not landed elsewhere?'

'No reports of it. But you never know.'

'We'll know in the morning.'

'Poor sods ...'

They returned to their barracks and Jacob fell into bed and felt it pitch and yaw as dry land does beneath the feet of a sailor who has spent too long lost on a drunken sea, and then sleep, oblivion, and all too soon the new day, abrupt wakefulness, empty beds further down the room, and at breakfast the blackboard still incomplete, and the visit of the Committee of Adjustment in mid-morning, the taking away of belongings and the changing of the sheets in anticipation of more new arrivals to toss into war's hungry gullet sometime later that day or the next. Ops were on again that night, and they went through the same routine, the test flight, the pre-op checks, the pensive lunch, the briefing and the final meal forced down into a churning gut. And then away to the planes and into the onrushing uncertainty of night.

***

Fifty miles away from where Jacob and the others are taking off again for Germany, Rose takes up her post for the night at her radio set in the control tower at her station, listening to the distant voices of her pilots as they sit in their planes at dispersal, their tension transmitting itself down the airwaves, the little coughs and verbal tics she has learnt to recognise so swiftly now that she can tell the men apart even when they have been at the station for less than a week and she has sent them out and shepherded them home only two or three times before their voices are lost forever.

One by one the planes depart and the voices fall quiet as distance hauls them out of reach, shoves them off the sudden cliff of night. The next that Rose hears of them are the early returns, skippers with planes that have developed a fault, an engine run down or a turret that has seized, and their voices are calmer now but uncertain with guilt as they land early without bombing the target. Then sometime after midnight the first reconnection, almost a rebirth, an everyday miracle, a plane coming home empty of bombs, the wireless operator calling for help in finding the base in the low-lying fog, an engine alight and the petrol down low, the flight engineer's voice over the intercom too as he adjusts the fuel settings in a desperate attempt to conserve the last drops for his plane in the fog, and the bomb-aimer's voice coming up from the nose, 'The flare path, I see it, skipper, I see it!' and Rose calling out again, almost crying out to her men now down the airwaves, guiding them in, then the skipper's voice saying something about a burnt boy at the back, 'Get the blood wagon ready, the rear gunner's burnt bad,' and then a hacking cough brought on by the stink in the plane, and the engines audible, a gentle roar intensifying, a growing glow in the sky from the flames from the engine, the glow getting lower, and then they are down but the undercarriage has gone, the plane lurches sideways and tips up on a wing and cartwheels across the field and the fog is dispersed and the radio falls silent as the blast from the explosion shatters the windows and flames light up the back wall of the room where Rose sits strewn now with glass, and again she wants to cry out but she suffocates herself in calm, listens out for another who is in touch with her now from somewhere high above, strung out on Benzedrine and calling for help, appealing to her now to call them on in, and down they come, down through the fog. 'The flare path, I see it,' says someone again, a short-distance echo of what has just been, and Rose finds her hand clenched in a fist because the voice sounds like Jacob's but she knows it's not him, that he is away somewhere else being guided on down by another petrified girl whose brow will be as furrowed and wet as her own, ploughed all to hell with worry, and then the engine noise roars past as the plane touches down and she sees its shape flashing by, silhouetted by the blaze from the earlier one, and she turns back to her radio and listens out for the next. And later on the fog has gone, the sky full of stars and the voices less tense, and she is guiding one in, just seconds from home, when streaks of sudden light brighten the sky, tracer bullets now from a German intruder, and the Lancaster catches light and explodes as it hits the ground and before Rose goes to bed that night she picks the glass out of her hair and she prays.

SUMMER 1943

Vera broke the news of her intentions to Norman as he sat slumped in his armchair in the sitting room, drinking his bedtime milk. The windows were open to the meadow at the back, the lights off, the blackout curtains pulled back. Bright moonlight lit up the field and Vera could see his profile silhouetted against the bluish glow as he raised the mug to his lips. A warm breeze shifted the curtains. He did not respond to her news, took another sip of his milk, then put the mug down on the side-table.

'What do you mean you're thinking of going out to work?' he said at last. 'What about the little one?'

'She's nearly seven now, Norman. She's at school during the day, and all I do is stay at home and bake and cook and clean and go up to mum and dad's. I can't even go and see Rose any more now that she's gone away.'

He looked at her for a moment, then turned his gaze towards the window again.

'And we agreed, didn't we?' she continued. 'We talked about it years ago, that perhaps one day it would be for the best. And the extra money would come in handy.'

'I earn enough for the family, Vera, that's my role, not yours. Your place is here.'

'But I'm lonely, Norman. Rattling around in here all day on my own. And there's a war on, you know – I've got to do something useful, do my bit.'

'You're useful at home, Vera. I don't want my wife going out to work. It's demeaning, I won't bloody have it.'

'You won't have any choice soon enough. When Daphne's seven, I'll have to get a job, it's the law. They'll send me to a munitions works.'

'They won't.'

'Of course they will. And you won't be able to stop them.'

'I'm not having it, I tell you. I provide for this family and I want my wife and child at home.'

He drained his mug and closed the window and went to bed. As Vera trod up the stairs later on, she heard his snoring from the bedroom and she undressed and put on her nightclothes and lay in bed beside him and finally she fell asleep as the summer dawn lit the edge of the curtains. He rose early and she woke to the sound of the news on the radio in the kitchen and Norman filling the kettle. She went downstairs and helped him with his breakfast.

'I'm serious,' she said finally. 'I'm going to find a job before they send me to one of those dirty armaments factories.'

'You're not.'

'Yes I am! I must!'

'No you're bloody well not. Vera, you knew you were marrying a farmer, I told you I was a simple man.'

He pulled on his boots and slammed the door on his way out. He returned at lunchtime and did not speak a word and when he came home in the evening he spoke kindly to Daphne but ignored his wife and ate his dinner alone and then washed and went to bed.

Vera fretted for hours before she raised the issue again the following week.

'Norman, I have something to tell you. I've found a job.'

Silence.

'I said I've found a job. I'm going out to work.'

'I heard you.'

'Well then?'

'What sort of job?'

'In a sweet shop.'

'That's really going to help the war effort.'

'Life has to go on, you know.'

'Where is it?'

'Woodstock. You know it, the one we went to the day after our wedding.'

'That old place.'

'I start next week. I'll be home by the time Daphne finishes school.'

'I never dreamt I'd see the day my wife had to go out to work.'

'Norman, it's for the best.'

'I wouldn't say so.'

He pulled on his boots and closed the door and went to his animals in the fields, and he did the same the following week as Vera was readying Daphne for school before her first day at work. Vera left Daphne at the school gate where the headmistress stood on sentry duty and counted the children in. Daphne let go of Vera's hand and ran towards the school-room door, then turned and waved and dashed inside. Vera walked to the stop and waited for the Oxford bus. She fidgeted with her watch strap and adjusted her scarf and checked the contents of her bag and thought of Norman stalking about the fields in his silent brooding rage. His mood had worsened as the day approached and he had not slept a wink the night before, sitting up again until dawn in the armchair by the sitting room window and leaving the house without a word when the cattle began to stir. Then she thought of Mr Bell, the shop owner, with his bristling moustache the colour of red squirrels, darting little eyes with the air of a fox and a smile to go with them. He was in early middle-age but looked rather older and she had seen him take on a military bearing that day at her interview when the delivery van turned up and people queued in a squabbling line with their ration coupons ready, eyes wide as gobstoppers and mouths like acid drops as they jostled about in the queue.

'Come on now, boys and girls,' he had said. 'Calm down, calm down, you'll all be served eventually.' And he tossed a mint imperial casually in the air and his mouth closed around it and the red squirrel moustache twitched as he sucked on the hard little sweet.

Vera waited for half an hour and finally she heard the bus's squealing brakes and she hopped aboard and took a seat by a window near the front. She watched as the bus trundled along the top road through Enstone, up and down the slopes and round the bends that ran through wheat fields yellow in the sun. As the bus drew up the hill past the Blenheim estate grounds and the long dry-stone wall where fat pheasants sat in winter, she rang the bell and jumped off the bus and hurried across the road to the sweet shop, the bell rattling a harsh welcome as she rushed in. The place was empty but she could hear footsteps in the back-room and Mr Bell calling out, 'I'm coming,' then the sound of his big bunch of keys jangling upon his belt as he walked.

'Oh, hello Vera,' he said, glancing at his watch. 'Been having a problem, have we?'

'I'm so sorry, Mr Bell, I really am. You see, I …'

'Don't worry, my dear,' he interrupted. 'Don't worry, I understand. Whatever it is, I understand. Now come into the back-room and I'll get you kitted out.'

He passed her a pink cotton apron and introduced her to the scales and went round indicating the sweets arranged in large glass jars upon rows of shelves and explained to her the rules about the ration books and the little tricks that people would try in order to sneak another ounce of cough candy or sherbet lemons. When the first customer arrived he slipped into the back-room and listened as Vera served and he smiled at her attentive repetition of the customer's request and the sound of her feet shuffling one way and another across the floor as she searched for an elusive jar.

'No, over there, dear, over there,' said the customer, Mrs Davis, a pug-faced widow who always wore crocodile-skin shoes she had bought in Paris in the 1920s and carried her purse in an ostrich-skin bag.

'You're the new girl, I expect?' said Mrs Davis, lowering her voice as Vera tipped the sweets into the scales. 'Just tip a few more in there, will you?'

They heard a sharp cough from the back-room.

'Well, perhaps not,' said Mrs Davis. 'I don't want to get fat, do I?'

Then she leaned forward and whispered, 'He's all right really, old Jingle. A good sort.'

'Jingle?' whispered Vera.

'Jingle Bell. Haven't you noticed his keys, jangling away on his belt all the time? You'll always know when he's around, that's for sure.'

Vera stifled a laugh and finished serving Mrs Davis and when she had gone Vera heard the jangle of keys as Mr Bell emerged from the back-room.

'Well done, Vera, well done. She's a bit of a sort, that Mrs Davis. We call her Tarzan round here, all that animal skin. Those crocodile shoes gave me a nasty nip once.'

He chuckled and took a sweet for himself and gave one to Vera and put the jar carefully back on the shelf and swept a trace of dust from the counter with an efficient flick of his finger. In mid-afternoon Vera served her last customer of the day and left Mr Bell jingling away behind the counter and rushed to catch the bus and cursed under her breath each passenger who lingered talking to the driver, delaying her onward journey, taking the bus closer to school closing time, and by the time three-thirty came the bus had not even reached Enstone and she imagined Daphne standing by the school gate waiting for her to come, and when she finally hurried up the hill it was quarter to four and by the gate stood the figures of a little girl with a satchel and the tall angular headmistress whose disapproving look put the cap on Vera's day.

As they ate their evening meal the ice thawed slightly and Norman asked about Vera's day and she slipped a small white paper bag onto the table and he looked inside and put one of the toffees in his mouth and smiled.

'I'm sorry, Vera,' he said. 'Forgive me.'

'Don't worry,' she said, and that was that.

The following day she left the house a little earlier and caught the bus without rushing and Norman walked Daphne to school and collected her later and he ignored the headmistress's haughty look and spent the walk home telling Daphne what the chickens had been up to and how one of the land girls had fallen in the pond.

That weekend, Rose arrived for three days' leave and she walked with Vera to the tea shop in town and they ordered tea and toast and squeezed onto a window seat.

'Have you heard from Jacob recently?' Rose asked as the sun streamed in and lit up her face.

'Yes, a letter came only a few days ago. He'd just been on his first op, I don't know where. I guess they're not allowed to say.'

'It could have been anywhere, there are raids nearly every day. Hundreds of planes.'

'How is it, Rose? On an airbase, I mean.'

Rose spread a meagre smear of jam on another slice of toast.

'Pretty awful really,' she said, and saw Vera's crestfallen look. 'I'm sorry, Vera. You know I've always been an honest sort.'

'I know, Rose, that's why you're my friend.'

'I don't know how they keep going, night after night, seeing all those other crews not coming back. But they go, so bloody scared but won't show it – press on regardless, they say, the chop will never get us.'

'But some make it through …'

'Yes, Vera, some of them do. Some of them make it to thirty ops. And some volunteer straight off for another tour, the bloody fools.'

'If Jacob volunteered for another tour I'd kill him,' said Vera, and they both smiled at the absurdity of what she had said.

'Will you see him when he gets leave?' asked Vera.

'Oh I do hope so. He's going to write as soon as he knows his dates. He said he'd take me somewhere he knows near Cambridge, a little place by the river.'

There was a pause.

'It's the real thing, isn't it, Rose? Between you and Jacob?'

'Of course it is, Vera, couldn't you tell? It's been there for ages and it's like nothing I've ever known.'

***

A hundred miles away in Suffolk, the Dog was bombed up and ready to go when Jacob took his place between Ralph and Charlie in the briefing room that afternoon. As the intelligence officer strode to the front to address the skulls, the blinds fell across the windows and the officer said in a loud decisive voice, 'The target for tonight, gentlemen, is Hamburg. And tonight, believe me, is a big one.'

Something between a cheer and a groan rippled across the room and the projector hummed its beam upon the screen and the intelligence officer outlined the night's work. Later that evening, Hairy Mary set the truck in gear and it pulled away across the airfield. Jacob sat in the back with Ralph and the others and another crew that had arrived the previous day and whose names he knew it would be a waste of time to learn just now, best wait and see if they were still there in the morning. Jacob watched the new men as they sat in the dark and he recalled the numb thoughts he had had in the moments before his first trip, thoughts he knew would be numbing them now. The weather had been hot and oppressive for days, the air growing heavy, building towards an almighty storm, and he sat sweating in his flying kit, knowing that when they reached cruising height the sweat would have chilled and his oxygen mask would be cool to the touch and still smelling of sick as he strapped it back on.

Approaching the German coast, Jacob crouched beside his flare chute, hemmed in by bales of aluminium strips, and he chucked them out in bundles at regular intervals, and as bombers across the stream did likewise the sky became a swirling mass of foil strips, throwing a protective sea of blips across the sky, shielding the bombers from the German radar operators and the night-fighters. A new navigational aid, H2S, showed the German coast in rough outline on a small screen in Charlie's navigator's compartment and Jacob sensed a confidence in Charlie's tone as he rolled instructions down the intercom to Ralph and in the nose of the plane, lying on his belly, Jacob watched the outline of the coast slip by as Ralph turned the bomber down the mouth of the Elbe towards the port city of Hamburg. The target was already erupting when they arrived and Jacob let the bombs go and watched pricks of light, orange and white and red, bubble up as high-explosive bombs blew the walls apart and he knew the incendiaries were showering down too onto the roofless, windowless buildings, bursting magnesium and phosphorous and petroleum jelly and burning rubber around the vicinity of their impact, facilitating the dispersal of fire and flame, and Don reported later that he could still see the city burning a hundred miles behind them as they sped home through the short summer night.

The following day, Jacob and the others sat in exhausted silence as the intelligence officer announced that the target for the night was Hamburg once more, and when they reached what was left of the city all they saw was the flicker of flames still burning beneath the drifting banks of smoke.

Jacob wearily let the bombs go and the Dog flew them home.

***

After two consecutive nights with every available crew in the air, operations were off the following day. Jacob and the others ate in the sergeants' mess, Ralph foregoing the more elevated air of the officers' facilities to be with his men.

'If these men are good enough to fly with me, then they're good enough to eat with me too,' he told the waitress as her intonation and her eyebrows queried his presence.

When they had finished and the mess hall was thinning out and their usual waitress came to take away their plates and cups, Don asked if she would sit with them a while.

'I can't remember the last time I sat and ate with a woman,' he said in mock desolation.

She was a pleasant-looking girl with auburn hair tied up in a bun and fine dark eyebrows that lifted slightly at his suggestion.

'But you've finished eating already,' she replied.

'Oh please, Millie,' said Don. 'Just for a minute or two.'

Millie sat down and they laughed and joked about an incident she recounted regarding a tray of eggs and a slab of lard and a tumble that someone had taken the previous day. The sun streamed in through the windows and lit up the grain of the table and Jacob noticed how fine and white Millie's skin looked against the golden brown of the oak and he saw that Don had noticed it too, that his hand moved a touch as if he wanted to take her hand in his own and hold it to his cheek, but instead Don made another joke and everyone laughed and she held her fine white hand to her mouth as she giggled and her eyes smiled at Don. As they stood up to leave, Don lingered at the table with Millie until finally he followed the others over to a grassy bank in the sun near the first of the Nissen huts. He lay down beside them and plucked a daisy from its stalk and began counting off the petals, 'She loves me, she loves me not ...' and Jim laughed and George called him a soft bugger and Jacob frowned.

'Don, you don't want to go messing with Millie,' Jacob said.

'Whyever not?' said Don, 'Didn't you see her eyes, the way she was looking at me, like I was a cream bun or something and she wanted to swallow me whole?'

'My dear Don, you have a rather fevered imagination,' said Ralph.

'Really, skip, a cream bun I was, I swear it. I saw it clear as day.'

'I saw it too,' said Jacob. 'That's what I'm worried about. Don't you know she's a chop girl?'

'Come on mate,' said Don. 'You don't believe that superstitious claptrap, do you?'

'Seriously,' said Jacob. 'Stratton was dicing with her and his whole crew bought it the very next night.'

'Jacob's right,' said Charlie. 'And before that there was that other fellow, you know the big Canadian guy, and the same damn thing happened, gone for a Burton the very next trip. Cream bun one day, toast the next.'

'Well it's a bit late now,' said Don. 'I've agreed to meet her for the bus into town this evening.

'For Christ's sake, Don,' said Jacob. 'Don't risk it. It's not just your neck that's on the block if you get the chop. We'll all be going down with you.'

They fell into silence and then Ralph spoke.

'Well, as skipper, I'm responsible for the safety of this crew, and I say that it's perfectly all right for you to see Millie this evening. However, you will need a chaperone to ensure you don't get up to anything with which the crew would not approve. So we'll all be going out with you. There can't be any harm in her drinking with us, just as long as it doesn't go any further than that.'

'Skip, I'd have invited you all to drink with us anyway,' laughed Don.

They met at the gate that evening and Millie arrived and they all got on the bus, a crowd of aircrew and WAAFs, and the bus hurtled out of the gate. The windows were open and the warm evening air rushed in and cast Millie's hair about her face and Jacob saw her looking at Don from beneath her auburn curls and Don looking back and smiling the smile of a man who knows he has been condemned and that his end is probably near, whether it be just around the corner of the next day or two weeks down the line or maybe three. Jacob watched as Don leaned his head out of the window and the wind swept over him and Don closed his eyes as the dipping sun brushed his face with gold, and then the rush of wind was interrupted and Don was opening his eyes again and Millie was leaning her head out too and was looking back at him, her face right up close to his, and Jacob thought of Rose and those times he had felt her soft breath on his face as she spoke, and then another song started up within the crowded bus, a raucous cacophony of voices bellowing out their sense of how good it felt still to be alive. The bus screeched to a halt in the nearest village and a handful of aircrew and WAAFs who had left the camp earlier to sneak in a preliminary pint squeezed on board and the doors closed and the driver gunned the engine and the hedges sped by again in a blur. They got off in the centre of town and streamed into the hotel across the road and soon the room was alive with the sound of voices and laughter and singing, the airmen in their best blue and the WAAFs in their severe, tight-fitting uniforms. The landlord lined the pint jugs up on the bar and filled them continuously and the bar never emptied and someone began playing a piano and Jacob looked across and saw that it was George and the singing started again and a little space cleared in the middle of the room where couples paired up and waltzed in time to George's dancing fingers and the tremulous warble of a Welsh flight-sergeant singing something that sounded entirely improvised in his native tongue, and then a more familiar song began and three dozen voices joined in, 'And the gunner in his turret, has got no fucking room! But he's got more room in there than in his fucking tomb!'

'They're singing about us,' said Jim, grinning at Don.

'To hell with that,' said Don. 'Here, get some more sauce down you,' and he pushed another pint into Jim's hand. 'No point in saving our money. We're not going to live long enough to spend it anyway.'

'Come on Donald, let's go and dance,' said Millie, and she took his hand and Don passed his glass to Jacob and winked as he followed her over to the space in the middle of the room.

'You don't really believe all that bull about chop girls, do you mate?' asked Jim.

'You can't be too careful,' said Jacob.

'Do you have a sweetheart at home, Jacob?'

'Of sorts. Reason enough to get through this war.'

'Well you should get stuck in here anyway, mate. You never know when you'll get another chance.'

He nodded over towards the other side of the room where Ralph and Charlie were with a group of WAAFs, Ralph talking vigorously as Charlie stared with his owl's eyes and smiled at something surprising he had heard.

'Come on Jacob,' said Jim. 'Let's have a wander over there.'

As they were walking across, Hairy Mary appeared in a flurry of red hair beside Jacob and slipped her arm through his and led him away to the dance floor, and he followed her reluctantly and held her politely but not intimately and he felt the occasional tug, a suggestion, as she tried to draw him in. The crowd thinned towards closing time and when the shutters came down the streets rang with shouts and singing. The bus drew up and they crowded in and a dim blue light lit the interior and the night air was still warm and humid and their bodies pressed together in a bobbing, sweating mass that swayed with the motion of the vehicle as it sped around the bends out of town, the songs that spilled from the speeding windows frightening the rabbits off the verges and into the hedgerows.

'You're all right, you are,' Hairy Mary shouted into Jacob's ear, and she took his head in her hands and planted a vigorous kiss upon his cheek and he put his arm around her and she rested her head on his shoulder and it bobbed up and down as the bus flung itself in and out of pot-holes. Beside him, Jacob watched as Don and Millie thrust their heads out of the window again and they grinned at each other as the wind sped through their hair and the moon cast the shadows of trees across the road. At the gate Don and Millie hung behind the others and by the guard house they stopped and gently kissed as Jacob looked back.

'Hey Don!' Jacob called out. 'I meant what I said. I don't want to get the chop on account of your knob.'

Don lingered, then turned and kissed Millie goodnight and ran to catch up with the others.

The next day ops were off again and Don and Millie met in the evening and walked down the lanes to the village pub where they sat and talked and imagined they were living a normal life again, a life in which people could meet and fall in love and contemplate a future unfettered by urgency or the need to cram experience into days or weeks not years, lest the years should never come. They walked back to the camp, the moon rising behind the woods, and they embraced in the empty country lane and they kissed in defiance of whatever the future might wish for them.

***

The following night the engines started up again towards dusk, gunning up the night with their roar, sweeping away the memories of quiet days. Ops were on and the target was Hamburg again. D-Dog shook as Ralph held the throttle at the runway's end, then the brakes came off and the Dog sped off into the deepening void as Millie stood with the others by the runway and watched the planes soar away until they were barely audible specks turning east. Then a bank of cloud swallowed them up and they existed no more and England existed no more for them, and all they knew was their hurtling crying machine and the song of the engines and the disembodied voices of their comrades over the intercom as the air turned cool and damp in the cloud. They emerged from the cloud into twilight, the first stars flickering on the threshold of night and the sun lighting up the top of the cloud layer with streaks of pinkish-orange cut through by blue-grey valleys. Away to one side Jacob saw another Lancaster lift up through the cloud, then another directly beneath them and another to starboard, and all across the sky the bombers crept up like beautiful black insects into the amphitheatre of the sky, huge and empty and wonderful, a place where only gods by rights should be. But a devil of a storm was stoking itself over Europe and they ran into it as soon as they crossed the enemy coast, the crack and flash from the flak-ships blanked out by the storm clouds. Rain sheeted through the sky, thrashing upon the dome where Jacob lay prone, a million rushing drops lit for brief instants by lightning bolts, and the thunder rose above the din of the engines and Ralph took the plane up but the storm was insurmountable, and he dropped the altitude but the storm could not be under-flown, and so they flew on through cloud in a sky thick with bombers, all attempting to avoid each other in the storm and the flak that was beginning to pock the sky. A huge flash of white tinged with orange and the bright red of flares erupted overhead and debris struck the Dog and she shuddered and flew on until the intensifying red bursts of flak and the smell of cordite and the faint orange glow through the cloud signalled their arrival over the target and Jacob bombed on the parachute flares through 10/10ths cloud and Ralph banked away onto the course for home. They cleared the storm thirty minutes out from the target and the night-fighters were waiting, picking off the bombers as they flew into the clear air, silhouetted against the lightning bursts and the flames of the city that had died.

Suddenly Jacob heard Don yelling down the intercom, 'Corkscrew port, go!' and a dark shape scudded by below, and the Dog dived away and she shook with the dull clatter of her guns as tracer fire from the fighter zipped past Jacob's dome, and then the smacking sound of cannon shells hitting into her somewhere unseen.

'Corkscrew starboard, go!' Jim was screaming now, then a long burst of fire and the Dog falling away again.

'I've got him!' someone was shouting down the intercom, and in the nose of the bomber Jacob saw the fighter trail away in a torrent of flame and he followed it down until a silent little blink upon the surface of the earth indicated its impact with the ground.

Then Ralph's voice, 'Rear gunner, what's happening back there? Rear gunner, I said what's going on? OK, radio op, back you go, go take a look.'

Then silence for several minutes, that burning back in Jacob's throat again, and then the sound of an intercom switch and George's voice, chucking up an oath.

'Radio op, what's up?' said Ralph, then a stream of oaths coming back the other way. 'Hey George, what the hell is it?'

'Leave it, skip,' said Charlie. 'He doesn't feel like talking just now.'

'I told you she was a bloody chop girl,' said Jacob.

'Bomb-aimer, maintain silence, will you?' said Ralph. 'And that's a bloody order.'

They landed as the first smudge of light smeared the eastern sky and they left the aircraft through the door beside the rear turret and in the half-light they could barely see what was left of Don and his guns, just a shape against the dawn, a shape that was not as it should have been. Then Jim was outside, peering into the turret, reaching in and pulling at something, then Jacob pulling at his arm, tugging him towards the truck.

'Come on, mate. You can't do anything for him now.'

'But we can't just leave him here, we have to get him out.'

Then Ralph was at Jacob's shoulder, pushing past him and pulling Jim away, and then six silent men were sitting in the truck as it bumped across the field, and they were in the debriefing room as Don's broken body was disentangled from the turret piece by piece, and at breakfast Jacob heard that they had hosed out what was left of him onto the grass in a stream of blood and bone and brain.

When Millie approached them in the mess they consoled her as well as they could, from a distance.

'I know what you're thinking,' she said, looking at Jacob. 'I'm a chop girl. Don't you worry, I'll keep away from you all now. I'll keep well clear until all this is over.'

And she burst into tears and hurried off into the kitchen.

'See what you've gone and done,' said Charlie. 'You've upset her good and proper now.'

'I'm not too fussed about that,' said Jacob. 'Just as long as she steers clear, that's all.'

Jacob noticed the ripples across the surface of Ralph's tea as the skipper's hands trembled almost imperceptibly.

'Jacob's right,' said George. 'No more chop girls, boys, or you're out on your ear. Right, skip?'

Ralph nodded slowly and he put his mug on the table to stop the shaking, but he knew Jacob had seen it, he had seen Jacob looking.

'You know, she was the first girl Don ever kissed,' said Jim. 'He told me that just the night before he died.'

'Poor old Don,' said Charlie. 'You can hardly blame him for taking the chance when he got it.'

They were assigned a new rear gunner, a former farmhand from Taunton. On his first night he woke the others with his shouting.

'No, not the cows, not the cows!' he repeated until Jacob leaned across and nudged him firmly in the ribs and he fell back into a fitful sleep. The next night was the same and he sat away from the others at breakfast.

'What's up with his bloody cows?' said George. 'A whole blooming herd of them by the sounds of it.'

The gunner was as silent in the truck on the way to the plane as he had been noisy in the night before ops. The first op they took him on was an uneventful trip to Kassel, the second a roller-coaster ride through the Ruhr's 'Happy Valley'. Over Essen an anti-aircraft shell burst close by his turret and a small shrapnel fragment made a small neat hole in the Perspex and a small neat hole in his head.

'That turret's bloody jinxed,' said Jacob. 'Two gunners gone in the space of three ops.'

Their mood was improved by the arrival of their next gunner. Alan Armstrong had completed a full tour already and he stood before them like a miracle now, still living, breathing and drinking beer after thirty ops.

'And at the start of my second tour,' he told them as he ordered them all another round, 'the ship got hit by flak on the run-in to Essen. The fuselage took flame, the heat seized the turret door, the plane was tipping forward, you know, a death dive, the real thing, and my back was cooking up in the heat. I hammered at that ruddy turret, shoved it all about, and finally it swung round and the door flew open and out I popped, like a pea from a pod, out into space, umbrella open, plane falling away, all of them with it too, all my lads. Couldn't get out, the buggers, spinning like fury it was, no chance of getting out of a thing like that, is there?'

'Then what?' said Jacob. 'Old Jerry and his hounds were after you, I bet?'

'Oh yes, my boy, but your uncle Alan is a cunning little fox. Landed in a field outside the city, pitch black, stank of pigs but it put off the dogs. I hid in a sty all the next day, washed myself in a lake that night, got rid of the stink at last, then off I went, a month on country roads in the pitch black into France, got picked up by the Resistance in Strasbourg, then back to Blighty via Spain and Portugal. They told me I'd like a position as an instructor at a gunnery school. No, thank you, I says, but they sent me anyway. So I gave it a week, then started to trash the place, couldn't live without the ops. Had got used to it, you see. And I'm a lucky type, the Jerries won't ever get me.'

'Well, we could do with a lucky gunner,' said Ralph. 'You're in, isn't he lads?'

'Too bloody right he is.'

They learned the value of Alan's cool experience on their first operation together when he saw an approaching fighter almost before it was visible to the eye, sent Ralph instantly into a corkscrew manoeuvre, and then shot the fighter down with a single burst when it persisted.

By mid-August their six-week spell was nearly up and they were due to start a week's leave the following day. They ate breakfast hoping for a day free of ops but the call came through in mid-morning, ops were on, and the usual ratcheting up of tension started from the moment they heard the news, slipping its grip around them through the day until it reached its peak in the truck out to the plane and in the final checks before take-off. Then the Dog took them away, up over the coast and out to sea, and they slipped into their in-flight rhythm. Half-way across the North Sea, Roland reported a problem with the fuel system, then the port outer engine juddered and stopped.

'We'll keep going,' said Ralph. 'We can get there and back on three.'

Then the starboard inner went out of kilter and Roland adjusted the fuel and it started up again, then stopped completely, then coughed and banged and struggled on.

'We'll have to abort, get me a course back to base, navigator.'

They landed and were confronted by the Station Commander in

the crew room.

'I take a very dim view of early returns, Andrews. A Lanc can fly on three engines, no problem at all.'

'But we only had two and a half, sir,' protested Ralph.

'Oh stop binding, Andrews. You displayed a clear lack of determination to reach the target. I won't tolerate boomerangs on this squadron. You'll damn well go out again tomorrow.'

'But sir, we're due to go on leave.'

'Frankly, you can damn your leave until you've all done another op,' and he stormed off.

They returned to their barracks and struggled to sleep as unspent adrenaline and disappointment hurtled through their veins. Jacob lay in bed and thought of Rose and the appointment they had made for the following day at the guest-house by the river in the countryside outside Cambridge, and he cursed the unavailability of the telephone, its booth chained shut until operations were over for the night. He lifted himself out of bed early to call her but she had already left her base and he slammed down the receiver and phoned the guest-house and left a message for her to expect him the next day instead, hoping, as he hung up, that he was not tempting fate with his promise. Three precious days they had planned together, and now one had already been lost and the other two might never arrive. He pushed the thought from his mind but it nagged at him throughout the morning and at lunch he dared not even glance in the direction of Millie lest she jinx him with a look alone, and at tea he noticed again the ripples in Ralph's trembling cup and he looked at Alan and his strange air of calm and the faraway unconcerned look in his eyes, and he was glad that one of their number had already overcome the insuperable barrier of thirty operations, living breathing proof that a miracle was an achievable goal, that survival beyond a single tour was possible, and survival beyond the duration of the war might then too be a prospect, just possibly, just a faint flicker on the distant horizon of the future, a glimmer of hope for a normal life no longer defined by fire and smoke and mayhem and long days of tension and waiting for the long black tunnel of night to swallow them up and perhaps, if luck was with them, spit them out again the other side of midnight. But a sense of unease, greater than usual, formed in Jacob's mind throughout the day and he noticed small signs, indications in what people said, that this would be his last flight, that this time he would not be coming back, that it would be his locker forced open by the Committee of Adjustment the following day and his possessions taken out and sent in a brown parcel to his family, preceded by the ambiguously worded telegram that promised nothing of certainty either way but bringing with it an expectation of the worst, and he thought of the letters he had received from Rose being sent back home with his belongings, where they would be read in the house opposite the place she had lived, beside the orchard filled with pigs with German names, and he thought of her again waiting for him near Cambridge, out of reach now that the telephone was off limits, the aerodrome now a cage of lost and hopeless souls living the final stretch of their lives in an agony of waiting-room hours. And then the waiting ended, and the truck arrived, and Mary's red hair seemed more vivid and beautiful than ever, and Jacob remembered what she had said to him as the bus sped back from the dance, 'You're all right, you are,' and he thought 'You're all right yourself, Mary dear, with your red hair and your hawksbill nose and your wonderful post-op smile as you wait for us by your truck to take us back for our mugs of tea.' And then he joined the others in the truck and Mary started it up and took them away to where the Dog was waiting. They got on board and took up their stations and the sound of Ralph running everyone through the pre-flight checks switched back and forth across the intercom, and the acceptance form arrived for Ralph to struggle to sign with his trembling hand and the door was slammed shut and the Dog's engines howled and they waited for the order to move off towards the runway, but the minutes passed and the order did not come and then a voice came over the intercom, 'It's a scrub! Ops are scrubbed,' and there was a cry of joy from somewhere in the plane and the order was confirmed and the engines were switched off and Mary was waiting for them again by her truck and within an hour as many crews as would fit inside the bus into town were on their way to a more pleasurable form of oblivion than the one they had been contemplating for most of the day. Jacob found himself next to Alan as the bus sped into town.

'I had the strangest feeling all day, Alan. I was sure, absolutely certain, that we wouldn't be coming back tonight.'

'Don't worry, son,' said Alan. 'I get that feeling every trip I'm on, and it's never happened yet.'

From the pub, Jacob phoned the guest-house and finally heard

Rose's voice somewhere distant down the line.

'Tomorrow, my darling,' she said. 'I'll see you here tomorrow. Hurry now, Jacob, hurry now, please.'

'I'll be on the first bus out in the morning. Goodnight, Rose dear, goodnight. And God bless you.'

***

He reached Cambridge in mid-morning and caught a bus to the village and walked the last half mile to the guest-house, the path beside the river hung over with long stems of grass that brushed his legs as he passed, sending butterflies red, yellow and white up into the air. He saw the house as he rounded a sharp bend in the river. A willow tree hung itself in the water and a cuckoo cast its voice across the meadow where red-brown cattle nosed through the nettles and Jacob looked up as he neared the house, with its roses fragrant in their beds at the front and the mauve clusters of wisteria hanging above the door, the open door with the flagstone floor beyond. He saw her in the doorway, Rose, wild Rose, beneath the canopy of flowers with the sun on her face and a smile that wiped away all his terror and uncertainty, and he stood before her and looked at her properly for the first time ever now, not the casual gaze of his childhood or the shy shifting indifference of his teens, but boldly, openly, seeing her as she really was, the woman who had grown up before him, who had waited for him until he joined her in adulthood, an adulthood of age beyond their years, of understanding born of extremes of experience and the clarity of urgency, of a need to notice all the details in case they should soon be there no longer, the flecks in her eyes, the dark summer specks and freckles that the sun lifted up on her cheeks, the scent of the soap on her skin, lavender and violet, and the honey-blossom wisps of her hair on his face, and the taste of her lips, her tongue, the sweet remnants of the strawberry she had eaten moments before, its little seeds in the soft secret recesses of her mouth, the hopeful thoughts she kept in quiet corners of herself, and the radiance of her love for him, a light that had built across the years, illuminating him now as they embraced beneath the flowers in the shadow of the cuckoo's call, in the sunlit beauty of summer, in the golden glow of peace, love and survival, the miracle of love's survival against the black hell of the burning night.

She took his hand and led him up the stairs to the landing, the elm boards uneven beneath their feet, the air fresh and cool after the heat of the garden, the light soft, hung with silence, just the sound of her breathing and the landlord's footsteps across the gravel outside. Rose paused by the door of the room at the end of the landing as a shaft of light lit the lace in the window.

'This is our room,' she said, smiling. 'I hope you won't think less of me ...'

She saw his puzzled look.

'... that you won't think less of me for not taking a separate room. I didn't really see any point in it, you see.'

'No,' he said. 'I don't think any less of you. I never will.'

They spent the day walking far along the river bank, out into the countryside where the labourers and the land girls were making up hayricks in the fields. A small flight of planes droned distantly overhead, on a training flight out towards the west. By the river they found an old mill abandoned years before and they climbed in through a broken window and explored the dusty rooms, finding small forgotten objects and items of furniture where the departing owners had left them fifty or a hundred years before, an old tweed jacket with a grubby sheen hanging on a peg on the back of a door, walnut shells gone grey in the fireplace, a spoon on the brick floor that clattered as Jacob's foot sent it spinning into the air, a scrap of paper torn across its middle, a half-formed footnote to the lives that had been lived here. Rose picked up the note and squinted at the faded words in the cool dim light.

'Dearest Joan,' she read. 'There is something I must tell you prior to my departure, something that I have always ...'

And there the words ran out of paper and the rest of the note remained unsaid. They found a pair of candle-holders on the window-seat in the top room, their candle stubs, snuffed out on some long-forgotten night, now thick with dust turned sticky with the wax.

'Shall we take them?' said Rose. 'I think they're Victorian. No one's going to miss them, are they?'

They ate at the guest-house and spent the evening in the garden as the light turned milky and the moon replaced the sun, and when they could no longer see they went to their room at the top of the stairs and Jacob lit the long-dead candles and the twin flames burned bright in the still air.

'Come here, Jacob, dear,' she said, as he turned to her and blew out the match. 'Come to me.'

And he went to her and she removed his shirt and let her dress fall away and then they were beside each other on the bed, the air warm upon their skin.

'It's been so long in coming, hasn't it, Jacob? This moment, I mean. I was afraid it might never arrive.'

'I was afraid of that too,' he said, and he kissed her gently. 'How long has it been, Rose, the waiting?'

He kissed her again.

'Oh Jacob, where do I start?'

'Let's start here, then, Rose, in the here and now. It's the only place for us now.'

'Yes, Jacob, nothing can take this moment from us, you know that, don't you? Whatever happens from here on in, this is ours forever.'

And then she was kissing him, all those feelings she had held within herself, unspoken or half-said for years, were flooding over him, drowning out the war, a dam breaking apart its walls. And then suddenly she was under him, and he was looking at her face, her face dark against the pale of the linen, her eyes and her smile a flare path in the gloom, guiding him in, calling him down, calling him home as if he were lost somewhere up there out of sight in the dark, and her hair thrown back on the pillow, swept back in the gale of love that the war had brought on, and when dawn came the flare path was gone, mist tripping about the open window and the candles spent and Rose sleeping peacefully in his arms, and the flares were burning bright within them now, the war could not put them out even if it might put out their lives.

The following day flung itself away more quickly than was fair, and the next night too blazed itself to pieces in its haste, and Jacob and Rose ate breakfast silently contemplating their parting. After breakfast she sat in the chair by the window and watched him pack his case, then they walked along the river to the road and caught the bus into Cambridge. They stopped for lunch at a café in the market square and drank their ersatz coffee and paid the bill, then sat a while longer, hanging onto each last moment together until the waitress cleared the table.

'It seems so long until your next leave,' she said. 'October, perhaps?'

'Yes,' he said. 'I should get another week after six more weeks of ops.'

They internalised their thoughts of what might happen in the interim.

'Let's see if we can make our leave coincide more fully next time,' she sighed. 'These two days have been marvellous, but how much better a week would be.'

A week, a whole week, an ocean of time for those accustomed to counting down their lives in hours not days.

'Yes,' he said. 'A week would be wonderful indeed.'

'But I don't know if I can wait until October,' she said.

'Will you have any leave at all before then?'

'Perhaps the odd day.'

'Come and stay near me for a night. The pub in the village has rooms. If we're lucky, ops will be scrubbed and no one will miss me then on the base.'

'Yes,' she said decisively, her mood lightening a touch. 'That's what we'll do. I'll send you a telegram as soon as I know.'

They waited together at the bus station and her bus came and took her away, back into the heart of bomber country, dressed again now in her stiff WAAF uniform, her top lip trembling a touch as she dabbed her eyes with a tissue and looked out across the flat countryside dressed in its green summer frock.

***

Jacob arrived in London that evening and met Harry Pollock at King's Cross. They found a hotel in the West End and spent the evening in a pub swapping stories of their operational lives so far and catching up on news of people they had known in Canada. They left the pub and walked back to the hotel through the blacked-out streets of London. The night was quiet, no planes overhead, the sky black and the streets lit only by the dim slits in the headlamps of taxis and the occasional car ferrying important officials about the capital.

'How many ops have you clocked?' Harry asked.

'Eight. Should have been nine but we turned back last trip out, engine trouble, and the Wing Commander chalked it off. Skip was bloody fuming. He couldn't have flown the kite there and back on two good engines. The Wingco virtually accused us of going LMF.'

LMF – Lack of Moral Fibre – the dreaded euphemism for a failure of courage, a cracking of the will. Jacob had seen a case the previous month, a skipper with three early returns in a row, whispers among the crew, minor trouble with an engine, then the turret hydraulics, and the last one unexplained. Rumours raced around the sergeants' mess at breakfast, a headless chicken laying eggs.

'Bugger all wrong with it, by all accounts,' someone said. 'Dropped his bombs in the sea and turned for home.'

'I heard they fell on a village up in Lincolnshire,' said someone else. 'They've been all over his Lanc this morning like rats, the Wingco and everyone.'

'He's had enough,' said Jacob. 'That's all'

'Poor sod, could happen to any of us,' said Charlie.

'Where's he now?'

'Getting his brevet unstitched, I expect.'

The following day the squadron had been called to parade. With an economy of words, the man was called before them and dispatched.

'You're a bloody disgrace,' the man heard in his ear as the Wing Commander tore off the wings he had worn on a dozen trips over Germany, lightly tacked back on now to facilitate the drama of the humiliation as the badge was removed. And then he was gone.

'To the Aircrew Correction Centre,' said George in the bar that night. 'Where the shit-house is always in need of a clean and the NCOs are shitty shites.'

'And the shitty shites have never been on shitty ops,' said Jacob.

'The shitty fuckers,' concluded George.

'If I start to crack, don't let me go that way,' said Jacob. 'Shove me out of the plane without a chute before you let me go LMF.'

'You won't crack, brother. None of us will. Not this crew.'

***

The next day, Jacob and Harry met up with Jim in London. They caught the train to Oxford, then the bus to Woodstock and Vera looked up as the shop bell rattled and she saw her brother standing in the doorway.

'Hello Vera,' he said, taking off his cap and smiling as she ran round from behind the counter and hugged him to her.

'Jacob, thank God you're here! It seems so long since I saw you.'

'It certainly does. You look great, Vera. I love the pink apron. Here, this is Harry, I told you about him in my letters, and Jim, one of our gunners.'

They shook hands and Jim made a joke about the names of some of the sweets, and Vera opened one of the jars and they dipped their hands inside and were all sucking on barley sugar when Jingle came back from his trip to the post office.

'Hello, what have we got here?' he said, laughing. 'All these uniforms. Have we been invaded? So tell me, which one of you is Vera's bomber brother?'

'This is Jacob here, Mr Bell.'

'Well done, Jacob, lad,' said Jingle, shaking him vigorously by the hand. 'Aim those bombs right on the Jerries' heads, eh? Right on Mr Hitler's bloody great Teutonic bonce, that'll teach him to come dropping bombs on us.'

'Too right, mate,' said Jim enthusiastically. 'We're giving old Adolf a right pasting, no two ways about it. We'll burn Germany end to end before we're done and they'll have bloody deserved it too.'

'Here you go, lads,' said Jingle, passing them each a small paper bag. 'Tell me the ones you want, whichever you like, fill those bags up with sweets, you bloody deserve them.'

They went for a walk around the shops and stopped at a pub for a beer which turned into two and then three, then picked Vera up from the shop and caught the bus to Chipping Norton together.

'There's a dance band at the Town Hall this evening,' said Vera as they walked towards West Street. 'You're all coming along, aren't you? It'll be great fun. Norman's coming too. You know how much he likes watching everyone dance, poor man, he so wishes he wasn't such a rotten dancer himself, feet of clay he has.'

'Oh yes, we'll be there,' said Jacob. 'Don't you worry about that.'

'They get so packed out, the dances,' she went on. 'Sometimes it feels like there are people from all the countries of the earth in our little part of the world now, American airmen, Australians, Canadians, Poles. They all speak so funny when they're drunk, sometimes you can hardly understand a word they're saying – and that's just the Yanks.'

Jacob and Harry and Jim spent the rest of the afternoon in the garden next to the orchard as Elizabeth ferried them plates of homemade cake, light on sugar but heavy on the butter made by Vera at the farm, and endless cups of tea, and they sat and smoked their cigarettes and talked with a certain bravado about ops and kites and squadron life while Elizabeth busied herself among the fruit trees within earshot, but when she had gone inside their conversation adopted a more reflective tone and it occurred to Jacob that if one had been eavesdropping now, the true nature of their lives might have revealed a fraction of itself to the listener. Later on, while Harry and Jim were lured by Alfred to the orchard so he could run them through the story of his pigs, Vera arrived with Norman and Daphne.

'Uncle Jacob!' Daphne squealed in delight, and threw herself at him. He picked her up and held her under one arm, then spun her behind his back and up onto his shoulders where she sat beaming, her chin propped up on the top of his head.

'You're getting to be a big girl now, aren't you?' he said. 'How old are you now Daphne? Six?'

'Six and a little bit.'

'Wow,' said Jacob. 'Six and a whole little bit! Are you coming to the dance this evening?'

She shook her head and giggled as if she had never heard anything so silly.

'Really?' said Jim, 'So who am I going to dance with?'

'Don't you worry about that,' said Alfred. 'There'll be plenty of young ladies happy to dance with an RAF chap like you.'

'Well what are we waiting for, then?' said Jim, winking at Harry. 'Let's go.'

When they got to the Town Hall the music had already started and they found an empty table and pulled up some chairs and sat and looked at the dance floor where a solitary couple were moving out of time with each other, holding each other in a way that suggested their intimacy was not yet complete. The man wore a uniform that leant him a certain bearing but also a formality in keeping with the music's sombre tone, and when the music stopped the couple went back to their place on the other side of the room and it was then, in the light of the wall sconces, that the reason for the awkward distance of their waltz was revealed, the man's right sleeve hanging limp and empty where his arm would have been before it was removed by the war.

Alfred and Norman came back to the table with their hands full of drinks, then Jacob fetched the others on a tray, and Alfred drank half his pint down in one long draw and offered his hand to Elizabeth and they joined the others who had begun to populate the dance floor. Alfred held Elizabeth close to him and Jacob nudged Vera and nodded towards them and they both grinned. Harry and Jim were discussing the details of the second Hamburg raid, comparing notes on their time of arrival over the target and the fighter activity on the way in and out and the planes they had seen coned by searchlights and blasted with flak. The music hammered out now, a strident ringing noise lifting others to their feet, and Jim and Harry struck up a conversation with a couple of Wrens at the next table and before long they had paired up on the dance floor and when their dance was over they sat together as the night slipped by in a blur of music and light and the sound of feet on boards.

'Let's dance,' said Vera to Norman, taking his hand, but he smiled his lack of acceptance and took another sip of his beer.

'I'm all right here, dear,' he said. 'I'm happy just watching.'

'Oh, come on Norman, just this once. Twirl me round the room, sweep me off my feet.'

'She thinks I'm bloody Fred Astaire, your sister does,' Norman said, winking at Jacob.

'Come on then, Jacob,' said Vera. 'Come dance with your sister,' and they were up and into the crowd and Norman looked on and took another swig of his beer and regretted his leaden feet and his ruggedness. He stood up and went to the bar and got talking to an American who was working as ground crew at one of the nearby airfields, and they found they had much in common having each grown up on farms, in South Dakota and County Durham, and they spent much of the rest of the night comparing breeds of cattle and sheep and methods of preparing feed for the winter, but eventually Vera intervened and persuaded Norman out onto the dance floor and they moved awkwardly around the room, Norman smiling apologetically each time his size 12s missed the beat or dropped themselves onto Vera's retreating toes, and when the piece ended he beat a quick retreat to the table and lifted his glass again to his lips, a barricade against further humiliation.

'You were wonderful, dear,' said Vera, and Norman grinned sheepishly and Alfred put his arm round him and then patted the back of his head and said something gruff and unintelligible.

They finally got home after midnight and sat up until late in the sitting room as Alfred got out his bottles of twelve-year-old Scotch that he kept for special occasions. By the time they creaked their way up the stairs to bed the birds were anticipating the dawn with their chirpings. The next morning, Jacob took Jim and Harry down to Elm Tree Farm and they went for a walk out across the fields to the wood at the top, past the land girls and the prisoners of war who were helping in the fields. They watched the German airmen as they passed, fighter and bomber pilots who had been shot down three years before in the Battle of Britain, and Jacob recalled the conversation he had had with one of them then, the one who had seemed so old but was probably not much older than Jacob himself. The Germans looked up as the men went by in their RAF uniforms and one of the prisoners made a comment and the others laughed and Jim made a coarse remark that was lost in translation. They went back for lunch at the Arbuckles' house where Elizabeth was getting the meat out of the oven and they sat down in the dining room and Alfred took up the two-pronged fork and the carving knife and started to slice up the pork. Elizabeth ladled on the vegetables and they began to eat and Harry commented favourably on the quality of the food and how it compared to what they usually got in the sergeants' mess.

'Yes, we're lucky out here in the country,' said Alfred. 'Still able to get proper food if we grow it ourselves, in spite of the rationing. I killed this one just yesterday, as I knew you were all coming.'

'What's this one called, then, father?' asked Jacob, and Elizabeth stiffened slightly in her chair.

'He used to call them all after British politicians, you know,' Jacob went on, looking at Harry and Jim. 'But then of course when the war started, it was the Germans' turn, isn't that right, father?'

Jacob grinned, suddenly boyish again, grinning at his gruff old man. Alfred smiled back at his son who had suddenly become a man himself, and he nodded.

'That's right, my boy. Dead right.'

'You've worked your way through Goering and Goebbels and Rommel by now, I should guess?'

'Oh yes, I've been through most of the generals now,' said Alfred.

'Would anyone like some more potatoes?' said Elizabeth.

'So now I've started on ...'

'Or carrots?' Elizabeth asked, rather urgently.

'So now I've ...'

'Alfred!' she said tartly.

'As I was saying,' Alfred went on, 'so now I've started on the cities. This one is Hamburg, no pun intended.'

Harry paused his fork just before his mouth and placed it back on his plate and took a sip of beer. No one spoke for a moment.

'Don't mind him,' said Elizabeth. 'He hasn't been the same since they shelled him at Ypres,' and Jim laughed and placed a large forkful of pork in his mouth.

'Well whatever it's called,' Jim said, 'it tastes bloody great.'

After lunch, Jacob and Harry and Jim walked into town and down to the common where the shallow lake froze up in winter, where Jacob had gone skating with Rose and William three years before. The conversation never strayed far from the war and their squadrons, and they debated the true nature of Arthur Harris, 'Butch' Harris, the chief of Bomber Command, a distant figure to the crews, rarely if ever seen around the aerodromes but an ever-present figure in their lives, the arbiter of who would fly, and how many, and where and how they would bomb, and when, and by extension therefore who would die, and what percentage of the bomber force could be lost on each operation without eroding its men and machinery to the point of ineffectiveness, five per cent a shade too high they had heard, though sometimes this percentage doubled or even tripled, but the crews went out night after night, whenever the weather allowed, and always a proportion did not return, multiples of six or seven at a time, crew-sized losses, and the lockers in the crew room bore scars and chips to their paintwork where they had been forced open to recover the belongings of those who had failed to return and had also failed to leave a key behind.

'What do you reckon old Butch is really like?' said Jim. 'Do you think he's really the tough old bugger he's said to be?'

'Can't see how he can be anything else,' said Jacob.

'Well he certainly can't be the artistic type,' said Harry.

'The artist of our destruction,' said Jim.

'Did you hear that story about him?' said Jacob. 'Speeding back to Bomber HQ at High Wycombe one night, stopped by a couple of police motorcyclists and cautioned. You should be more careful says one of the policemen – you might have killed someone. My dear boy, says Harris, I kill thousands of people every night.'

They all burst out laughing

'And then,' continued Jacob, 'they gave the bugger an escort home!'

They all fell about again, their laughter empty in the darkening void of night.

'Good old Butch,' said Jacob.

'Bloody Butcher Harris,' said Harry.

'And who's he butchering?' said Jim. 'Them or us?'

'Bloody both, I should say,' said Jacob. 'We're all for the chop in the end, us in the planes and them on the ground.'

'I'm not sure which is worse,' said Harry.

'It's all fire in the end,' said Jim. 'It'll burn you just the same whether you're in the air or under the bombs.'

'Cheery lot, aren't we?' joked Jacob.

'Oh yes,' said Harry, laughing. 'Right happy mob, we are.'

And they stood up and walked into town and spent the rest of the afternoon drinking heavily at the Fox Hotel and competing to see who could eat the most pickled onions from the jar on the bar, and who could be the last to throw up in the gents from the beer and the onions and the quiet constant fear that had really got a grip on them now.

***

They returned to their squadrons two days later, Jacob and Jim saying goodbye to Harry at King's Cross and catching their train towards Cambridge as Harry headed north to Lincolnshire. Jacob and Jim reached the airfield towards dusk, the sound of Merlin engines greeting them from beyond the rise in the land where the airfield lay, and as they walked through the main gate the Lancasters were taxiing around towards the end of the runway, one after another, then the green light flashed in the signals van and a pilot released his brakes and his plane lumbered past the crowd of ground crew and WAAFs who were standing by the runway to wave the planes off, and at the very end of the runway the first plane hauled itself off the ground and climbed quickly and banked away and another was already airborne behind it, then another, until they were all gone, a long line of planes heading for Germany.

The following day ops were on again, and Jacob went out with Ralph and Roland to check on the Dog as the fuel load went on.

'Looks like a maximum,' said Roland, as the fuel line spewed its contents into the tanks in the wings.

'The full eight hours,' said Ralph. 'Nice one to have first op back after leave. Best get popping the bloody Benzedrine.'

Jacob passed by the post room and collected a letter from Rose, smiling at the news that she had secured three days' leave in a month's time and would come down to stay in a room at the pub as she had promised. But such things would have to wait, and Jacob joined the rest of the crew for the main briefing at four.

'Hello, chaps,' said the intelligence officer, surveying the rows of skulls in front of him again now. 'Tonight it's a big one, the Big City,' and Jacob saw the curtain fall away from the map of Europe that covered the front wall of the briefing room, the lengths of red wool stretching out their route from the east of England, dog-legging at the turning points, then on to Berlin through bright red clusters indicating the flak that he knew so well now, the slow rise and sudden acceleration of the tracer shells as they passed him on their way into the infinity of the sky. Then the pre-flight meal, bacon and beans bringing back the sick taste of ops, shoving that feeling right back down his throat, and he swallowed it down and felt it hollowing away at his guts. The crew gathered in the crew room later to wait for the off and they sat and smoked and Jacob and George started an aimless game of billiards, caring little whether the balls hit the pockets, the money that they wagered meaningless currency until the morning came and they had earned another day in which to spend their winnings or regret what they had lost. George won anyway, as he usually did.

'Here you go,' said Jacob, tossing the notes towards him across the baize. 'Don't spend it all at once, will you?'

'Want to win it back?' said George, taking a pack of cards from the side-table on which he had let his cigarette burn itself to a stub, and they found a couple of empty chairs and sat down to see which way the money would travel this time. Jacob's gaze flicked back and forth from the cards to the other members of his crew who sat around on the chairs and sofas that were strewn about the room. He watched over them now, feeling their mood, little tell-tale signs he had come to know. Ralph's eyes glazed half-heartedly across a newspaper, but he was clearly only pretending to read, his thoughts wandering elsewhere as the edges of the paper quivered. Charlie sat with eyes closed, affecting indifference, but his face was drawn and grey and his lips moved just a touch, the hint of a prayer. Roland sat in silence and twitched. Jim just looked around the room under a blue-grey pall, one cigarette after another, an incessant consumption of smoke. Next to Jim was a gunner from another crew, coughing and yawning to excess, getting up frequently to visit the loo, then blowing his nose as if something had got itself inside of him and he had to get it out.

'He's for the chop,' Jacob thought. He had seen the 'chop look' before, and he knew it when he saw it. Those who had it knew they had it too, which only made it worse. But that was how it worked, a spell cast upon them, some sort of sign that tonight fate would turn its back, perhaps a gathering of rooks in a tree as the man took an afternoon walk, or the barracks cat choosing his bed upon which to leave a dead mouse or a carefully placed turd, or just a feeling, a sixth sense that this was the night that had chosen to claim them, the date upon which their names would be written, on which wives and families would ponder their end, and Jacob found himself thinking how Rose and the others would wonder at what exactly had befallen him, was it a fighter or a flak-burst or the weather or a failing in the Dog that had brought him down, and what had he felt when it came, was it a drawn out thing, with time to contemplate the end as the plane took flame and burned away slowly to the ground, the kind of demise he had seen attach itself so often to other planes and their men beside him in the sky, or was it a vertical spinning descent that pinned him inside too far from the hatch, or would it all come suddenly with no time for terror, just a single 88mm shell striking the open bomb bay on the bombing run, turning the thirty-ton Dog to vapour in the bright white blink of a burning eye? Then he noticed a man looking at him from the other side of the room, studying him, that curious knowing look, keening in, like a vulture around a thing that it thinks is going to die.

'He thinks I'm for the bloody chop,' Jacob thought, as he flung back the look. 'Snap out of it, you clot,' he told himself. 'Get rid of those thoughts.'

Then he realised that George had won another hand undisturbed.

'Bloody hell, George, you're cleaning me out tonight!' but his complaint was half-hearted, anaesthetised, another feeling numbed.

'Come on, Jacob, just one more hand. One for the road! We've got a few minutes left and I'm on a roll.'

'I'd rather not. My mind's not on it,' said Jacob. 'Don't want to leave the loved ones with no inheritance, do I?'

And his thoughts turned again now to the night to come and to how much he longed to stand up and walk out of this room and out of the camp, to take the first available bus to Rose, his Rose, she had told him so, the reason he had to get through this war.

But nothing could be done, ops were on and he had to go. The call came and he went to the crewing-up room and left his belongings in his locker, stuffed a few valuables and keys and last letters into the pouches that were provided, and when he had finished he watched other men doing the same and he knew that some of these belongings would be found the next morning by the men from the Committee of Adjustment who would come to force open the lockers of those who had failed to return, perhaps those unlucky lockers known to be so by the experienced crews, lockers that turned over their occupants with unusual frequency, impatient to be unburdened and empty again. But these lockers would be full again the following night when the sprog crews arrived and went out through the same door, not to come back.

Then Jacob went to the plane and bombed Berlin and was back before dawn. The new day crept in dim with a late-September fog that clouded the fields and the Lancasters stood barely visible at their dispersals and as Jacob crawled to breakfast with hopes of a day off ops he passed by the operations room to take a look at the board with the take-off and landing times of the squadron's planes on the previous night's raid. Dread letters were chalked next to two of the crews, FTR – failed to return – and he was suddenly aware that the brutal impact of the letters had gone. They had undermined themselves, had brutalised him past the point at which he might retain the capacity for feelings of loss, and he no longer dwelt on the barely-remembered faces of those who had gone, nor wondered at their demise. He simply offered them a mental shrug, wiped them from his memory, seven fewer names to have to remember.

He went off to breakfast to see if there were any eggs.

**

Then a letter came from Lincolnshire, from Harry, written to Jacob at the start of their tours, to be sent to Jacob in the event of 'something untoward', as Harry had always referred to it. And so Jacob heard directly from his friend, after the event, that he had been lost and that their short friendship had meant a great deal to him and that he hoped Jacob and he could both have made it to the end of their tours and remained friends after the war, but that this would not now be possible, and that he hoped Jacob would make it to thirty ops and would remember for many years his good friend Harry.

The next trip was to Turin and when the target was announced a cheer went up across the briefing room.

'Pleasant little trip there and back,' said Ralph. 'Nice view of the Alps on the way.'

'Yes, off to see the ice-creamers,' said Jacob. 'Light flak, static searchlights, we'll be dropping the bombs at our leisure.'

'None of them are easy,' whispered Charlie.

'I was only joking, Charlie mate,' said Jacob.

'It'll be easier than bloody Germany, that's for sure,' said Ralph.

'Best not tempt fate though, lads,' said Charlie. 'We wouldn't want to get …'

'Shut up, will you, Charlie?' said Jacob. 'We're trying to follow the briefing.'

The trip to Turin was as uneventful as Jacob and Ralph had predicted. Next came a 'gardening' job to the Baltic, the bomb-load replaced by 'vegetables', floating mines to hamper the German Navy as it emerged from its ports. Then three bad trips to Germany – Hannover, Mannheim, and Bochum – the Dog returning from the last of these minus a wing-tip that had been shot away by flak, but Jacob entered the debriefing room in high spirits. Rose was arriving the following day.

They met at the gate at lunchtime and spent the day walking through the fields and woods nearby, the calls of the pheasants echoing through the fog from somewhere among the trees, and then they returned to the pub and ate a modest dinner and went to the room that Rose had taken. She had brought the candles they had found in the abandoned mill-house near Cambridge and she lit them and placed them in the window and turned off the lights and the candles burned down to nothing during the night.

'What will become of us?' she said, as Jacob dressed in the grey light of morning, but her question was overtly rhetorical and it went unanswered. She got out of bed and padded over to him.

'It was sunny once,' he said. 'Do you remember that, Rose, do you remember those days?'

'Yes, I remember them,' she said. 'And they'll come back for us, Jacob. Keep the sun inside you and those days will come back.'

'But there's no sun inside me now,' he said. 'I've filled up with smoke,' and the image lodged itself in her mind and she felt the little wick of flame inside her too as she clutched him to her, felt him burning.

Outside, fog still cloaked the countryside and the branches of the trees were black and dripping. Jacob left for the airfield to check on ops for the evening and he met Charlie and Jim at breakfast.

'Ops are on,' said Jim.

'You're joking,' said Jacob, sitting down next to him. 'They can't send us out in this muck. We won't be able to take off, and if we take off, we won't land.'

'They say it's going to clear up later,' said Charlie, but his night-owl eyes were disbelieving.

The fog had not lifted by the time of the briefing, but shortly after it began to disperse and the planes took off into the milky gloom. Rose stood in her WAAF uniform with the others by the runway's end and watched the planes go, and she lay awake in her room in the pub as the candles flickered into the early hours. Finally she heard the distant hum of the first returning plane and she stood by the window as the noise intensified and the giant shape of a Lancaster bomber passed overhead, and as it roared down onto the runway another was audible away in the distance, then a few minutes later another, this time with its engines howling out of sync as it landed. Minutes passed and another came in, and she stood by the window and counted them all down, eighteen in all, and when the last was home she went back to bed and slept until morning. The next day the fog was back and ops were off and Jacob returned to the pub and found Rose beaming as he came into the room. They went into town for the afternoon and then spent the evening together again, and then the night, and then the morning came hurrying in and they stood at the bus stop, Rose with her overnight bag and Jacob with his toothbrush. The bus arrived and Jacob pulled Rose to him.

'I'll see you again soon, my darling,' she said.

'Yes, my leave is due in three weeks.'

'I'll arrange things so we can spend it together.'

'Please do your best, my dear.'

'Don't worry, Jacob, I will …'

She kissed him and stepped up into the bus and Jacob watched her face dissolve behind the glass as the mist stole her away.

AUTUMN AND WINTER 1943

The next three weeks dragged to their conclusion in a world of half-light and night, the days shortening as autumn drew in and threw its grey squally mists across the flatlands of Suffolk. Jacob and the crew waited all day with tautening nerves, going through the wearing gears of pre-op rituals, the tightening of the stomach that refused to accept lunch, the briefings and the specialist sessions for the navigators and bomb-aimers, the pre-op meal of bacon and beans, and the donning of their flying clobber in the chaos of the crew room, men flying off the handle at the loss of a glove or the temporary misplacement of a lucky scarf, others sitting silently and fully kitted-up, dragging hard and long on a cigarette, then chucking it away half-finished and lighting up another one straight away. Strained laughter erupted somewhere over by the door, an excessive reaction to a feeble joke, then silence again, and then cursing and the furious repeated slamming of a locker door, and the sound of the trucks arriving outside, their doors banging and the incongruously cheery executioner's voice of a WAAF calling her crews out to die. Then the bumpy ride across sodden tracks to the far-flung dispersals where the Lancasters waited like big black birds, poised for the night as real birds sang and then settled themselves down in the darkening woods nearby, and then Jacob stepped inside his big black bird and it closed its wings around him and he became part of it, its fate and his own indivisible now in the face of the night, and he waited for the off as the engines coughed then roared and the airscrews turned several revolutions and then spluttered into spinning life, the blades invisible now as they spun, and still the crew awaited the order to go, but it did not come, the operation was scrubbed, the cancellation of the trip left until the last possible moment in case the fog should lift and let them up into the sky. And so the bird let them out again into the suddenly quiet night and the truck took them back to the crew room, exhausted by the anticipation, demoralised at having invested the day with torment and then not to add another op to their log, another step towards thirty, aware that the next day would bring the same fears and tensions and perhaps, at the end, the trip that would finish it all.

In the bar after a cancelled op, Jacob saw the imperceptible trembling of Ralph's tea cup magnified now into a visible shaking of his pint-jug of beer, sometimes held in two hands to keep it still, then after four or five drinks the trembling subsided and the Ralph of the pre-war years peeked out into the room and Jacob remembered him as he was when they had first met mere months before, mere months that might have been a lifetime. And then the beer really took hold and Jacob and the others, still soaring on fear and adrenaline, piled the mess chairs against the walls, and up they climbed, up atop the chairs, supporting each other as each man in turn flipped himself over and planted his feet on the ceiling and took two or three footsteps across it as the others held him there, and then he fell and the others tumbled down around him, laughing and roaring and delighted at the sight of their footprints on the flat white ceiling – footprints, thought Jacob, as he lay on the floor with the rest of the crew stretched out around him, that would still be there long after the men who put them there had been blown to smithereens in the flak-hacked twinkling red-glow skies of Germany.

Finally three more weeks ended and Jacob and his crew reached another week's leave, the next waiting room in their operational life, another chance to disappear into the country, far away from this other life, this life of waiting for the paused hand of death.

Rose stood waiting for him beneath the clock at Cambridge station and he hurried over to her and they fell into each other's arms as the clock struck above them. They stayed a night in Cambridge and a night in London, then travelled up to Chipping Norton, Rose at her grandmother's and Jacob in the house across the lane, and apart from the night-time, when decorum dictated their separation, they spent each day together, alone at times, at others in the company of Norman and Vera or Alfred and Elizabeth, and they were each for the other a prism through which they could interpret this strange place again, this place they had left behind when squadron life consumed them, this place inhabited by their former selves and by loved ones to whom they could not talk of the details of service life and who would not have been able to understand it anyway. They travelled back again together on the penultimate day of their leave and spent the night again in Cambridge so that they could leave their parting until as late as possible the following day, and when the parting came it ripped their guts from their bellies and sent them hollow and bereft towards their separate destinations.

'Next time we see each other, my tour might well be over,' Jacob said as he turned away. 'Just ten more ops now.'

'Just ten more ops,' she said. 'Each one might as well be a lifetime.'

By mid-November, four more ops had been and gone, four more red and black nights of terror and flame, and alongside them many more scrubbed trips that held the crew at a pitch that rubbed their nerves raw. Ralph's nerve sometimes now held only until the end of the bombing run and the long steady pause while the photo-flash recorded the accuracy of the bombs, but after he banked the plane away from the target and they were into the cover of darkness away from the searchlights and the fiercest of the flak, he would slip grey-faced and sweating from his seat for a spell on the rest-bed behind the wireless set and Jacob would come up from his place in the nose, his bombing duties done, and take the controls and follow the course Charlie gave him and point the Dog towards home. Ralph would sometimes retake the controls for landing, and the crew said nothing afterwards, the secret stayed with them, an understanding that they would function and survive as a crew or not at all, and if this meant helping each other across the personal barriers they each might encounter, then that is what they would do.

***

Winter now placed its hands around the airfield and subjected it to its variable caress, clear harsh frost-hung days segueing into star-strung nights that invited out the Dog, and the moon lit up the target by the bend in a shimmering river or a black mass of suburbs stretching out into the blue-grey softness of the countryside, the blue-grey and the black then lit by the orange glow of the fires that ate away the town and touched the belly of the Dog with its colour and its heat, the twin lights of moon and fire illuminating her trawl across the sky through the fiery blooms of flak and sister planes that were disintegrating into flames. And then home again beneath the moon, the fire gone out except for the pale glow of exhausts from her Merlin engines and the burning of exhausted men's desire to survive another day, then a sudden re-ignition of flame two miles in front of them as a wounded bomber drops too fast, out of control in its urgency to feel the ground again, and it explodes on the runway, the crew's delirium at touching down just an evaporation of their last explosive drop of hope. And on other days, winter brought a milky balm that hung itself across the airfield, a quiet white blanket of relief, a thick mist bringing a scrub and a delirious bus-ride into town for condemned men relieved of their duty of slaughter and suicide for at least another day. And then the Battle of Berlin, the Big City, flung far away across the German map, approached in force through 10/10ths cloud and bombed blind for nights on end, sky-marker flares over the aiming point, a red-orange suggestion in the murk the bombers' only visual contact with the target, searchlight beams lighting up the cloud-base, a translucent shroud hanging above the burning city as teenage gunners at their ack-ack guns followed the passage of the bombers, small black insects skating across an illuminated sheet of glass. And in the air the Dog flew blind and Jacob noted the sudden glow of collisions, bombers falling to the ground in pairs, bombing accidentally their brothers who flew too close below. And on the ground beneath him the conflagration, the people in their shelters along the tortured corridors of his Benzedrine-fuelled imagination, the corridors in which he repeatedly turned out the lights as some dread hand kept turning them back on, forcing him to see them, those people down below as the cellars turned to ovens and they roasted slowly, were cooked not burnt, or asphyxiated by a fire too greedy to spare any oxygen for their lungs, found the next morning by streak-faced rescue crews, all sat in a row in their catacombs, untouched by blast, perfect little bodies but perfectly dead all the same. And Jacob could see them still at dawn as he fell at last exhausted into bed and tried in vain still to turn out the lights.

***

Suddenly they approached their twenty-ninth op, the mythical twenty-ninth, the penultimate one that they knew had claimed so many crews before, but they were confident now in their machine and each other, men fused to metal in a common cause, men fused to each other, moulded by experience and necessity and a bond of love that would last them a lifetime, however short or long that lifetime might be. So they helped each other, Charlie prodding George at his radio with his long ruler to keep him from dozing off on the long run home, Jim and Alan twin gunners, four drug-widened eyes scouring the night for fighters, Roland lightening the mood with his gallows humour as he adjusted the fuel settings, Jacob helping Charlie with map-reading and ground identification through the glass eye of the nose-cone, Ralph hauling himself across the barrier of his fear to step into the cockpit once more and grip the control column so hard, in an attempt to control the shaking of his hands, that in the morning after a long trip he woke with cramp in his fingers and when he stepped from the plane his mouth was red with blood and when he looked in the mirror he saw that he had bitten his bottom lip black and blue. And when Ralph had overcome the mounting dread of the outbound flight and the flat-steady terror of the bombing run and finally turned the Dog for home, slipping now into a paralysis of silent gibber and fear, Roland took him to the rest-bed by the main spar and laid the blanket over him, patting his hand and telling him his work was done, and Jacob took the controls and flew the Dog home, rejoicing in the fulfilment of his dream, the thing he had promised the woman in the haberdashery store when he was eleven years old, though she had refused to believe him, that he would be a pilot one day and would fly around the world and back again. He brought them home from their twenty-ninth op, and at the debriefing the crew kept their silence as they always did about the fusing of roles that had taken place in the air.

The thirtieth trip was delayed by heavy early-December falls of snow, and the crew drew in closer to each other, a hermetically sealed unit that lived and socialised almost exclusively together now, Ralph joining his sergeants in their sub-standard accommodation, the corrugated hoop of a Nissen hut, devoid of insulation and warmed by a coke burner in the middle of the room for which they were provided with insufficient fuel. On flightless days they took walks into the trees at the far end of the airfield and brought back firewood to feed the flames, and when the flames demanded more, or when a night on the beer had stoked their imaginations, they took to dismantling old chairs and shelves and fed these to the fire instead, huddling around the glow of the flames as the damp and the cold in turn huddled up around the backs of the men, shivering in the greatcoats they would still be wearing when they crawled into bed. They spoke of their last operation, the thirtieth one, where it would be and how it would go and what they would do thereafter. Six months away from operations was the prize, half a year, a hundred and eighty days of life, an almost uncountable number of hours and minutes into which they would squeeze the realisation of a lifetime's ambitions, perhaps a marriage, even the promise of a child, the re-establishing of family ties and a reconnection with the places from which they had come, a chance to reassess their hopes for their post-war lives, should such a thing be feasible after all, six months bringing duties no more threatening than a posting to a training unit, squeezing other young crews through the sausage-machine so that they could be grilled by fire, consumed by the greedy night. But all that must wait. First must come the thirtieth, and then, God willing, the birthday party that Ralph's parents had been planning for their prematurely aged son and his mates, a long weekend together in their beautiful house by a lake in the Surrey countryside to celebrate the completion of his twenty-second year, a privileged existence now ravaged by time and fear and guilt. The birthday approached, Ralph a Christmas baby born between the Nativity and the cusp of the New Year, but the weather would not oblige and it kept the door to the six-month spell of life locked behind a chain of snowstorms that swept in across the North Sea and the flatlands of East Anglia and Suffolk, and before they could conclude their tour Christmas Eve dawned with a slight lifting of the cloud and the ground staff were set upon the runways with their shovels and their spades. They dug away the snowdrifts in search of the black road beneath, and the sound of shovels scraping across tarmac carried across to the mess where the airmen sat and ate their breakfast on long benches, sitting shoulder to shoulder as the sound of the shovels grated on their nerves, like the shovels of grave-diggers scraping at stony ground that was about to become a tomb, the dark womb of the earth into which they would be returned from high up in the sky by gravity's clutching hand.

'They can't possibly send us up tonight,' said Ralph, his hand jiggering his fork about in erratic pursuit of the last beans upon his plate. 'It's Christmas Eve. We can't bomb on Christmas Eve, for Christ's sake.'

'They didn't bomb last Christmas,' said Charlie.

'Old Butch must have been feeling soft,' said Jim.

'Yes, all sentimental,' added Jacob. 'But they'll send us this year, just wait and see.'

Roland stirred his tea vigorously and shrugged. 'Can't do much about it anyway, can we?'

'We'll be fine,' said Charlie. 'They won't send us tonight. I've got a good feeling about it.'

'Like that time we got shot up over Essen?' said Jacob. 'And the Dog came back with twenty holes in her belly.'

'Yes, just like that, now you come to mention it,' said Charlie. 'But we got back all the same.'

'Well tonight we're going nowhere,' said George. 'They'll keep us waiting and then they'll pull the plug at the last minute and we'll be at the Christmas dance instead. And Sally Simms is meeting me there.'

'Sally Simms?' said Jim. 'You spawny sod!'

'No word of a lie.'

'Then we can't possibly go on ops.'

The day dragged by and shortly before the main briefing the news came through – a scrub. A cheer went up, the shovels were put away, and the men went to their quarters to prepare for the dance. The night began with a prayer, then carols in the mess, food served by the officers to the lower ranks, Ralph winking at his men, then drinking and dancing and a different kind of song took hold, sung from the heart in a tone lost somewhere in a no-man's land between jocularity and lament, 'Every fucking evening at half past fucking eight, you can hear us on the runway with the throttles through the gate, get up you big black bastard, we're twenty minutes late, and we've got to bomb the Ruhr in the moonlight!'

Charlie had drunk more than he was accustomed to and Jacob watched his face turn slowly grey and then blush a glowing pink and Charlie fell slowly into silence and a frown stitched itself upon his brow.

'What's up, mate?' asked George, who had noticed it too. 'It's Christmas Eve, sup up and sing.'

'I've just been feeling it recently, that's all,' said Charlie. 'When's it all going to end, when will we be free? I don't know if I can carry on like this any longer.'

'Of course you can,' said Jacob. 'You've got no bloody choice. And it's just one more op now.'

'I could always go LMF.'

Jacob gripped his arm. 'No Charlie, you can't do that to yourself, and you can't do that to us. We won't let you.'

'I might not be able to help myself.'

'We'll bloody help you, then.'

'I was supposed to join the clergy, you know,' said Charlie. 'Before the war that was the plan. How could I ever be a priest after all this?'

'Because you're saving the world, son,' said George. 'Not even Jesus Christ could do that.'

'That's right,' said Jacob. 'After all this is over it'll be move over Jesus, Charlie Appleforth's taking his place by God's right side.'

Charlie grinned at the thought and as another carol started up, George and Jacob joined in loudly and Charlie mouthed the words.

'In the deep mid-winter, frosty wind made moan, earth stood hard as iron, water like a stone, snow had fallen, snow on snow ...'

Outside, as the carols were sung, the big black bastard Lancasters sat beneath their white caps of snow and listened. Finally, on the 29th, the Dog barked as the light began to fade and the engines howled their way into life, and the door slammed shut and George tapped Charlie on the shoulder and said, 'By God's right side, son,' and Ralph placed his trembling hands on the control column as Jacob settled into the nose and the green light flashed in the van and the little crowd of well-wishers waved them on their way and the Dog loped along the first yards of the runway, then gathered speed and lifted her pregnant bellyful of bombs into the air and they set course for Berlin, the Big City for the big send-off. The flight path betrayed the bomber stream to the radar eyes of the watching defences and the night-fighters swarmed around the bombers on the inward leg and the flak went up, a curtain of fire hung across the sky, and the Dog took them through the buffeting blows that lifted her fifty feet and dropped her down again, and Ralph gripped the controls, his hands drained of blood and his cheeks glowing white in the night, then the eerie blue tinge of a master searchlight beam brushed the Dog's flank and she shrugged it off, but it came again and pinned her in its glare and then more beams, bright white slaves to the radar-controlled blue, fastened onto her and the Perspex canopy became a solid white box of impenetrable light and Jacob felt the sensation of being suddenly motionless in the air, suspended in a bright white static void, and then Alan's urgent hollering filled his ears down the intercom, 'Corkscrew port, go!', and Ralph hauled the plane down hard, then up and across and then down the other way, the Dog twisting this way and that in a desperate attempt to fling the searchlights from her back, and the flak flew up through the searchlight beams and burst all around and the stink of cordite filled the cabin and then suddenly they were out, the white turned to black, the searchlights groping after them but the Dog slipping away, and the night was just darkness with a glowing orange heart and the dark shapes of planes.

'Where the hell's the target gone?' said Ralph.

'It's to starboard now, slightly behind us,' said Alan.

'We'll have to go around again,' said Ralph. 'Fuck.'

He banked the plane away in a broad arc, outside the curve of the approaching stream, then tucked back in towards the end of the flow of planes. Ralph could hear the Master Bomber overhead, circling the Big City as he guided the planes in on the flares.

'Bomb on green! Bomb on green!' he was calling. 'And cut out the bloody creep-back! If I see any of you shirkers releasing early ...'

Creep-back, the phenomenon of bombs released slightly too soon by terrified men unwilling to fly straight and level any longer, the bombs sent away a second or two too soon, falling before the target, then another doing the same a little way behind, each time the bombs creeping further back from the aiming point, sometimes leaving a line of fires five miles long extending into the countryside outside the city.

'I said bomb on green! On green! And ignore the bloody flak! It won't hurt you, you know!'

Ralph pressed on towards the green-eyed city centre and then Jacob sent the bombs down and the Dog leapt up as the weight was lifted from her, and the Big City became small and dim behind them as distance doused the flames and Jim and Alan in their turrets heard brief bursts of 'Merlin music', choirs of angels and classical instruments playing in harmony, an auditory illusion created by the constant roar of engines, and as the music filled their ears they watched the glow of the city finally dim then extinguish itself, like the dwindling flame of a candle that has been lit too many times. And suddenly darkness, a fire gone out, Jacob at the controls and the gunners cramming down the Benzedrine and Ralph beneath the blanket on the rest-bed crying silent tears that he would dry away for landing, and George tuning the wireless to a music station as the Dog crossed the English coast, and the crew singing *Abide with Me* in unison as the night let them go and the Dog brought them home and the wheels kissed the ground with passion and longing and Jacob thought of Rose as he brought the plane to a stop and the engines sighed themselves into silence and the only sound now was of crewmates breathing life in again over the intercom. Hairy Mary flung the door open and clean air flooded through and it flushed away six months of hell and let life back in and life wrapped itself around them and pulled them out of the bomber and into Mary's arms and she put them in her truck and hurried them away, leaving the Dog alone and surrounded by winter grass.

Back in the Nissen hut, Jacob lit a candle and spoke a Godless prayer, a litany of future hopes, as George shovelled coke into the burner and Charlie sat on the next bed and talked about his father and Roland lay down and closed his eyes in thought, and Jim and Alan sneaked over to the WAAFs' quarters where Sally Simms and Hairy Mary might let them in for cups of tea but nothing stronger. A little further down the track in the officers' quarters, Ralph Andrews looked at himself in the mirror and pulled down his bruised and bloody lip and stared into his own eyes and wondered where the confidence of youth had gone and how he had become, in half a year, a grey-eyed shell in Air Force blue with a foxhound's bloodshot eyes and hands too shaken to sign his name on the aircraft acceptance form. But he had survived, and so had his crew, and that was an achievement beyond the reach of all but a few, a small percentage of men who were either very good or very lucky or very much both. And it occurred to him at last, for the first time, that today was his birthday, a day of celebration, the symbolic start of life, and he took off his shoes and lay on the bed and turned out the light and let the day slip away into sleep.

The crew spent the next day beneath a lifting cloud, laughter now flowing from sources other than the gallows and bitter irony, and in the evening they packed their cases and made use of the phone calls they had booked, informing their loved ones of their survival. Jacob spoke to Rose in hushed and grateful tones, the echo on the line casting his gentle words back at him down the wire, mingling with her own sweet incantations, the promises and the exultations and the joyous sign-off lit by the prospect of proximity the following day.

***

Jacob and Rose met at King's Cross, another couple in a crowd of people uniting and separating, pairs and groups at different stages of the journey on which the war was taking them, and individuals who had already lost themselves to the conflict, or had lost their kin or their meaning and who stood on the platform in groups of one, just a greatcoat and a suitcase and a faraway stare fixed somewhere on the memories of what had been and could never be again. A small boy walked down the platform with a canary in a rusting wire cage, a patient bird awaiting the erosion of its prison by time and its longed-for flight away from the reach of the small boy's hand and his peering face. Above the trains it would fly, high up into the vaults of the station where it would smack its head repeatedly against the glass canopy, thirty times in all, and then follow the pigeons out from under the rafters and away into the blue of the sky, a trilling speck of yellow escaping the gaze of the world. It sat in its cage and regarded Jacob and Rose with its black ball-bearing eye as they pecked each other on the cheek and then wrapped themselves in a full-blown soaring kiss, and the crowd milled about them and the boy and the silent caged canary disappeared and Jacob looked into Rose's eyes and they smiled, broad beaming unbridled smiles, and they kissed again.

'Come on Jacob, mate,' said Jim. 'We've got a train to catch and a party to attend and it's New Year's Eve.'

Jacob turned and grinned at his crewmates, Charlie the night-owl, Jim and George standing with Sally Simms and Hairy Mary, her hair stuck out in red streams, Roland with his wife and kid now, set just aside from the group, holding the young one in his arms, and Ralph Andrews with his officer's cap pushed back upon his high forehead and his tall thin figure stooping forward to say something to Roland's son, the baby boy laughing at first, then crying and burying his head in his father's shoulder, and Roland and Ralph sharing a subsequent joke.

They reached the Andrews' house in late-afternoon, riding up the long drive in a pair of cabs hired at the station, the cars' dimmed-down lights just beginning to cast pale beams upon the road as darkness fell, the engines purring smoothly, and Jacob knew that away east in the flatlands Lancaster engines would be revving up for the night, their crews already at their stations and contemplating the night to come, and in the taxi Jacob heard the conversation surge and pause as the men's thoughts flicked back and forth between what they had left behind and what lay in front of them now. As the tyres crunched across the gravel drive, the lights in the house went on and the black-out curtains were quickly drawn. Around the house stood oak and elm, tall and bare against the winter sky, and down by the lake a line of alders leaned their heads across the water as if peering at their own reflection, and a little way out a pair of punts floated, tethered to the bank by lengths of chain. The four tall chimneys of the house reached almost as high as the tops of the trees, sending plumes of smoke into the thinning sky. Mrs Andrews threw the front door open and hurried down to the car as her son stepped out and she looked at him silently, arms outstretched, and he held her tight and heard her whisper something soft and desperate in his ear. Mr Andrews came down the steps, dressed in his weekend gear of cords and brogues and a checked shirt topped by a green velvet waistcoat and a matching tie. He went around shaking hands with all the crew and kissing the ladies on the cheek and making small welcoming noises as he did so, then clipping out an order to the Springer spaniel to stop jumping up and muddying the uniforms of the guests. Then he picked up a suitcase in each hand and ushered everyone inside and took them all to their assigned rooms, Roland and his wife and son all in together, then the men in pairs, and Rose and Sally Simms and Hairy Mary in the big room that looked out across the lawns at the back, over the reed-fringed lake and the woods and the pasture beyond.

'Better than our usual digs,' Jacob said to Charlie as they put the suitcases down and sat opposite each other on soft beds thrown with chintz. They put their clothes in a large mahogany chest whose drawers had been scented with lavender oil, the same oil that had been sprinkled upon the pillows to encourage restful sleep, and a fire burned in the grate, the dry logs sending sparks up the chimney in little popping bursts.

In the oak-panelled drawing room they gathered and Mr Andrews brought two bottles of sherry up from the cellar and everyone drank a toast, first to the survival of the crew, then to the two lost gunners and to second-tour Alan Armstrong who could not be with them now, and then to Ralph Andrews and his twenty-second birthday of the previous day, and the evening passed in an oasis of civility and calm, a silent world surrounded by countryside and water and woods, and the only sound at times was the fire in the grate and the creaking of the old house as it adjusted itself to its warmth. After dinner, Mrs Andrews invited Rose and Hairy Mary and Sally into the morning room to see the tapestries she had worked up over the previous year, hunting scenes depicting men in skirts on horseback in pursuit of wild boar, and others of red-coated huntsmen behind a pack of hounds, and a large one of a skyscape, successions of black four-engined specks far away among the clouds, the English coast behind them and the dark clouds of Europe stretching out ahead.

Midnight came and Mr Andrews brought up a bottle of 1928 Port and one of Scotch and they all toasted the end of 1943 and the onset of '44, the year perhaps that would end the war. Later on, when everyone else had gone to bed, the crew went out to the lake and drew in the punts on their lengths of chain and pushed themselves off into the darkness, drifting out into the centre of the lake where the water lay flat calm and the mist swirled about their heads. They pulled the punts together and lashed them into a single floating platform and they talked of what they would do if they ever made it back to civvy street, then turned to their impending separation as they went their individual ways to training units up and down the eastern counties, a six-dog mongrel litter dragged up together but sent away now to strange and separate homes.

'I've been thinking,' said George. 'I'm not sure I could stand six months in a training unit. I mean, I think I might miss ops in a way.'

'Are you completely mad, George?' said Jim. 'You're going to miss ops?'

'Well, I've kind of got used to the way of life. And it's what we've been trained for, isn't it, to kill the Hun, to bomb the bloody Jerries out of the war as quickly as we can, to get the whole thing over and done with?'

'Give it a week and you'll be all right,' said Jacob. 'I think I could get used to being off ops, no problem at all.'

'Really, though,' George went on. 'I've been thinking I might put in for a second tour straight away.'

'They won't let you,' said Jacob. 'Everyone needs a rest after thirty. Even Butch recognises that. And anyway, if you go straight back, you'll be finished before us and we'll have to get a sprog in to arse about with that radio of yours.'

'Yes, we have to do this together,' said Jim. 'We started it together and we'll see it through together to the end. Isn't that right, skip?'

'That's exactly right,' said Ralph, with something like a sigh. 'We get the crew back together in six months and we do another twenty, and then we're free. Does everyone agree?'

Jacob, Jim and Charlie nodded and grunted their drunken assent.

'Well, all right,' said George. 'I guess I can wait for a mob like you boys.'

'Roland?' asked Ralph.

'We'd understand, though, Roland,' said Charlie.

'Yes, it's different for Roly,' said Jacob. 'We can't expect you to leave the wife and the little 'un if you get the chance not to go.'

'Yes, sometimes they let married men take on other duties after the first tour,' said Ralph. 'It might be for the best, you know.'

'No boys,' said Roland. 'I'll be with you, I'll be going too. Don't you worry about that.'

Jim slapped him on the back and the sound echoed away across the lake and back off the far-bank trees.

'Good old Roly,' he said. 'Fair play to you, mate. Fair play.'

They sat in the punts for another hour, singing their Air Force songs and swigging from the bottles they had brought, and they returned to the house as high as kites and woke the household as they stumbled into the hall and banged about in the kitchen making sandwiches and playing ball with the dog, and Jacob found himself thinking of D-Dog over Germany, flying on New Year's Eve with another crew, no doubt, dodging the flak as the moon shimmered silver on her wings, her bombs falling away like big black fish swimming down into the depths of the sea, someone else watching them go now, not him.

Hairy Mary came down first, poking her head around the kitchen door as the spaniel chased Jacob across the red tiled floor, snapping at the tennis ball that he shielded from its jaws with his feet.

'Jacob, stop tormenting that poor dog,' she said, her hair wilder than ever now, flung about her head by sleep, tipped up behind her by the raised collar of her dressing gown.

'Have I ever told you, Mary, how much I love you?' said George. 'How beautiful you are?'

'Shut up you daft bastard,' she said. 'I know you don't love me really.'

'I do Mary, honest I do,' he said. 'For taking us out and bringing us back, night after night.'

'With your cheery smile and your questioning eyes,' added Jacob.

'Stop messing about, lads,' she laughed.

'That's right, Mary,' said Charlie. 'With your cheery smile and your questioning eyes. That's what Don always said about you.'

'And your scary hair,' added George, taking another swig from the whisky bottle. 'Your scary hair and your wary stare.'

'Scary wary hairy Mary,' said Jacob, and Charlie giggled and George put an arm around her and then another, and pulled her in gently and hugged her and kissed her on the cheek. 'See, Mary, I love you dearly.'

'Poor old Don,' she said.

'Yes,' said Jacob. 'Poor Don. One kiss from the chop girl, and that was that.'

George began to sing softly under his breath, 'Don't kiss that pretty girly, Don, you'll be a long time gone ... don't kiss that pretty girly, Don, even if she's top ... don't kiss that lovely girly, Don, kiss away the chop ...'

And Jacob and Jim drummed a lilting rhythm upon the kitchen top with their fingers, and George hummed the tune again and Jim went silent and sat in the chair by the door and put his head in his hands.

'Fucking hell,' he said, in a voice the others could barely hear, and Mary went over to him and he felt her blood-red hair fall across him as her arms closed around his narrow shoulders and he wept for the friend who had entered his turret whole that night and left it as pulp and fragments.

Rose and Sally had come down now and they all left the kitchen and went to the drawing room where the fire still glowed and Charlie took a newspaper from the rack and wafted air upon the fire and stoked the flames and Ralph took Jacob into Mr Andrews' study just across the hall to show him his father's collection of Victorian oils, pastoral scenes thick with sheep and shepherds and wild windswept hills. But when they turned to the surgeon's desk they saw a different set of pictures laid out upon the leather top, a series of black and white photographs of young men in RAF uniforms, wings still upon their breasts, their strange passive haunted eyes staring from faces shorn of eyelids and lips and brows, their noses stubs of flesh, their skin pulled taut and scarred across the place where their cheeks had been and up across the bare dome of their scalp, their mouths frozen in lipless joyless smiles. Burns victims, men of air who had become men of flame, their absent faces partially reconstructed by the skilled hands of Mr Andrews. And others too, civilians, women and children with the same strange ageless staring eyes and melted features, victims of the Blitz, burnt by phosphorous and petroleum jelly and plain old raging fire.

'These shouldn't be here,' said Ralph.

'Yes, it's not even Burns Night …'

'Very funny, Jacob.'

'It doesn't make any difference, seeing these,' said Jacob. 'It's not as if we didn't know what this was all about already.'

'He never wanted me to go,' said Ralph.

'That seems fair enough. No one can really have wanted all this shit for their son.'

Later on Ralph heard the front door close and saw two figures pass in front of the window. Jacob and Rose walked down the path towards the rose bower and they sat beneath the rough old boughs and Rose touched Jacob's face with gentle fingers, then with gentle lips, and her eyes spoke to him silent words beyond the reach of mere linguistic constructs. She saw the tears in his eyes and she squeezed his hands in hers and lifted them to her face and placed her lips upon them, once, twice, three times, then held his palms against her cheeks and pressed her face into them.

'Don't cry Jacob, my darling,' she said. 'There's no need.'

But the tears rolled down his cheeks and inaudible sobs lifted his throat up and down.

'These hands have killed thousands, Rose,' he whispered. 'Bloody thousands …'

And he attempted to withdraw his hands from her grasp, but she held them tight and kissed them again and again and then she held him to her and felt his body lift and fall as he wept, something dying in her arms.

1944

New Year's Day came in bright and clear and Jacob woke with his head still spinning from the night before. He looked across to where Charlie sat propped up on pillows, reading one of the copies of The Lancet that Mrs Andrews left dotted around the house when they overflowed from Mr Andrews' study.

'Morning, Jacob,' said Charlie. 'Interesting article, this, all about the causes of renal dysfunction.'

'Liver failure might be more appropriate after what we drank last night.'

In the kitchen they joined the others and drank copious amounts of milky tea, and then they went for a walk across fields full of sheep, the animals scattering away up the hill at their approach. Everyone went their separate ways at the railway station, promising to keep in touch and to see each other again in six months' time if not before. Jacob and Rose went to Cambridge, then out to the village where they had stayed the previous summer, along the riverside path to the guest-house with the willows outside and the flowerless climbing rose above the door. They stayed two days and went again to the mill-house where the candlesticks had been and they sat in the window-seat of a ruined room and watched the stream flowing under the arch and out across the fields and back into the river thirty yards away.

'What will this year bring for us, Jacob?' Rose suddenly asked, as they looked across the bare winter fields.

'Who knows – who can say what even the next month will bring?'

'But can we live our lives regardless? Shall we make our plans despite the war?'

'I think that might be for the best.'

'So let's make our plans. You know what I want, don't you Jacob?'

'Of course, my dear. Of course I know.'

'And you want the same?'

'More than I dare to admit.'

'So let's do it, darling.'

'When?'

'As soon as we can.'

There was an urgency in her voice.

'Spring would be nice.'

'Can you wait that long?'

'We'll both have leave in February.'

'February, then,' she said.

'Yes, Rose dear, February. I'll start arranging things as soon as I get back to Chipping Norton tomorrow.'

They parted again at the station, Rose heading back to her airfield and Jacob to Chipping Norton for the remaining week of his leave.

They married in late-February in St Mary's Church in Chipping Norton, Jacob in his new officer's uniform for which he had been commissioned the previous week, travelling down to London to be fitted out in his Burberry coat and Van Heusen shirts. He stood near the altar as Rose entered the church in a simple white dress, Daphne just behind with a posy of snowdrops, and the little girl stood next to her godmother and her only remaining uncle as they took their vows and kissed in the light of the stained glass window, beneath the gaze of the loved ones at their backs and the members of the crew who had managed to get away for the occasion. Then they paused for photos by the church door and walked up the hill into town to the Fox Hotel where they ate and drank and danced away the war.

When Jacob returned with Rose from their short honeymoon in the West Country, a telegram from Ralph was waiting for him. The Dog had been lost the previous week over Germany.

'Poor old Dog,' said Jacob. 'Poor bloody Dog.'

And he felt the tears coming, the loss of a machine welling him up now for the first time in months in a way that the loss of men could no longer do.

'Still, we wouldn't have got her back anyway, would we? She was someone else's now.'

The next day Jacob and Rose left for London, then on to Cambridgeshire where Jacob had been posted as a bombing instructor at an OTU not far from Rose's airfield. They slipped back into their old lives of separation and longing, waiting for a forty-eight-hour pass so they could meet in a room somewhere above a village pub and remember that they were man and wife again.

***

Months later in the bar at the OTU, Jacob and another instructor drank too much and got talking to a group of Australian recruits who were finishing their training before being posted on ops.

'So what's it really like, sir?' one of the recruits finally asked. 'On ops, I mean.'

'You'll find out soon enough,' said Jacob. 'And then you'll know.'

'But is it as bad as they say?' asked another.

'No, it's not all that bad. Just keep your wits about you and you'll be OK. Now do you boys play cricket?'

'Sure do, sir.'

'Well wait there, then.'

Jacob winked at the other instructor and came back with a bat and a ball.

'Right, get that fire extinguisher over there as a wicket,' he said. 'And you lot over there, where are you boys from?'

'Lancashire, sir.'

'And you?'

'Kent.'

'Right then,' said Jacob. 'England against Australia.'

'No thank you, sir,' said one of the English lads. 'We're just having a quiet pint. We'll be off in a minute.'

Jacob marched over to the men.

'What?' he bellowed. 'When your country calls, you bloody jump! Now get out there on that wicket and wait for the toss.'

The men looked at him. 'Sir, but ...'

'Move it! Now you, you marsupial chaps, forget the toss, you can bat first. England will bowl. And you there, Shorty, you can be Don.'

'But I'm a bowler, sir.'

'I don't give a fuck, I said you can be Don. Bradman, that is. Now get over there while I bowl you some bloody bodyline. And here, don't forget the willow.'

He chucked him the bat and the other instructor laughed and

lobbed the ball to Jacob and he came in off a long run and hurled the ball into the floor and it reared up and passed the man at head height and cannoned off the wall at the back, knocking a picture to the ground, shattering the glass. The batsman paused, then steadied himself and waited for the next delivery. It hurtled up and struck him full in the chest, doubling him up.

'Strewth, are you all right?' asked one of his mates.

'Of course he's all right,' said Jacob. 'Just a glancing blow, isn't that right? Isn't it?'

'Yes, that's right,' said the man, but the next ball struck him full on the head and knocked him cold.

'Come on, sport!' said another. 'That's not bloody fair.'

'Not fair?' said Jacob. 'Not bloody fair? You'll have to be tougher than that when you get in a fucking Lanc!'

The Australians gathered around their friend and one poured a pint of beer over his head and he came round and they laughed weakly as Jacob and the other instructor attempted to cajole them into continuing the game. When they refused, Jacob grabbed the bat and took a series of blows as his mate fizzed the ball at him down the length of the room and the recruits muttered to each other under their breath. They did not know that later that night Jacob would retire to his room and lie in his bed with his knees pulled up to his chest and feel the hot slick of tears as they burned their way across his face in the silence of the night. Nor did they realise that this instructor who guided them through their training was a worn-out ops man who had somehow cheated the odds and reached the golden milestone of thirty operations and the unimaginable expanse of time and continued existence that six months away from front-line service promised. After months spent crouched on the knife-edge of readiness – months when each take-off would likely be his last, when he saw each night planes beside him disintegrate into huge balls of sudden black and orange, or sprout wicks of flame from a flak-struck engine that became a long tongue of fire as the plane gradually tipped into a dive, and other planes were caught like metallic little moths in the searchlight cones up which the ack-ack poured in bright tracer streams until the moth puffed white and was gone – after months spent living this strange half-life, in which sixty per cent of his comrades were already retrospectively statistically dead, this life more intense than anything he had ever or would ever know, a parallel existence lived against hopeless odds while his peace-time self waited in vain in the triage room of the future for his own return, after all this, he bore a peculiar kind of madness, a heightened something that demanded more from the world than an ordinary life can provide, and so he behaved like an animal that has been brought up tame and then exposed to the wilderness, a knife held to his throat too long, and now he missed the knife, could not breathe without its edge, and he still feared but also craved the hurtling rush of the take-off and the bright white terror of the searchlights and the utter companionship and loyalty that only other ops men and his own clannish crew could provide. Released at last from the torment and tension of the operational squadron, he now could not wait to rush back to it, to step again into the dirty cramped innards of his whale, to set off together full tilt down the runway at dusk, to climb up and out over the cold grey North Sea and into the waiting arms of the enemy.

**

The six-month spell at the OTU came to an end and Jacob had two weeks' leave. He spent two days at home, Alfred silent in his acceptance of his son's return to operations, Elizabeth doubly proud now that he had achieved the rank of Flying Officer, and Vera delighted to spend time with her brother before he went to his new squadron. They walked into town and passed the haberdashery where Vera had bought the wool for Norman's gloves in the winter of '34.

'Did you see her?' Vera asked Jacob after they had passed. 'Looking at you like that through the window. She looked so down about it, seeing you're a pilot now, just like you told her you'd be.'

'I'm not a pilot, Vera. I'm a bomb-aimer.'

'But you are, Jacob. Near enough, you are. She looked so glum I nearly laughed, so glum to see you hadn't failed.'

'But in a way I have …'

Airmen of more junior rank saluted Jacob as they passed and when the next group approached, he tugged Vera's arm and they ducked in under the arch by the Cooperative store.

'What's wrong Jacob?' she asked. 'What's got into you?'

'I don't want them saluting me, that's all. It's just a uniform. There's nothing special about me just because I've got this bloody uniform.'

They watched the men pass, and then went to the Church Army Forces Club where they ate spam rolls and talked to the soldiers and airmen there about the 'big show' that everyone knew must be coming, and the freight trains that rumbled ceaselessly through Sarsden Halt, heading for the south coast loaded with tanks, and the transport planes that passed overhead, Dakotas with black and white D-Day stripes upon their wings.

And then back to Elm Tree Farm and suddenly it was time to go, Jacob turning to wave as always beneath the arch of the bridge that sat across the road at the bottom of the hill.

He spent the remaining week of his leave in a guest-house near the airfield where Rose was based and they caught brief moments together and one single uninterrupted day and night when they spoke again about the future, approaching the subject at oblique angles, then veering away from it as the present intruded and they sought refuge again in their intimacy, and then it was over and they went back to their life of six months before, separated by fifty miles by day and what might as well have been a lifetime of flying by night.

***

The knife was at Jacob's throat again as he sat with his old crew – Ralph, Charlie, George, Jim and Roland – in the mess on their first evening back at their new squadron. Alan Armstrong had completed his second tour in their absence so they were allocated a new rear gunner, the son of a miner from Ashington, at eighteen the youngest member of the squadron. Their first raid back was a daylight op over Normandy, easing the way for Montgomery's British Second Army in the beach-head along the northern coast of France. July and August brought more daylight raids in support of the invading Allied armies, but as summer turned to autumn the emphasis shifted back to the cities and the strategy of bombing Germany out of the war.

Jacob watched the USAAF Flying Fortresses leaving vapour trails across the daylight hours as they flew out in their defensive box formations, little fish flashing silver flanks in the distant sky, their fighter escorts high above, and then at dusk he got inside the crew's new Lancaster and set off again into the German night to finish the work the Americans had started in the day. Targets came and went,

Darmstadt, Frankfurt, Moenchengladbach, Dortmund, Kaiserslauten, Bochum, Bremen, Duisburg, Brunswick, Essen, Düsseldorf, Gelsenkirchen, Freiburg, Karlsruhe ... on and on they went and suddenly it was winter and the bombs continued to fall and the planes fell out of the sky and the carousel of empty beds on the morning after ops continued to spin, rotating men in and out of the squadron at random, luck overriding skill, and Ralph's nerves went again, and Jacob again sometimes fulfilled the role of home-leg pilot and the crew's operations mounted and at last they flew their fiftieth, the twentieth of their second tour, the end of their obligation, finally they were free, permanently so, free to leave the war behind and resume their lives away from the front-line – but something held them, would not let them go, and in the pub on the night after their second tour expired they drank too much and agreed that the job was not yet done and that they would carry on until it was, and so they left for a month's leave having agreed they would be back again thereafter and they would finish the war as they had begun it, flying together, dying together if necessary.

'Rose is going to fucking kill me,' said Jacob, as they left the pub, but he knew he had no choice, it could be no other way.

'Stay with me, Jacob,' Rose said, when he told her he would be going back. 'Let the others go if you must, but stay with me now. You don't have to go, you've done your bit, more than that, more than anyone could expect. Stay with your wife now, build a proper life with me, not this life of waiting and worry.'

'But Rose, I have to go, don't you see?'

'No, Jacob, you don't. Who do you love more, them or me?'

'Please, Rose, please don't think of it like that. They'll think I'm yellow if I drop out. The war's nearly over, I'll make it through, don't you worry about that. I'll make it back to you, I promise you I will.'

'I feel like I've lost you already, Jacob. Over and over, so many times.'

He kissed her, a passionate guilty kiss of love and longing, and then he caught the train back to bomber land again.

JANUARY 1945

It was a cold Sunday morning, frost still on the grass in the Cotswold fields outside, the breath of the cattle forming small clouds in the sunshine down by the pond where the ruined reeds hung red-brown and limp in the mist. Vera tore a piece of grease-proof paper from the roll and wrapped it round the left-over lamb from the previous night's dinner. Meat was hard to come by for most, but out here in the country there were ways and means. Norman worked hard and deserved the perks of the job, the occasional lame lamb dispatched early in its life to end its suffering and provide for the family table, or the pheasants snared in the woods and carried home in the lining of an ample coat.

Vera could hear Jacob talking with the others in the sitting room across the hall. They spoke in quiet clannish tones, so different to the night before when they had returned from the pub roaring drunk and high on life. Now they could feel the tug again of their other life, thoughts turning to the train back to London and the flatlands of Cambridgeshire, farming country before the war, bomber country now. Vera tied string around the bundle of lamb, kissed it, placed it inside Jacob's suitcase in the hall, and went into the sitting room. Jacob was standing by the fire next to Norman, laughing at something Ralph had just said. Vera smiled at him as she came into the room and she went and stood by her brother. He balanced his cigarette on the stone hearth and left it there as he brushed a stray speck of ash from his RAF blue. The men all wore the Pathfinder flash now, an elite badge worn by the best and most experienced crews whose responsibility it was to locate and mark the aiming point for the main force, dropping red and green marker flares or brilliant magnesium white to light up the target area, illuminating it for the hundreds of bombers heaving up behind.

'Vera, my dear, you make the most excellent tea in all of England,' Ralph was saying. 'Jacob has brought us to this little nest of serenity

171

several times now, and each time I look forward to the Sunday morning tea more than anything else you can possibly imagine.'

'Everything except the beer,' chipped in Jim.

'Ah, yes, of course,' said Ralph. 'The beer. And your father's violin, his many merry tunes.'

'And the sentimental ones,' said Charlie. 'I like those ones best.'

'I like those ones too,' thought Jacob, and his mind went back to late the previous evening, well past midnight, when the fire had burned itself down to embers in the grate and the rest of the crew had already gone upstairs to bed and he had stayed beside the fire, talking with his old man.

'We'll be off to the Ruhr again, father. Tomorrow night, I expect, or the evening after that.'

'I know, son.'

'Will you do something for me, father? Before you go, will you play the violin for me, when I take myself upstairs to bed?'

'Of course I will.'

'It will help me sleep, you see. And I need all the sleep I can get.'

Alfred nodded.

'Play all my favourite tunes for me, father. *Danny Boy* and *I'll Be Seeing You*, and all the rest.'

And as he went up to bed he turned and wished his father goodnight, and as he pulled the covers up to his chin he heard the catches flick back and the bow running across the strings at the base of the stairs, stirring up the notes, and the tunes he loved drifted up to him and he settled back to listen but all too soon the night had stubbed them out. And now, in the sunlight of morning, he stood and took a last drag on his cigarette. He put it out and placed it on the mantelpiece.

'But we won't be back here much more, I'm afraid,' Ralph was saying to Vera. 'The war's in its final throes, everyone can see that now.'

'Well you can still come for tea when it's all over, dear, don't you worry about that. And you'll all be able to stay as long as you want then, I'll fill you up with cake like all your birthdays have come at once.'

'We'll certainly look forward to that, won't we boys?'

'We sure will, skip,' said George and the others nodded and then there was a pause and someone said the words that had been on their lips for an hour now, in the back of their minds since the minute they had arrived, 'I think we'd best be on our way.'

They gathered in the hall and said their thanks to Vera and Norman and put on their coats and stepped out into the icy air, Jacob with his suitcase full of meat, the lion and the lamb. The gravel crunched under their feet as they walked down the path past the patch where the strawberries grew in June, then across the yard and out of the gate and along the lane that led towards the railway bridge where Jacob would always stop and turn and wave at the figures, Vera and Norman and Daphne, and they would always stand by the porch and wave back as Jacob turned away out of sight beneath the bridge, but on this morning, for some reason, or perhaps for no reason at all, as they looked on in the sunshine and the frost, Jacob did not stop and turn around, he did not wave, and life swept him away again beneath the question-mark arch of the bridge.

Vera went to the sitting room and her eyes fell on the cigarette stub that Jacob had left on the mantelpiece. She tucked it into her apron pocket, poked the fire, placed a fresh log on the glowing coals, and began sweeping up the ash that had escaped from the grate.

'Daphne, go and get me some more logs, will you?'

Her voice was unintentionally harsh.

She heard the girl's footsteps tracking down the path, towards the log-pile that was propped against the wall of an outbuilding and covered by a rough corrugated metal sheet. She saw Daphne rummaging among the logs, then taking a handful of stones from the gravel path and chucking them down onto the metal roof, and she heard their hard staccato rattle, the sound that Jacob had used to convey the impact of flak fragments against the fuselage of a Lancaster on the bombing run.

That night, before she went to bed, Vera placed Jacob's cigarette stub in a silver case, already bluish with age, and tucked it under her pillow as Norman snored beside her. She lay awake as the bed reverberated in the dark and she imagined Jacob already away over Germany in a throbbing, roaring, hurtling plane, coned in the searchlights and pitted with flak and cannon shells, and she wondered when the war might permit her to see her little brother again.

**

Vera heard from Jacob again a fortnight later, his letter arriving on a wet Monday morning, dropped through the door by a postman soaked to the skin in the rain. She took it into the sitting room and read it standing by the window looking out over the sodden grey-green fields where Norman walked head bowed behind his animals in the murk. The gutter above the window had sagged with the weight of the water and a steady stream cascaded onto the gravel outside as Vera read the letter.

Dear Vera and Norman and Daphne

Well here I am back to work again after a very enjoyable leave. I was so very pleased to see you again recently at the farm and was also very pleased to see that you are all doing fine. How is work at the shop going down, Vera? You should be quite an expert by now. And Norman, backing the winners still at the bookies? I'm sure I've told you this before, but I am so pleased that he has got along so well with his job since he took over the farm before the war, and I hope you will have many, many more happy years together – but I guess it is fruitless just hoping when you know for sure already that everything will be OK. I guess I'll tell you something now you never knew before, Vera – you remember just before you were married when I was only about 11 years old and Norman and you used to get me to bed at night. Well I used to wish that when I got to be a man I would be just like Norman, and I am still wishing the same – but I guess there's not much chance of that now. I reckon you are the luckiest, Vera – you got the best fellow in the world and that includes everybody.

I am not so content here as I was on my previous tours but I think I'll be able to stand it. I have quite a decent billet but the food is the biggest complaint. Still, there's no one getting really good food these days but we hope it won't be long now. The weather has been awful ever since I came here – it has done nothing else but rain. I must say I am getting heartily sick of it all, the whole damn thing, but I am so busy with my work that there isn't much time to dwell on all that, and really I can't complain as I am keeping quite well considering it all.

Well, I think I've talked plenty about myself and I shall close now. Hoping to hear from you again soon. Hoping this letter finds you all in good health. I will write again shortly.

Your loving brother, Jacob

***

Jacob and the others were the last crew to enter the briefing room. They had been lingering in the mess after lunch, contemplating a cold February night off ops, when the Wing Commander came in flapping.

'Right then chaps, we need another crew for tonight. Barnes has had to drop out, broke his bloody ankle falling off a bicycle playing silly buggers. If I hadn't seen the x-rays I'd have sent him away LMF.'

'We'll go, won't we boys?' said Ralph.

The others murmured their approval.

'Good show, chaps,' said the Wing Commander. 'Main briefing's at three. Bombing leaders and navigators meet at two.'

'What's the gen?' asked Jim. 'Anyone see the gravy going on?'

'Just a squirt,' said Roland.

'A short hop, then.'

'The Ruhr, no doubt.'

'Happy bloody Valley again,' said Jacob, and he lit another cigarette. 'Oh well, at least we know our way there and back by now.'

They took their seats at the briefing, the less experienced crews watching them as they sat down in the seats everyone knew to leave free for them at the back, the senior crew in the squadron, nearly sixty ops behind them, a cheating of the odds several times over, their Lancaster, B-Beauty, outstripping even the crew in her luck and resilience, sixty-two white bombs painted like tears on her cheek below the pilot's window, 'Black Beauty' daubed beside them, the night-horse that always took them out and back again, standing in the field by day, nose in the air, then headlong into the night.

The curtains were drawn across the windows, the screen tugged away from the map at the front.

'The target tonight, gentlemen, is Dortmund. The Hansa benzol facility, north-west of the city. Some of you chaps may have been there before.'

'A military target, then,' whispered Jacob to George. 'Thank goodness for that.'

'Same net effect on the war,' said George.

'Still, good not to be bombing the civvies.'

'None of them are fucking civvies, Jacob. They're all in it together, so to hell with the lot of them.'

The route out took them over the Dutch coast and then suddenly they were on the run-in to the target, the master bomber overhead, guiding them in, Jacob in the nose, fussing over the bomb-sight and the selector switches, the target looming beneath him, edging itself inside him now, eating him away, the way it always did. Then Charlie breathing out adjustments to the course, his voice down the intercom like a ghost, Ralph responding in word and action, adjusting B-Beauty's path, setting his fear aside until the bombing run was over, Roland hurling out bundles of foil strips to scramble the German radar, searchlights lamping up the sky, light flak tracing slow-motion streams of red and green, accelerating as it passed. Then a plane struck away off to starboard, a little lick of flame along the fuselage becoming a stream then a deluge, the flares inside the belly of the pathfinder igniting, dripping bright gobs of light, the plane dipping away, bleeding red and green fluorescence from its guts, spinning down like a Catherine wheel, and Jacob in the front of Beauty, concentrating now, the target coming near, then the aiming point in his sights and he is suddenly cold, and his flares are going down, Christmas trees of cascading light, and the bombs drop away and the plane lifts then settles, freed at last of its bombs. Ralph banks them away as a torrent of flares from other pathfinders goes down, then the intense white light of fighter flares bursting apart the night with their glare, and Beauty is fleeing headlong now, racing towards the darkness, Ralph's hands shaking violently upon the control wheel, flak bursting beneath, then Jacob coming up from the nose and taking the controls as Ralph goes back to the rest-bed, looking back as he goes, guilty and wrong but forgiven all the same, and Jacob is guiding Beauty now, loving her, taking her away from the target, that thing he never wants to see, slipping away beneath him now, another bad glow in the memory and he is leaving it behind.

But then a judder, a ripping sound, like gravel, gravel on a corrugated metal roof, explosive shells raking along the underside, the rear gunner shot to pieces, a leg ripped off at the knee, wind raging around his shattered guns, and Jim silent too in the other turret, slumped in his harness, all but dead, his heart spraying his life away, wasting it all over the ribs of the fuselage, blood hissing on the searing metal of the burning plane as a torrent of flame is sucked down its steel tunnel to where the other gunner sits already burnt black. And then another shrieking pass by the Ju-88, incendiary shells ripping through the mid-section, the wireless set bursting into flames, George bursting apart at the seams as the cannon shells tear through the fuselage, in and out of him, up again into the night through the shattered metal above his head, his blood soaking Charlie's desk, turning the maps and charts blood-black in the light of the flames, the angle-poise lamp throwing its bulb now towards the roof, Charlie on the floor with his oxygen tube around his neck, struggling to throw it off, and Ralph rising from the rest-bed and crawling through slime towards the cockpit where Jacob and Roland struggle to hold Beauty level as she tosses her head and throws her reins and demands to be allowed to let herself fall, tired of the whip, tired of fighting through the fire and the night just to go out again the next day, trailing her mane of fire behind her, shuddering now, shaking again as more shells rip into her guts and another fighter homes in on the blaze and pumps more death inside her, strips of Window cascading up through the cabin in the rush of air that pours in through her wounds as she fills up with smoke.

'We've had it, lads!' shouts Jacob over the intercom. 'Bale out! Bale out! And get out quick!'

Ralph is in the cockpit now, looking up at Jacob from his place on the floor, then standing and staring at him as the foil strips swirl around and glycol from the tank in the nose sprays about and Jacob shouts at him repeatedly.

'Get out!' he shouts. 'Fucking get out!'

Ralph tries to grab the control wheel, tries to haul it back, but Jacob hands him off and Roland pushes him hard towards the hatch at the front and Ralph goes down the step into the nose, kicks the hatch away, sits on the edge, looks back, drops out into the freezing night. Jacob shoves Roland away too and Roland jumps and Jacob is alone now with the dead men. He stares behind him at the blazing interior of the fuselage. He hauls at the wheel, pulls Beauty level, then stands up and steps back towards the navigator's desk and slips on something soft that glistens and seems to be moving still, and he bends down and holds his face close up next to Charlie and hears him whimper, or perhaps it is just the gurgle of the blood that bubbles up in his throat, specking Jacob's face red with spittle as Charlie coughs and tries to say something, then coughs up again and speckles him more. Beauty is pitching forward again now and Jacob lurches back to the wheel and pulls her level and holds her steady then lets her go and returns to Charlie but he

Christopher Jory

will not cough for him now, does not whimper or gurgle, and the blood does not bubble up in his throat but lies flat inside his mouth, flat black ink inside a well from which no more words can come. Jacob looks now to where George is a dark bundle by the main spar and he steps towards him, slipping in a hot slick of blood and slither that is beginning to simmer and burn, and he takes George's gloved wrist and tugs, pulls him towards him, feels him light beneath his grip, realises he is pulling only half a man, the hips separated from the waist by a cannon shell or a ripping piece of fuselage, and Jacob lets go and slips, then stands and moves again towards the main spar to get at the gunners, but he cannot get across it, Beauty's metal burns him, burns him through his flying suit, and the flames really get a grip on him now, force him back, and Beauty is tipping again, tipping away down, and he slithers across to the wheel and hauls it back and Beauty shakes, a great wracking judder as an engine disintegrates and hot shrapnel comes zinging in, and she lurches to one side and bows her head and Jacob is aflame and he takes a last look at the dark shapes that were Charlie and George and he stumbles down the step to the bomb-aimer's dome and he sits beside the hatch, burning he is, burning beside the selector switches and the bomb-sight through which he has seen his war, nights of criss-cross streets of orange, the city's lattice-work kissed by the silent crump of bombs thousands of feet below, and he pushes his flaming feet through the open hatch and the wind wrenches his burning boots away and he thinks again of Rose, his Rose, the reason he had to get through this war. Then he drops bare-footed out into the freezing night and is whipped away beneath Beauty's blazing belly, feeling the rush of the flames that envelope her now, and he tugs at the cord and feels the sharp pain in his groin as the parachute pulls free from its pack and he hangs in the air, suddenly aware that his head is on fire, and he pulls off his flying helmet and sees it tumble away alight, the stink of burnt skin and hair filling his nose, and he watches Beauty slide away now, tipping away down, and he looks for more parachutes to bloom, a mushrooming of hope, but there is only the cascade of flame, becoming smaller now with distance, fading and brightening as it passes through layers of smoke and out again, and then Beauty winks at him, a final acknowledgement as she extinguishes herself against the ground. And then nothing, just the night and the rush of the wind and the ripple of bombs a mile away and the searchlights reaching into the sky and the

178

voice of the bomber stream overhead.

The winter wind, a biting February gale, sends clouds scudding past and the smoke from the fires drags its way across the burning town where the bombs have fallen, and the suburbs around the benzol plant burn and the wind carries Jacob towards the flames, the buildings clearly visible beneath him now, individual ruined rooms in roofless homes, hurrying figures thrusting out their clod-hopper legs as they run, and bombs exploding still, crump, crump, crump in long lines, and Jacob follows them down, towards a dark space between the buildings, a dead park perhaps, the winter trees black and bare, and he passes the rooftops and suddenly he is down, in the middle of the burning town where dogs are barking among the bombs. He throws off his chute and touches his head, feels the hard bare scalp and the hot place where his face used to be, and he tries to blink but his eyelids are no longer there and the sulphur from the burning buildings stings his eyes and his tears run in streams, and he runs across the park and huddles between a low wall and a bench as the ground jumps and quivers with the continuing blasts, and he covers his eyes with his hands and bends his head down between his legs and he waits. The first wave of bombers has passed over now and he waits for the second, and when they and their bombs have passed he listens to the sound of their engines receding into the distance, the flak belt on the edge of town still pumping shells up into the air, a plane streaming flame coming down a mile or two away, and then the planes are all gone and he is alone with the enemy. The people begin to emerge from their cellars and Jacob runs along beside the low wall to the edge of the park, burning streets in every direction, people milling about, and he looks for a uniform, a soldier to whom he can surrender, his chances of survival greater in their hands than in those of the civilian population. He turns confused down a side-street, dazed by the heat and the light and the thumping in his head and an unidentifiable stabbing pain in his chest and something agonising in his groin, and he sees a woman staring at him and he bows his head and hurries on, hearing her voice behind him.

'Terrorflieger!' she is screaming, and he looks quickly back and sees others looking at him too, then a man walking quickly, gesturing to others, and the group is behind him now, shouting, a hubbub in his ears, and he feels the first blow fall on the back of his head, and he raises his arms and another blow knocks him down and he falls to his knees and he hears the people arguing, one holding another back, then a woman coming in from the side, flinging a brick upon his head, and then a man kicking him down and smashing a boot into his face and stamping on his skull, and another with a crowbar hacking at his legs, and then a uniform nearby, a policeman perhaps, gesticulating, then a sneer and the uniform walking away, and a man with a rope, the rope forced around his head and he is dragged to his feet, the rope pulled tight around his neck, and a man is trying to fling the rope over a pole, but the rope is too short and keeps falling to the ground, and the blows rain down on him again, and then the rope is torn off and a chain is put in its place and pulled tight, and he feels the grating of the chain links as they slip over the top of the pole and he feels the tug on his neck and his feet lift off the ground as the chain around his neck drags him up into the air. As he hangs there he sees the figures a few feet below, furious contorted faces shouting up at him, then some uniforms hurrying in from one side, and he thinks of Rose and he silently begs her forgiveness for having left her again, and he remembers his words, 'Rose will fucking kill me,' and then the chain begins to close off his throat and he tries in vain to scream in this place that is grey and hot and broken.

**

The loss of Jacob's crew was noticed first by the squadron's other ops men, smear-faced and smiling weakly, cigarette smoke and banter in the crew room before the earnest debriefing, the reporting of planes they had seen going down, and then the post-op breakfast in the dark as the sound of a straggler roared in, the bacon and eggs swimming in grease on the plate, the chink of cutlery against the white, then the ops room where the padre and the Wing Commander and Squadron Leader stood by the board with its list of names and take-off times and two arrival times not yet filled in, B-Beauty and one other. And then the morning came, the blanks on the board blotted now with FTR and no news of landings at other stations, just the question-mark sky and the forgotten tunnel of night slipping into the past from where secrets were never revealed. Then the closed lockers were forced open, chipping off paint along metal edges already twisted and bent, and the belongings taken away to be posted to those concerned, and the laundry-bags that had been hanging along the wall outside the mess were removed, their fresh clean contents needed now by others, then the Committee of Adjustment pulling up in their van outside the men's quarters and the faces at the windows and the other men on their beds as the places were cleared, photos and books and letters collected and put in bags and taken away, the beds stripped and empty, the men erased. Then the telegrams were written and sent and in Chipping Norton the postman walked down the path to Mill View Cottage, whistling and then suddenly stopping as he saw what he was bringing, the crests and the badges, the end of something young, and he knocked on the door and Elizabeth opened it and smiled at the postman, then saw what he held in his hands, took it in her own, and as Alfred came down the stairs he heard the thud as she fainted and her head struck the floor.

Alfred's footsteps across the gravel, the knock on the door, brought Vera to her feet and he saw her and Daphne at the window side by side, the smile and then the change of look as Vera saw the colour of his face and the hang of his mouth and she sent Daphne upstairs and pulled the door open, and Vera knew, Alfred did not need to say a word.

'It's Jacob,' she whispered. 'He's gone, hasn't he?'

Alfred passed her the telegram and she took it gently, sat on the trunk in the hall and read it through.

Deeply regret to inform you that your son F/O J. Arbuckle failed to return from operations over enemy territory stop pending receipt of written confirmation from the air ministry no information to be given to the press stop letter follows

'He might not be dead,' Vera whispered to Alfred. It was more of a plea than a statement. 'Sometimes they get out.'

'Not many get out of a burning Lanc, do they? That's what he always used to say. Not enough room in the bloody fuselage.'

'How's Mother?'

'In bed. The doctor's given her something to calm her.'

'And how are you?'

'Don't ask …'

Daphne was looking down from the bend in the stairs.

'What's wrong, Mummy?' she said. 'Is it Uncle Jacob?'

'It's OK, dear. He's just going to be away for a while.'

'For how long?'

'For a while.'

Daphne ran down the stairs and out through the door and across yard. Vera heard the sound of stones from outside, gravel being flung against the corrugated roof of the log store, Daphne picking up another fistful and flinging it hard against the metal, then again, repeatedly, harder and harder until Vera came out and took her in her arms and carried her back into the house. Then Vera called Norman in from the fields and she told him the news and he sat in the kitchen for a long time in silence and he was there again that evening and it was then that she heard him sobbing.

At Mill View Cottage, Alfred took down his violin from the shelf in the kitchen.

'I'll never play this again,' he said to the doctor as he was leaving. 'Don't really see the point any more.'

He removed the strings, placed the instrument back in its case, flicked the catch shut, went round to the out-house, and put the thing in the cage where Jacob's birds used to be. Then he locked the door of the cage and threw away the key.

In Cambridgeshire, Rose collected her mail from the post room, an envelope with Jacob's writing in curiously faded turquoise ink, as if left in the sun to pale, and she amused herself for a moment with the thought that it was the brightness in him, the sunshine he represented, that had faded it in the act of writing. She was smiling as she opened the letter as she walked down the corridor, then her hand went to her mouth and her eyes shaded over, the sun going out, her hands shaking now as Jacob had told her Ralph's used to do. She sat on a bench outside and felt the damp in her bones and her lungs gasp for breath as she read again the letter dated two months before.

Dearest Rose

I write this letter to you from the past, to comfort you in the present, to wish for you a bright future. You will hear the bare facts of this news from others, but from me you must hear what lies behind my going. I know that you could not understand why I left you again when I was at last free to stay. I had done my bit, I know, but I could not let the others go back without me. Because, you see, after everything we had been through together, I would never have forgiven myself if they had gone out alone and failed to return. I know too that this caused you to question my priorities, to question even my love for you. But believe me, my dear dear Rose, I have loved you, loved you more than words can say, and you must forgive me for going away from you now. I had no choice in the matter, you see, I did what had to be done, to see things through to the end, with hope always that we might build a lifetime together when all this was over. That is the thought I cherished above all others, to survive to the end, to make it back to you, not those temporary snatched nights of leave, but permanently, with all our lives ahead of us still. I have written and thrown away so many of these last letters to you, my dear, throughout my service, each one updating my feelings for you, for I never expected to survive so long and I would not have wished to leave you with out-of-date sentiments, small things compared to that which I feel for you now, this mighty thing that joins us together. But the letter you hold in your hands now is the very last, the thing that must join me to you now, and the one in which I must tell you that I will not be coming back to you after all. So please, Rose, forgive me for going, for leaving you again when I knew I should have stayed. And put me behind you, darling, remember me of course, but look to your future and build another life for yourself, the life that you so deserve. Stay wild, Rose, stay true to yourself above all others, for that is why I loved you before I even knew what love was. And remember that I have lived both my dreams, to fly like a bird and to love you, both equally, and I know my life has been made worthwhile by both, but above all by what you meant to me.

Fly a kite for me on the hill above the farm sometimes, won't you my darling?

Your loving husband, Jacob

That night, Rose stood by the runway to see the planes off, then spent the following hours in the control room listening out for the returning crews on the radio set, the voices of the wireless operators tired but unemotional as they called in for their landing slot, then the dark shapes drifted down in the night and when the stragglers were in and all had been counted down, Rose went back to her room and lit a candle in the Victorian holder from the mill-house and she let it burn down as she lay awake and alone in her bed in the gloom. Then she took the pack of woodbines that Jacob had given her in Cambridge.

'For when you need them,' he had said, and she had known what he meant but pretended not to.

'I won't need these,' she had said. 'Not now, not ever.'

'Take them anyway, just in case you do …'

And she took one now and slipped its end between her lips, leaned her neck towards the flame and lit the tip, sucked at the light until a glowing, burning thing joined her to the flame. Then she sucked hard and the thing glowed orange like a burnt-through lump of coal when the night is nearly done, and she breathed the smoke down, choking herself, then another gasping draw, her lungs inflating, filling up with smoke, then the smoke expelled in the direction of the candle and the candle going out and the only light now was this burning little thing that glowed for her in the dark.

***

Vera returned to work the following week, no funeral to punctuate the grieving, just the open question of the telegram. Jingle brought her a cup of tea and they talked about the weather and the behaviour of the customers, skirting around the monster in the room, the beast upon Vera's shoulder that whispered Jacob's name in her ear and punctuated her conversation with silence, vacancies into which words would not come. Then Jingle went into the back-room to sort out the stock and Vera heard the jangle of his keys, the metallic rattle, and she began to transfer the sweets from jar to jar as he had asked her to, weighing them out in the scales first, their hard little bodies clattering into the metal tray like gravel, sweet gravel again on metal, and she heard the voice again in her ear and the beast bearing down upon her shoulders, and she took a fistful of sweets and flung them down and they bounced across the floor, then another, yellow ones this time, hurling them across the room, a spray of hard little sweets, bullets clattering into a fuselage, sherbet lemons, acid drops, mint imperials, yellows and reds and greens and whites, bright flares going down, little bombs, and Vera fell to her knees as a customer pushed in through the door, the hard little things digging at the flesh of her knees as she wept, then Jingle hurrying up behind her, 'It's all right, pet, come on now,' and his arm around her, nudging the grumbling beast away.

***

Alfred stood by the dry-stone wall, running the blade of the scythe

184

across the edge of a stone, a steady rhythmic scraping as the pigs stood beneath the bare trees on the far side of the orchard. They knew the sound and what it meant, and as Alfred lifted himself over the wall the pigs ran to the far corner, Himmler and Goebbels trotting along at the back, Churchill, the dominant male, jamming into the others with his heavy flank as they ran. Elizabeth watched through the window in the side of the house and for the first time she understood her husband's actions in the pig-pen, the source of his rage and the reasons for its silent expression. The scythe swept up to Goebbels' neck and the animal squealed and struggled and then stopped and Alfred looked up and saw Elizabeth looking at him through the glass, and he knew that she felt the same sickness in the pit of her stomach, and she turned away and Alfred dragged the animal across the orchard and into the out-house where it hung from the rafter as he shovelled out its guts.

***

A month after B-Beauty went down, Pilot Officer Ralph Andrews walked in through the door of the crew room and sat at his place at the table by the window and lit a cigarette and listened to the voices of the men on the other side of the wall. Then the Medical Officer came in and sat next to him and they spoke. Ralph told him nearly all the details, of the night-fighters and the flames and his vague recollections of baling out, the gunners left dead in their turrets, the others last seen at the hatch or in the chaos of the cockpit, and he omitted the detail as to who had been flying the plane, not lying as such but permitting the assumption that he had stayed in his seat until the end, and the arrangements that his dead crew had made were a secret they would keep forever now.

'There's been no word of the others?' he asked again, to a shake of the head, and the ash fell from his cigarette as his hand trembled again.

The Medical Officer placed a hand on his arm to quiet him, then listened as Ralph recounted his descent to the ground, the days of evasion, walking by night until he heard American voices on the far side of a river, how he swam across and was saved. Back in England, they had tried to discharge him, but he insisted he go back to the squadron, to see it through to the end.

'Are you sure you don't want to call it a day?' asked the Medical

Officer as Ralph's ash dropped away again from the tip of the cigarette he had not lifted to his lips since he lit it. 'You've done your bit now, fifty-six ops is a hell of a total.'

'No, I'm going to see it through. It's what the others would have wanted.'

He took off two days later to bomb Cologne and he remained in his seat throughout, his voice steady but his hands shaking visibly, the flight engineer casting frequent glances across to his new skipper. The following week the Ruhr, first Essen and then the next night Dortmund again, then four more ops, the last in mid-April to Potsdam, just one plane lost out of five hundred as Germany faded from the war, and then two weeks' leave at the house by the lake in Surrey, long days in the punt on the water drifting, head thrown back, looking at the sky where the birds wheeled above, the first hatch of insects upon the water and the dimples of small fish kissing the underside of the lake-top with their rubbery lips, sucking down the insects that skated on the glass in the sun, and long evenings in the study with Mr Andrews, talking over the events of the last two years and flicking back through the photos of childhood and adolescence, and then a request, reluctantly met now, to see his father's photos of the burns victims again, Ralph looking into their features and wondering if this was how his crewmates had been, faces melting in the heat, was this how Jacob had looked as he spiralled away down at the controls of Ralph's plane?

Then suddenly the German surrender and VE Day, a party falling across the nation, and Ralph found himself in the village pub where his first crew had always gone on nights when scheduled ops fell victim to snow or fog or a sudden intrusion of mercy. As he looked around at the WAAFs and the ground staff and the multitude of others who had kept the airfield churning out its planes, and at his own new crew, ten ops into their first tour, just weeks in the air but aged beyond their years, he thought of the ones he had lost, of Jacob and Charlie and Roland and Jim and George, and Don and the other tail gunners, and dear old Dog and Beauty and the holes in their skin, and he felt suddenly old and alone in the absence of friends, surrounded by new strangers who knew a part of what he had experienced but not all. He had no one now with whom to share the memories and the burden of what he had seen and what he had become in the night skies over Germany, a shell of a man, a tough strong shell but hollow inside all the same, an emptiness that no years could fill, an empty vessel now until the grave, and he lifted his pint and toasted them all inwardly, and he drank the beer down in one long swallow and then he joined in the song of victory that the others were singing.

MAY 1945

On 13th May 1945, Alfred Arbuckle dressed himself carefully in his Sunday best, then adjusted the tuning knob and the volume, shifting the set towards the window to receive the words more clearly, then sat down next to Elizabeth, stiff-backed together on the settee but alone with their thoughts.

In Cambridgeshire, Rose was in the mess where the aircrew sat as the radio was turned up high above the buzz of conversation and laughter, and she lit a cigarette as Winston Churchill's resonant voice cranked into gear.

'It was five years ago on Thursday last that His Majesty the King commissioned me to form a national government of all parties to carry on our affairs. Five years is a long time in human life, especially when there is no remission for good conduct ...'

A ripple of amusement drifted across the room but Rose just sucked hard on her cigarette and watched the end glow orange, orange as a town that was dying beneath the bombs.

'... for a while our prime enemy, our mighty enemy, Germany, overran almost all Europe. France ... was beaten to the ground ... The Low Countries ... were subjugated. Norway was overrun. Mussolini's Italy stabbed us in the back when we were, as he thought, at our last gasp. But for ourselves – our lot, I mean, the British Commonwealth and Empire, we were absolutely alone ...'

A murmur of agreement ran across the room around Rose, and Churchill moved on to the debt owed to Fighter Command in the Battle of Britain five years before.

'In July, August and September 1940, forty or fifty squadrons of British fighter aircraft in the Battle of Britain broke the teeth of the German air fleet at odds of seven or eight to one. May I repeat again the words I used at that momentous hour: Never in the field of human *conflict was so much owed by so many to so few ... but conjoined with the Royal Air Force lay the Royal Navy, ever ready to tear to pieces the barges, gathered from the canals of Holland and Belgium, in which a German invading army could alone have been transported ... With the autumn storms, the immediate danger of invasion in 1940 passed ...'*

As Alfred bowed his head and tightened his grip on Elizabeth's hand, Churchill noted the resilience of the residents of Britain's bombed-out cities.

'... then began the Blitz, when Hitler said he would rub out our cities. That's what he said, rub out our cities ...'

And Rose heard the shouts go up from the men around her, indistinct voices raised in protest, then a solitary voice above the din, 'We rubbed you out instead, Adolf!' and then raucous laughter and someone shouting 'Shut the fuck up, I'm trying to listen'.

'... blitz was borne without a word of complaint or the slightest sign of flinching, while a very large number of people – honour to them all – proved that London could take it ...'

And the Merchant Navy's role was praised, and the listening men of Bomber Command nodded in appreciation, but Rose sensed some of them shift in their seats at Churchill's sudden switch from the air to the sea.

'... my friends, when our minds turn to the North-Western approaches, we will not forget the devotion of our merchant seamen, and our minesweepers out every night, and so rarely mentioned in the headlines ...'

Next it was the turn of those at home, the factory workers and the Home Guard, still no mention of Bomber Command, and Rose reached for the fresh pack of cigarettes she had bought that morning and she struggled, in her agitation, to spark up a match.

'... in our munitions works, which were becoming very powerful, men and women had worked at their machines till they dropped senseless from fatigue ...'

And Churchill moved on to the Army and its land campaigns overseas, and Rose whispered under her breath, 'What about Jacob? What about him?' and at Elm Tree Farm, Norman stood up and said to Vera, 'I've heard enough of this, he's not even going to bloody mention them,' and he walked out of the kitchen and closed down another part of his heart.

'... *we have played our part in all this process by which the evil-doers have been overthrown ... we marched many miles and never knew defeat ... last year on June 6th ... poured millions in from this Island ... the Somme and the Rhine all fell ... France was liberated ... Germany lay open ...*'

And then Churchill shifted his attention from these shores and considered the alliance with the Americans and its role in the future.

'... *and it may also be said that never have the forces of two nations fought side by side and intermingled in the lines of battle with so much unity, comradeship and brotherhood as in the great Anglo-American Armies ...*'

'To hell with all that,' Rose said to the man next to her, and he nodded.

'Sod the bloody Yanks!' roared Alfred a hundred miles away in Chipping Norton. 'What about my boy?!'

And as Churchill's speech drew towards its close, Alfred stood up with a face like thunder and the men in the bomber stations looked around the room at each other or down at their feet or out of the window with their mouths set hard and their eyes on the sky, and Churchill concluded with the end of the conflict and the future of the post-war world.

'... *I told you hard things at the beginning of these last five years; you did not shrink, and I should be unworthy of your confidence and generosity if I did not still cry: Forward, unflinching, unswerving, indomitable, till the whole task is done and the whole world is safe and clean.*'

In Chipping Norton, Elizabeth filled the kettle and fired up the flame on the hob as high as it would go, and Alfred went outside in his Sunday suit and best brown brogues and swung the scythe into Churchill this time, tears streaming down his face as his prize pig fell at his feet and its blood poured into the ground.

And Rose lit another cigarette and left the sergeants' mess where she had been sitting, saying goodbye to a flight-sergeant she had coaxed through the last month with tea and kindness and quiet companionship, and she walked out through the gate of the airfield and across a field of flowers and never went back.

***

Ralph flew a Lancaster for the last time three weeks later, on a 'Cook's tour', a flight over German territory for ground crew and WAAFs and others who had worked throughout the war at the airfields without ever seeing the enemy or the effect their work was having on his cities. Now they saw it clearly in daylight from a steady run at 5,000 feet, an ideal height for a panoramic view, and in the daylight now Ralph looked out on the endless expanse of burned-out buildings, street after street of empty shells, barely a roof anywhere, walls half-standing or gone, chimney stacks burned black, hardly a living soul in the streets, just the occasional black-clad figure pushing a cart or a pram beside a bend in a grey river, then out again over the suburbs, flattened too, houses and factories gone, and the countryside pocked with craters, then out across green fields to another town where the scene repeated itself.

Ralph was discharged in June and returned to Surrey and the house by the lake from where he made journeys across the country on his motorbike to visit the families of the crew he had lost, long hours on the road dissolving some of the clutter from a mind burdened with memories, contemplating an unexpected future, an unscheduled desert of time ahead of him now, a stark contrast to the last two years in which his life had dissolved itself away one day at a time and the short-term nature of things had augmented their intensity, the song of a thrush heard on emerging from a bomber at dawn, the soft lips of a girl, the brush of her breath upon his face, the hoppy taste of watery beer and the saltiness of the bacon at the pre-op meal, the wet nose of the squadron dog and the sound of its whimper as the crews left for the trucks, these temporary treasures stitched like stars upon the curtain of night. Now his uncertainty was different, a question mark not over whether the future would come, but what it could possibly contain and what could be done to fill these unexpected years.

In Chipping Norton, Alfred and Elizabeth heard the motorbike coming down the hill and they invited Ralph in and talked about Jacob and the night that it had happened, and the months beforehand, the operations they had been on and the nights they had spent together in the Dog and the mess and the pub, and the others in the crew, and how they had really been brothers. Then Alfred took him across the road, past his orchard, empty now of pigs, young apples forming on the trees, and he left Ralph at the gate to Rose's house. Rose had only ever seen him in his RAF uniform and in the company of Jacob, and to see Ralph now in cords and a jacket and a polka-dot tie disconcerted her, like meeting a stranger.

'Let's go and see Vera,' Rose said suddenly. 'Jacob's sister. You remember her, of course?'

'I certainly do. The best tea in England.'

'I'm sure she'll want to hear all the things Jacob wasn't able to tell her during the war.'

Ralph got on the motorbike and Rose sat sideways on the pillion seat and they roared up the hill and down the lane to Elm Tree Farm, then walked side by side up the path where strawberries were growing again, and Rose knocked on the front door and smiled at Ralph as they waited.

'How many operations did Jacob fly in the end?' asked Vera as they sat in the room overlooking the fields at the back.

'Nearly sixty,' said Ralph.

'That's plenty, isn't it? Far more than he had to, I mean.'

'Yes, more than was it was fair to expect.'

'He knew he wasn't going to make it,' she sighed. 'You could tell that in the end – the way he talked, it was obvious.'

'None of us thought we would survive, not if we ever really thought about it.'

'But you survived,' said Daphne airily, sitting at the end of the sofa nearest the door.

'Yes, indeed I did.'

'Oh, I'm sorry, Mr Andrews,' said Vera. 'Please excuse her.'

'That's perfectly all right,' said Ralph. 'Well, I think I'd better be on my way. It's a long way back to Surrey.'

'Will you give me a lift?' said Rose. 'Just up the lane?'

'Of course, it would be my pleasure.'

'You've left the Services, haven't you?' she asked when they had gone outside.

He nodded.

'Me too,' she said. 'It was the hypocrisy.'

'Churchill's victory speech?'

'It makes me so damned mad. People are starting to talk you down already and the war in Europe's barely over.'

'I don't really care,' he said. 'My job was to beat Hitler down.

That's been done.'

'But, you do care. I can see that you do. How could you not?'

'Bad memories, that's all.'

'Do you want to see the airfield at Moreton-in-Marsh?' she asked, with sudden forced brightness. 'It's not far, and it's a nice day for a ride.'

Ralph gunned the engine and they sped up the lane and out along the Worcester Road, the warm air rushing past as the motorbike sped along, and Rose clasped her arms tight around Ralph's chest so as not to fall off as they flew over the bumps together and for a moment she had the sensation, just for an instant, that the man to whom she was clinging was Jacob. But then the moment passed and Jacob was gone and Rose almost let go as she saw again that it was Ralph to whom she was clinging now.

Ralph went for a job interview at an insurance firm the following week but they turned him down. As he was leaving, the receptionist, a lady in her fifties in horn-rimmed glasses, called him over quietly.

'You were in Bomber Command, weren't you?' she said.

'Yes, I was.'

'So was my son. A word of advice,' she said, 'and I do wish you well. Take Bomber Command off your CV. Not everyone agrees with what was done over Germany, there are a lot of agendas, people don't understand.'

'Thank you,' Ralph said. 'I appreciate your concern.'

'It is well intended, I can assure you,' she smiled.

'I'm sure it is,' he said quietly. 'But I was in Bomber Command, and it's bloody well staying on my CV whether people like it or not.'

1950

'My heart is my engine,' she had told Jacob. 'And love is my fuel ...'

And the tank was filling again now, his tank, not hers, though he hoped to fill hers again too. It was hope that was filling him now as he buzzed along, zinging along the lanes he had known when he was young, where they had walked in the early days, when something was emerging and they knew that it was. He rammed the bike up through the gears, thought of Norman too, Norman as he had held the bike for him, grinning him in, grinning him in to try it.

'Take it, Jacob,' he had said. 'It's yours.'

He had been speechless, Jacob, when he saw the thing, the gleaming black and silver, the exhaust and the black leather seat, and the speedometer, all the way up past the ton and into that realm where he would feel he was flying.

'But it's brand new, Norman?' he had said. 'You can't give me this. It must have cost a bomb ...'

'Take it, son, you deserve it, you bloody do.'

And Jacob had taken it straight out, in spite of the cold, a freezing February fog bleeding up in the hollows, dusk settling in as the headlight went on, then Jacob in the saddle, and the noise of him fading off around the hill and along the Churchill Road.

And now, four months on, he was buzzing again, buzzing with a thing he had not known for years, since he could last remember who he was and what life's purpose could be. And now he had found it again, Norman had forced it on him, made him see.

'I'll take you to see someone tomorrow,' Norman had said. 'Someone to pick you up, to put you together again.'

It was her, it must be her, the one he had lived for, longed for, recovered for, and the one he knew he should not see, to be fair to her, leave her be. But Norman had insisted, Norman knew what was best, he usually did.

'Get yourself down here at nine and we'll be there by noon.'

Three hours? Could she really have gone that far?

'So who then, Norman? Is it her? So far away, three hours by car?'

'You'll see when we get there,' Norman smiled.

Jacob knew it must be her, but Norman would not say, must have felt the name would cause Jacob to shrink away again, like he had since he got home twelve months before, shying away from her, leaving her be. So no confirmation, just anticipation, just bittersweet hope for Jacob, led towards her now, to something he knew he should not do, to be fair to her, better let her go. But now he could not stop himself, the thought of her sucked him in. Twelve months since he had got back, five long years without her, he had lost himself in the interim, found himself again, a version of him, of what he had been, the only version he could be now, the version he did not want her to see. But the pull was there, and so he relented and he loved it again, the thought of her, daring it, daring life to let itself back in, a little miracle to turn him around.

He revved the bike down the hill to Elm Tree Farm and across the yard, Vera at the window, Norman on the doorstep already, dressed for the day in a tweed jacket and tie, and his best brown brogues shone to a shine you could see yourself in.

'Let's go, then, Jacob?'

'Let's go, Norman.'

They stopped for coffee off the A34, then down through the roads Norman had memorised on the map, the names and numbers, ticking them off as he went, and Jacob sensed the tension in Norman as something neared, the silences lengthening, his eyes fixed on the road. And then the turning, off the main road, through a Surrey village, familiar somehow but from another season, something he had seen before in the dark, in a New Year's dusk in the war, and then they were pulling up the gravel drive, the brick-built house at the end, four tall chimney stacks sticking themselves into the sky, almost as high as the tops of the trees, and the shimmer of the lake, and then Norman pulling the car down through second and first and coming to a halt, not by the door but away to the side, thirty yards away.

'But why here, Norman?' said Jacob, desperate. 'Why bring me here, to Ralph's house? I thought it would be her, isn't it her?'

'Go on, lad,' Norman said as he patted him on the knee and the door of the car shifted open. 'I'll wait for you here. Take all the time that you need.'

'Thank you, Norman,' said Jacob, uncertain, and he stepped out of the car and he felt Norman watching him, watching him walk across the gravel now, towards the house, painful, limping, something broken that has been carelessly repaired by hands whose heart was not in it, bodged together, so no one could fix him now, not even her, whatever Norman might say, and certainly not Ralph, so why bring him here? To confront him? To forgive? Jacob was wiping away his hope now, the hope that had sprung from reunion, but with it the guilt was going too, the guilt he had felt at the thought of her, of reopening the wounds she would have healed, the ones she must have buried since he had gone, covered them over with scabs, cracked and weeping things to pick at slowly down the years until they really began to heal, only for him to go and lose his discipline and go and see her, to pick them off again and set the wounds weeping. But the problem now was Ralph, sprung upon him suddenly it seemed. Perhaps it would be better this way, the way Norman had planned it, no time to brood before the reunion, no time to plan what to say to the man who had left him there, left him burning in the plane, his plane, the skipper's ship, burning by the hatch over Dortmund, Jacob burning himself away to nothing at someone else's post before he left the dead ones to it and jumped. Then four years of absence, an absence within himself, nothing there, then his own re-emergence, something peeking out again, but now suddenly Ralph, the prospect of him, thirty yards away, behind that heavy door. And what to say? What could he say? I forgive you, skip, for what you did? I forgive you for leaving me this way, burnt away now while you got off Scot free, sailed away down, left me there? Oh yes, I loved the flying, loved the Lanc in my hands, and I pushed you away, I wanted to save you. But you didn't have to go, did you Ralph, you didn't have to leave me, not when it really came to it, not at the end? Twenty yards now, limping in, limping towards the door. So let me see, how to do this, nice and direct perhaps ... Ralph, it's me. Do you remember? Your old mucker. Thank you bomb-aimer, top job, let's go home, what you always said. Yes, Ralph, let's go home, I'll take you there, like I always did. You sure made it didn't you, Ralph, you sure made it home? And a lovely house it is, the lake at the back, the punts where we sang away our hearts that New Year's Eve, counting ourselves down to nothing together, the punts lashed up, holding us all as one, you and me and Charlie, George, Jim, Roland, all of them, all gone now, all burnt to fuck as Beauty went down. Ten yards, Ralph, slowly does it, let me think now … five yards … and what should I say, when I see you, what words will come? Will you recognise me, when you look me in the eye, will you see those nights in me, the ones we spent together, or will the nights we've spent apart since then blind me from you? Your heavy door's in front of me now. Oak, your father said, oak like us then, young and strong, indestructible, warping now, more than a hint of rot around the edges. Will your father be here too, the surgeon with those photos that he left on the desk that night, the burns victims he treated, carefully rebuilding them in a way that the German didn't bother rebuilding me? Perhaps that's Norman's plan, perhaps it's your father he has brought me to see, a magician, a reconstructionist, someone to put me back together again now, properly this time where the German would not. So I'm at your door now Ralph, alive still, oceans of time before me, but all alone now, alone in all this time, time that life will not snatch away from me as it threatened to do any day back then when I had it all, everything I needed, companionship and love, and too little time to live it in, too little time replaced by too much now, nothing to fill it with, no one left to fill the void. Now the heavy iron knocker, the one shaped like a fox's head with the worn-down nose where people have gripped it, rammed it down against your door, my hand on it now, lifting and falling, calling you, Ralph, calling you now.

Jacob waited on the step, then lifted the knocker again and let it fall, more gently now, uncertain. Then a noise inside, someone coming down the stairs, and a familiar sound in the hall, that cough, the one he recognised from all those nights he had spent with the person who coughed that way in the war. The cough stilled him, and he glanced back at Norman in the car, looking, peering out through the rain-specked windscreen at the figure on the doorstep, the boy he loved, waiting, watching for the horrified reaction, another potential sin for Norman to judge her by.

Then the door was open and she was there.

She looked at Jacob, right in the eyes. And she knew before he spoke, he didn't have to say a word.

'It's you, isn't it?' she said.

'Yes.'

'Jacob?'

'Yes, Rose. What on earth are you doing here?'

She paused, began to speak, stopped.

'May I come in?' he said.

She stepped back and let him into the hall. He remembered the room off to the left with the leather chairs, the study to the right and the Victorian oils and the desk where the photos had been that New Year's Eve, left by Ralph's father in an attempt to dissuade.

'Please,' said Rose. 'Come through into the kitchen. I think I have to sit down.'

They sat at the table and stared at each other.

'My poor dear,' she finally said. 'What has happened to you?'

'Landed myself in a spot of bother, that's all …'

He tried to smile but no longer had the face with which to do it, just a wrinkling of the thing that served as a nose, the suggestion of a twinkle in an eye, the old Jacob in there somewhere, the canary trapped inside its cage. She saw him looking at the thing on the window sill, the Victorian candle-holder from the mill-house near Cambridge.

'Our light,' he said, picking it up, putting it back again. 'No candle in it now?'

'I don't really use it any more. Haven't done for years.'

Then his eyes were on the photo in the silver frame, just as she was reaching for it. Too late, so she left it there and paused.

'Not that?' he said.

She looked at him.

'Not that? You and Ralph?'

'Jacob, I'm so sorry. If I had known …'

'But Rose …'

'Why didn't you come sooner? If only I'd known …'

'I couldn't have come. And it's better this way, really it is.'

'You say that like you really mean it.'

'I do.'

'But if I'd known, I would never have … things could have been so different. They would have been, for sure.'

'It would have been no life for you. Not now, not with me this way.'

'Let me make you something? Tea? Are you hungry? There's some cake …'

'Maybe a cup of tea, thank you.'

She put the kettle on and stood to hide it as the flames licked its base. Then the kettle's shrill whistle, a scream. They took their mugs out into the garden and sat beneath the bower where Rose had held him that night in the war.

'Do you remember when we last sat here?' she said. 'That New Year's Eve? I think of you every time I sit here.'

His face moved, that twinkle in the eye again, rattling his cage.

'Yes, Rose. How could I forget that? There's a whole lot I don't remember, but I remember that night. I remember the good bits mainly, you know, less of the bad. I don't remember much about the night we came down.'

'Ralph's told me some of it.'

'Yes, I expect he has. I woke up in hospital a month later, feeling like bloody death. They'd smashed me all about when I landed, the townsfolk. Can't blame them, I suppose. The military saved me, so the doctors said, got me in the nick of time, carted me off somewhere, then into hospital. Couldn't remember my name, some bugger had stolen my dog-tags when they tried to lynch me. Tommy Bomber, the surgeon called me, wrote it on a sign above my bed. Kept telling me about his family in Hamburg, how they'd lived there until that time in '43 when we smashed up the bloody place. He lived through it, none of the others did. Decided he'd make me pay, could have rebuilt my face better than this but didn't. Said I'd dropped anonymous bombs from twenty thousand feet, now I could live without a face.'

'Bastard.'

'Well he was actually quite a cultured man. An amateur poet too, he said, spoke excellent English. Just hated my guts. He gave me a letter before he went – bit flowery if you ask me. I'll show it to you sometime, I've got it at home. I read it nearly every day. I've been back a year now, you know.'

'A year? But the war's been over for five.'

'Couldn't remember my name, could I? When the real Tommies came in April '45, found me in the hospital, they couldn't work out who I was and I couldn't tell them. They knew I was RAF, bits of my uniform hadn't burned, but Tommy Bomber's not much of a name to find yourself by, is it? Well they sent me back to Blighty anyway. In a Lanc, of all things, with a load of other boys, POWs they'd picked up on the road. I was in hospitals around London for years, then a convalescence home. Then bits began to come back, broken memories, names, then my own. They came down to get me, Norman and Vera. Wanted to check me out before mother and father saw me. Father's heart's not what it was.'

Rose reached out a hand and touched his face with her fingertips and he closed his eyes and sensed her on his skin, skin that could barely feel, then her breath on him, up close, and he opened his eyes and she was there, and she kissed him, on one cheek, lingering there, uncertain, then the other, his forehead, the thing like a nose, then she took his hands and lifted them to her and kissed them too. Over and over again.

'You look wonderful, Rose,' said Jacob. 'Better than ever, you really do.'

'Jacob, I love you still. You know that, don't you?'

'Thank you, Rose. I mean, after so long, that's very kind of you.'

They sat together as the drizzle cleared and a watery sun lit up the clouds.

'I can leave Ralph,' she finally said. 'He'd understand. I'm sure he would.'

'No, Rose.'

'Yes, Jacob. Why not? We didn't know. If we'd known, it would never have been.'

'No, Rose. You can't. It's better this way.'

'Then why did you come?'

'I had to see you. I held out as long as I could. A whole year. But I couldn't wait any longer. I'm sorry if I've caused you inconvenience. I should never have come.'

'No, Jacob. Don't think that. Please don't think that.'

When he left she watched him walk across the gravel towards the car where Norman stood, leaning now against the passenger door, waiting for the boy. He put his arm on Jacob's shoulder and Rose saw him saying something, then looking towards her as he held the door open and he helped Jacob in as the rain started up again. She closed the door and leant against the wall and heard the tyres on the wet gravel as the car pulled away down the drive. She placed her hands upon her belly, held them against the bump, the growth, the growing little piece of Ralph inside of her. Her back slid down the wall and she slumped on the floor and pulled her knees up into her chest and she felt her body lift and fall as she wept but there was no one there to hold her.

**

Rose hacked furiously at the mulberry bush with her clippers. She had found another empty bottle hidden away beneath its branches and the bush was paying for it now. Ralph would be home soon, and then she would give him what for. Or perhaps she would ignore it as she usually did, for what good was intervention when things were so wrong? No, she would leave things undecided until he walked through the door, would let her mood decide, her heart would tell her what to do, the usual way. She stopped her hacking and picked at the place where the thorns had got her the previous day, picked off the scab. Then she looked at her watch. He would have landed by now, tucking his usual purchases – a bottle of whisky, a bottle of gin, and two hundred cigarettes – into his suitcase and catching a taxi from the usual place, the driver pointing the bonnet towards the Surrey countryside.

Ralph had been with the airline for two years now and Rose knew he was valued for his calm authority in difficult flying conditions and regularly reproached for his love of a drink or two. His bosses had warned him the previous year that the latter must be curtailed. She had found their letter, hidden away in his desk, and he sought help at a clinic with some success, but the reprieve could only be temporary and when he was off duty for a few days she knew he would be back at the cabinet and half-empty bottles would find their way into the unlikeliest of places, under the bushes by the patio, hung overboard from one of the old punts on the lake by a long length of fishing line so that it drifted concealed in the water – chilled and ready to serve – or behind a copy of the complete works of Shakespeare on the top shelf in his father's old study.

Rose heard Ralph's taxi approaching now along the avenue of trees and then the twist of his key in the heavy oak door. From where she stood out of sight in the kitchen she could smell the lilies he had sent her the previous day, the usual peace-offering ahead of his return, their perfumed pink fronds bowed over the side-table on which they sat in their vase in the light airy hall. Two or three flies buzzed about in the sunlight that was streaming in through the door at the end. Off to one side was the oak-panelled study lined with books. On the other lay the sitting room, with a leather armchair each side of the fire where they sat on winter evenings when he wasn't flying. His frequent trips did not bother her now, she had been used to far worse in the war, and she had recently read that commercial aviation was even safer than travelling by car. It was the motorbikes that most unnerved her now, even if when she was younger she had liked to ride at speed, sitting behind him with her arms round his chest and the wind in her hair as they flew along country roads together. In the year after the war, he had made frequent trips to see her, his behaviour somehow dutiful, harbouring an obligation the reason for which she could not quite perceive, and she had sensed in him something lost and alone, something that reminded her of Jacob – perhaps it was the way he spoke about what they had done in the war, the language the men shared, the kites and the prangs and the wizard shows, and that look in their eyes sometimes, that faraway look. This comfortable familiarity hung its sticky web around her and though she pushed the spider away it was inevitable, the first fleeting kiss, then the longing – for Jacob or something that somehow resembled him – and the guilty relief when she heard the engine returning again the following week, revving up the engine of her heart, stoking it with fuel, low-grade fuel but fuel all the same, and she ignored the disapproving looks of Alfred and Elizabeth from across the street and Vera's pointed questions, and Norman's absolute refusal to see her, to let her set foot near Elm Tree Farm. And when she came down to talk to Vera one day, Norman answered the door and spat out the words, 'So soon? How can you forget Jacob so soon?' and he slammed the door shut in her face.

'I haven't forgotten him,' she said when Vera came to see her later. 'That's just the point, I can't forget him, I have to fill the void and Ralph is the closest I'll ever get to being with Jacob again.'

Now Rose heard Ralph pushing the door open, then the sound of him placing his case on the floor in the hall where he always left it, his footsteps past the lilies, and then he was in the room and Rose was there, in a worn-out summer dress and a hat and a bunch of fresh-cut flowers in her hands, held in front of her like a wedding posy or a wreath.

She was still young until you got up close and saw the lines that life had left upon her face, the Ganges-delta of creases around each eye, a little map of sadnesses etched out by the erosive power of tears.

'Hello darling,' she said lightly. 'How was your trip?'

'Average,' he said. 'A bit of light turbulence over the Alps, nothing more than that. Oh, and the route took us over the Ruhr, all lit up like a Christmas tree. And bloody Perkins was asking about the war again, how could we have done it, all those women and children down below.'

'Ignore him, dear. He's just an air steward. He should stick to serving Martinis.'

'That's exactly what I told him. Anyway, darling, we should be getting ready, we've got this do tonight. I told the taxi to come back at six. We need to be there for seven.'

Ralph made himself a long drink and Rose heard him opening the door onto the patio overlooking the lake as she went upstairs. She sat on the bed and took the small picture frame from the shelf and looked at the photo, the slightly blurred black and white image of Jacob in his uniform sometime in 1944, the year they had married. She touched the glass with a fingertip and held it there for a second as she always did and wondered now what might have been, if only she had known. Then she put the photo back on the shelf and slipped out of her dress.

Ralph heard the rush of the shower and he went back into the kitchen and made himself another drink, slightly stronger this time, and he sat down again in the late afternoon sun. He wondered what the evening would bring, good memories and bad he supposed, perhaps a few faces he knew, morphed by years that had sprung upon them suddenly. He had been in touch off and on with one or two members of his last crew and he had always said he intended to make it along to another of these squadron reunions one day. He heard the shower go off and he drained his glass and went upstairs to prepare for the night ahead.

The reunion dinner started slowly, a room of squadron men with their wives, distanced from the events of five years before by more than time. The world had changed and they lived cut off now from those with whom they had shared the fuselages of bellowing planes. But as the drinks were served and the food followed up behind, they found themselves sucked back into the experiences they had shared, if not with the particular men they were talking to now, then with others just like them, and the memories flooded back and the controversies were aired, the moral arguments about the bombing and the way the country and its leaders had rejected these men, turned against what they had done in their name, and a sense of injustice filled the room alongside the companionship.

Then someone stood to make a speech and a ripple of laughter floated across the room at a wry observation that he made and Rose saw Ralph looking at her, but she was lost in her thoughts, only half listening, and she already knew all the arguments anyway. They made no difference to her now, they could not bring Jacob back whole, could not put him back together again the way that he had been. And when she pictured the men of Bomber Command it was not Ralph she saw, but Jacob, her Jacob – Jacob as she most liked to remember him, in that damned uniform of his, leaving her at the gate of the airfield as he went to join the others in his billet, turning away from her in a sense forever that time while Rose went to pack her things in their regular upstairs room at the pub, a wife packing herself away to become a WAAF again; and Jacob as he was on their wedding day in 1944, his face lit up by the prospect of extended leave punctuating the period between his first and second tours; and that day on the farm with the kite in the wind, laughing together as they tugged it this way and that in a piece of sky that was blue above their heads; and skimming stones when he was a boy and she was almost a woman, down at Pool Meadow where lost coots called to each other across the lake in the dusk; and that first time, not long after he was born, a dim and distant memory, a little bundle of wrinkled flesh in a cot in the top room behind the Victorian glass of the window at the gable end above the pigs and the orchard. And what a thing that little bundle of flesh had become, what meaning he had given her, then and now, a strange haunting constance that had been with her always, even when he had been away in Canada and who-knows-where over Germany – especially when he was who-knows-where over Germany – and after he had gone he was still there too, he was with her this evening, really with her, even more than the flesh and blood that was sitting physically beside her now, this flesh-and-blood Ralph who she had once admired and been fond of but who could never be that other thing that Jacob had been, perhaps still could be again, that magical other thing that could not be explained or understood and had no need to be. She noticed Ralph turn and smile at her again and she smiled back as she always did and he turned away and nodded as the man making the speech listed the erosive effects of the bombing on German resolve and her capacity for the continuance of war. Rose looked around the room at the men, several tables of them, most now slipping towards lives of comfort, a milestone most of them could never have expected to see, a milestone Jacob had been denied and Ralph had for some reason been destined to achieve, and she wondered again, why him, why had it been him who escaped from the plane, not Jacob, even though Jacob had been in the nose, the bomb-aimer, nearest the escape hatch, and Ralph had been at the wheel. The persistent thought came to her again, that Jacob had been cheated out of it, cheated out of it somehow by Ralph, and she herself had been cheated too, cheated out of a life with Jacob by the man who sat beside her now. But she pushed the thought back into the black box in which she kept it, that dark little place that she did not want to see, that place where the truth had been recorded – she preferred the truth now in dormant form. And she reminded herself that it was of course for all of them that she had at first lobbied and written and chivvied, to her MP and the Prime Minister, and anyone who might listen, that it was on behalf of them all that she so hoped there would one day be recognition, the recognition they had been denied, recognition and forgiveness, though forgiveness was not the right word, and not just for Jacob. Yes, not just for Jacob, for all of them, even if above all for him, for all of them, even for Ralph. Even? Where had that word come from? He wasn't so bad, she thought, she shouldn't be so harsh – she had admired him, was fond of him once. That must mean something. She repeated it to herself again – she was fond of him, admired him, used to anyway. But then the dark little box of truth creaked its lid open again and something uncomfortable began to slip out and so she slammed the lid shut and lit another cigarette and sucked the smoke down and poured herself another full glass of wine and took a long swig and then took Ralph's hand in hers.

She zoned in again now to a speech that was winding down towards its conclusion, recounting the importance of the bombers in clearing the way for the land forces after the invasion of France, and Rose found herself looking around the room again, commenting to herself inwardly now on the wives who accompanied their men this evening, the lucky ones, those who had clung on to their men beyond the limits of the war or had met them in the post-war years, and she saw their broad smiles and their happy sparkling eyes and enthusiastic applause and her own clapping slowed and then stopped, like the slow winding down of the propeller of an engine that has run out of petrol and died.

'My heart is my engine,' she had told Jacob. 'And love is my fuel ...' But when had the fuel run out? When had it gone? That first time, when his plane was lost and the days went by, one more dawn, one more dusk, no news, just three letters, FTR, failed to return? Or was it the telegram, the uncertain one, the presumption of loss, lost over enemy territory, no word to be given to the press? Or the later telegram, the confirmation, premature though it now proved. Or that knock on the door at the house by the lake in Surrey the other day, Jacob there again on her doorstep. What was left of him.

Ralph was quiet in the taxi on the way home from the dinner and Rose took his hand in hers again.

'Who was that chap you were talking to at the end of the dinner?' she asked.

'Bill something-or-other. Bomb-aimer.'

He slurred his speech slightly. He had drunk more than he should again, she thought. So had she.

'A bomb-aimer? Like Jacob ...' Rose said.

She regretted the comment as soon as she said it, but Ralph ignored it or pretended to.

'Yes,' he said. 'We were working out which raids we'd both been on. Quite a few towards the end of the war, it seems – he started his tour in January '45 and was tour-expired by early April. That was a pretty intensive period of punishment we were dishing out then.'

They sat in silence as the taxi accelerated along the outer lane. She guessed Ralph was thinking about Jacob too now, but he shifted the subject when he spoke. She squeezed his hand, a reflex. It was warm, hers was cold. It had always been that way, this difference between them. The taxi sped along in the orange glow of the streetlights.

'Do you think we did wrong back then?' he asked suddenly. 'It does bother me sometimes.'

'No, I'm sure you didn't do wrong,' she said. What was he suggesting? How could Jacob have done anything wrong?

'It was a pretty awful thing, though.'

'Plenty of awful things happened back then. You had a job to do and you did it, that's all.'

'I suppose so,' he said.

The taxi pulled up the drive and along the avenue of chestnut trees and Rose walked up the steps as Ralph paid the driver. They went into the kitchen and Rose put the kettle on the hob.

'I think I need another drink,' said Ralph. 'Would you like one?'

'Maybe a small brandy,' she said, knowing she shouldn't.

He poured the brandy from the decanter on the chiffonier and passed it to Rose and then took a tall glass for himself and shovelled in some ice and filled in the gaps with whisky. They went out onto the patio and sat in a pair of chairs beneath the wisteria. Ralph stretched out his legs and drained his glass, then got up to make himself another and she watched through the gap in the curtains as he filled the tumbler and tipped the liquid down his throat, then filled up the glass again. He came and sat next to her again and lit a cigarette. She noticed the glowing ash quiver in his trembling hand. He saw her looking.

'Chilly isn't it?' he said, grinning in that way that always annoyed her now.

She had become accustomed to the tell-tale signs that the war brought on when it intruded again on his thoughts. It was normally only the alcohol that invited it in. After a heavy night she would find specks around the house where he had sat with a cigarette, unseeing eyes retracing long-lost events, his hands twitching the ash unseen to the floor, the empty bottle tossed into a hedge afterwards to be found the next day by the gardener.

Rose recognised the signs now.

'So did you enjoy the evening?' he asked at last.

'It was the same as last time, wasn't it? The same arguments, the same controversies. You get tired of hearing the same thing after a while. But it's so unfair, how people speak so badly of you all these days, like you were criminals or something, like you should feel guilty for what you did.'

'It's hard to face the truth sometimes, isn't it?' he mused, after a moment's pause.

'What on earth do you mean?'

'Nothing really.'

'Look Ralph, let's not talk about the war now,' she said. 'Let's talk about what we're doing tomorrow.'

'No, no, let's talk about the war some more,' he said. 'Tonight of all nights I think perhaps we should.'

'Come on Ralph, darling, let's just …'

'No, let's not just … when you said in the taxi, you said we had a job to do and we did it …'

'Yes, that's right.'

'I'm not sure that's correct, strictly speaking. In my case, I mean.'

'What on earth are you on about? You flew far more ops than most.'

'Yes, but the others …'

'It wasn't your job to die, Ralph.'

'But Rose, there's something I've never told you.'

'Well maybe it's best you don't tell me now, then. You're far too drunk and so am I.'

'No, really Rose …'

'Ralph, you're drunk, leave it to the morning.'

'No, Rose, no, I can't leave it till the morning. The morning might never come.'

'Don't be ridiculous, dear, it's nearly morning now.'

But he did not laugh in response as she had hoped he might.

'Listen to me Rose,' he said, leaning across towards her so that his face was close to hers and she could smell the deadening breath of spirits as he spoke. 'That night over Dortmund, what really happened Rose, I wasn't flying the plane, you know that don't you? I wasn't the pilot then.'

'What do you mean you weren't flying the plane? Who was?'

'Jacob was.'

'Why on earth was that?'

'I wasn't well, hadn't been for a long time. My nerves were shot, you see. It was the flak and the fighters, Rose, they got to me in the end. I flew the plane out but I didn't always fly it back, not after the first twenty ops or so. Once we'd bombed, the thought of the fighters on the way home, sometimes I just couldn't cope. So Jacob helped me out.'

'Jacob flew the plane?'

'He never told you? He said he wouldn't. A family secret, he called it. What's in the family stays in the family, he said.'

'No, he never told me. Not then, not since.'

'Not since? What do you mean, not since?'

'Oh my God …'

She looked at him, horrified at what she had said.

'What, Rose? What?'

'He's come back, Ralph. He's come back at last, he's come back from the war.'

'What the hell do you mean?'

'He survived, Ralph. Oh, he isn't the same at all, but he's back all right. They sent him home in '49, what was left of him. He's burned Ralph, burned away, inside and out. But he's still Jacob. He's still my Jacob.'

'Good lord,' said Ralph. His voice came clear and flat and low, barely a whisper now, and he bowed his head and waited for her to put an arm around him and stroke his hair like she used to do and tell him it did not matter now, too many years had passed and life moves on, but she sat still and quiet and when he looked up he saw tears in her eyes and her tears overflowed and rolled down her face and she stood up and went into the kitchen and took a napkin from a drawer and dabbed at her eyes. When she looked up, Ralph was in the doorway.

'Tell me all this doesn't matter now, Rose. Tell me, please.'

'Ralph, I'm sorry ...'

'Please, Rose.'

'Ralph, I'm so sorry, I can't.'

'He always meant far more to you, didn't he?'

She shook her head.

'Didn't he?'

'I was meant to be with him, that's all,' she sobbed. 'And I was cheated out of it.'

He approached her and attempted to place an arm around her shoulder. She looked up at him, her Ganges-delta eyes now flooded with tears and clogged with the black silt of mascara. She eased his arm away and spoke in a raised whisper, as if her mouth were ashamed of the words that it uttered.

'How the hell did you have the gall not to tell me about this before, about Jacob flying the Lanc? Isn't it the skipper who stays with the bloody plane?'

'Rose, that's not fair.'

'Do you think I could have married you if I'd known?'

He stared at her blankly.

'Well, do you?' she cried, and she hurried away up the stairs and

Ralph heard the bedroom door as it closed.

He went out onto the patio and walked across the lawn to the place by the alders where the punts lay tied up and he slipped the chains out of the mooring and stepped aboard and pushed himself out into the middle of the lake. He felt for the length of fishing line and pulled it up to see what was on the end. Gin, half a bottle, the label had come off in the water but he knew the shape. He unscrewed the cap and held up the bottle and tipped a long stream in the approximate direction of his mouth and felt it splash upon his face and into his eyes. He cursed the wasted liquid and held the empty bottle over the side of the punt and pushed it under the surface, letting the air bubble up out of it until the cold water had filled the empty vessel and he let it go and the bottle fell away to the silted-up bed at the bottom of the lake. He lay back on the punt's cold hard boards and watched the clouds scud across the moon and saw the vapour trails of departed planes high above, dispersing now in parallel lines, floating apart up there, never again to meet, a strip of silent sky always between them now.

***

The first time Jacob and Rose met after that was for tea. Rose drove up to Chipping Norton when Ralph was away overnight with BOAC, somewhere down in Italy. Then out into the Cotswolds with Jacob on the bike that Norman had given him, Jacob revving the engine hard as they tore along the lanes, Rose clutching her arms around him, burying her face in his back, breathing him in, a happiness in her lungs, clearing out the smoke. They stopped at Chipping Campden, left the bike by the medieval market and found a tea room. Tentative and whispering they sat, Jacob and his girl, aware of the gaze of the others, their eyes burning in on him, Jacob dipping his head as he stirred his tea and Rose glaring back at them when she knew he could not see, wanting to say something, to put them right, but not wanting to cause a scene, fearing embarrassment, for him more than for her. And Jacob not caring, just glad to be there, with her, with Rose, the reason he had got through his war, his Rose again now for an hour or a day, husband and wife again, pretending to be, as if they had never been stolen away. And then out again to the bike with a bellyful of scones and Rose with her face buried again in the folds of his jacket as the wind ripped at her hair and the wasps flailed by and flecked her, and her arms again around his chest, a thing that she thought could never be again, and he could not see her now, could not see her tears.

After that she came whenever she could, and she was thrilled at Ralph's promotion to long-haul flights.

'That's wonderful, darling! I'm so proud of you.'

Wonderful to be gone for three days, into the car and up into Oxfordshire and down to Elm Tree Farm where Jacob stayed when she was there, and in the top room they lay together in the still of the night and when she woke she found him in the chair by the window, looking out over the fields where Norman walked among his cows, Norman thinking as he walked, thinking of Jacob and Rose and how a wrong can sometimes be a right.

***

'These are for you, son,' said Norman one day after Rose had gone. Jacob took the cage. The birds sat together. One looked at him, rolled an eye, cooed.

'Just like Eric and Penelope,' Jacob said.

'That's what I thought.'

'Where did you get them?'

'Where I get everything. From the wood.'

'Thought so. Thank you, Norman, they're marvellous.'

Jacob took the birds up to Mill View Cottage and put them in the out-house's empty cage and closed the door. Upstairs in his room he took out the box of eggs he had taken when he was a boy, when Norman showed him where to go to find the best ones, clambering up the trees together, Norman gripping a branch beneath him, waiting to catch him should he fall, and Jacob peering into the nest, taking one egg, leaving the others, and Jacob's smile when he saw the thing, the specks and freckles, like the specks and freckles that the summer sun lifted up on Rose's face, and he would take it and pass it to Norman, and they would walk home together discussing the best way of putting a hole in each side and blowing out the thing that was in it.

Jacob divided his days now between Mill View Cottage and Elm Tree Farm. He kept his gun at the farm, the gun that Norman had given him.

'I've bagged many a brace with this,' Norman said. 'Had it for years. It'll do you well.'

And Jacob used it in the woods at dusk, navigating the paths that Norman had shown him in his youth, the roosting points and the low boughs with the fat silhouettes dark against the trees, the searchlight beam of Jacob's torch and him peering down the sight in the dark, the flash of the gun and a flying thing falling now, tipping away down, a burning bird, and the rummage in the nettles, their sting on his skin not bothering him now, nothing there to feel it, and Norman down the hill in the farm washing off the smell of muck and hearing the gun and little nervous ripples slipping across the water of the bath, Norman's physical response to his wondering if he had done right to give him the gun, might Jacob have used it on himself this time, blowing away the face he had been left with? But no, he concluded, as long as there was Rose there was hope, and he must find a way to persuade the boy that he and Rose must be together again. Then the sound of knocking on the door as Norman was dressing, and Vera in the hall, letting him in, Jacob's voice full of the wood and what it gave him now, life again, breathing it in, and the birds on the table and Vera cutting out their guts and their feathers plucked out, loading up the kitchen table with their beauty, Jacob and Norman swigging as they plucked and Vera bustling around above. Then the birds going in the oven and Jacob thinking, dwelling on it, watching the roasting birds, roasting golden brown until their skin cracked and spat with fat the way skin does in a burning plane. The way it does in a burning building too, he knew that too. The doctor had told him so, what it was like beneath the bombs, in the firestorm, Hamburg 1943.

***

It went on this way for months, stretching into a year, then two. Always the same toxic mix of happiness and grief, a love hauled back from the edge of death, kept alive on life support, suffering, better perhaps to let it die.

'I'd still come back to you, Jacob,' she said. 'Even now.'

'With the little one and everything?'

'Yes, everything.'

'But you can't.'

'I would, for you I would.'

'It's impossible, Rose. It's a dream, let it go.'

And then that last time, in 1952, at the house in Surrey, Ralph away again, Jacob turning up on his bike, the kid left with a baby-sitter for the afternoon, Rose and Jacob out on the lake in the punt, heads thrown back and staring at the sky. Like they did when they made love, when they were young.

'Jacob,' she said at last, as the swallows dipped and turned above the lake. 'Jacob, you're going to have to take me back. Take me back or you won't be able to see me again ...'

'Don't do that to me, Rose. Please don't do that. Let us carry on like this. It does no harm, Ralph needn't know. And it's not as if I'm a threat to him.'

'But you are, Jacob. You are. Because you have my heart. You always have.'

'Rose, I'm so sorry for the bother I've caused you ...'

'Oh, life's such a bind sometimes, isn't it?' she said. 'What it does to you.'

He nodded, hesitant now, broken.

'So then, Jacob. Take me. Take me back or lose me.'

'I'll think about it,' he said at last.

But he knew it was impossible. He would not condemn her to that, to life with him, forever with him. But nor could he stand the thought of life without her, after all he had been through, so he left without resolution. He took the bike up through the gears, tearing at the road, at the wind, into the wrong lane and over the breast of a hill, howling out her name as the lorry hurtled in and he ducked back out of its path at the last moment and his howl was drowned out by the roar of the engines and the lorry's horn and the hammering about that hurtled through his head, that mad pumping, the pumping of a heart run wild, and back in Surrey Rose felt her heart winding down again, fuel running low, truth filling up her engine now with emptiness, the emptiness of certainty, the certainty of what his answer would be to her foolish ultimatum. And so she decided that she would have to bend, she would have to give in, to accept him on his terms if she could not have him on hers.

But how could he have known that, as he spent the following days out in the woods, overloading Norman's table with pheasant and rabbit and hare? He waited, waited for her next letter, but it was delayed, the Royal Mail going down the tubes. So out on the bike again, tired of the gun, tired of the game, out along the Churchill Road and into the fog, then past Kingham and into the wolds, along the wrong lane around the bends and over the hills. And then the other vehicle, not a lorry this time, just a small slow-moving car. But Jacob was really travelling now, he was really going home, and the speed did the job.

Norman took the call.

'It's the police,' he said to Vera. 'They said I'd better go.'

'Oh, my God. Who is it? Father?'

'No, let me see to this, Vera. I'll be back shortly.'

Then Norman's slow trawl out into the countryside, going steady, up through the gears as he always did, less happy with machines than with beasts. Then finally the little gathering on the road in front of him, pulling the car over, the policeman's hand upon his back, gentle, almost a caress.

'Yes, it's him,' said Norman. 'Let me take him.'

'You can't, sir. There's a protocol.'

'Let me have him, I said. I don't want to leave him here in the road.'

'I'm sorry, sir. He has to stay with us. I'm sorry.'

Norman put Jacob's personal effects on the kitchen table when he got home and went up to Mill View Cottage to break the news to Alfred and Elizabeth. Elizabeth's head hit the floor again when she heard, the second time Jacob had done that to her with his going.

'He let his birds out today,' said Alfred. 'The ones you gave him, Norman. The pigeons. I thought that was an odd thing for him to do.'

They went round to take a look. The cage door was open.

'They're not in the tree either,' said Alfred, looking up.

'They won't be,' said Norman. 'They've gone for good, haven't they? They were wild ones, those. Were never meant to be in a cage anyway, I suppose.'

Vera phoned Rose with the news and that evening she drove up to Chipping Norton, leaving Ralph and the little one on a pretence. She sat with Norman and Vera, perched on kitchen chairs, silent for a while.

'This was in his pocket,' Norman said at last, passing Rose the letter. She unfolded it, saw the gothic handwriting, read it through as

Norman watched her.

Dear Tommy Bomber

Let me explain to you how it was, what you did in July 1943, how you took my life away. Four times you came to drop your gifts. Or was it five? I lost count in the end, lost count of the days, of the bodies. Of the limbs, the ones I saw and the ones I removed. The people I buried, the bits of them. The first night was bad enough, but when you came back again, I forget now, the second time or the third, which was it now, the firestorm? You can probably tell me, Tommy, you had the best view, up there, looking down, twenty thousand feet or so. A panoramic view, I would suggest, no? Beautiful perhaps, all that orange light, silent down beneath you. You could feel the heat in your belly through the skin of the plane? I heard that was so from captured airmen, the ones I was meant to save. Imagine that, Tommy, heat rising twenty thousand feet into you? How must it have felt to be in there, to be in the cellars just ten feet underground? Did you think of us then, down below, in the fire? It was hot Tommy, the weather I intend to mean, hot and humid already before you came, perfect weather for a tinderbox. And when you came back again the hot humid weather was still hanging over the city and a strong wind was blowing, fanning the flames that remained from your previous raids. Seven hundred bombers over our little city, though it seemed like more, swarms of you, in little more than an hour, swamping the defences with how many tonnes of bombs? Two thousand? Three maybe? The fire service was already dispersed and stood no chance against the volume, the intensity of the bombing, the time-delay fuses. And the cookies, those big ones? How quaint of you, that name. And the incendiaries, always the incendiaries spreading fire. Innumerable fires took hold, the roofless buildings acted like chimneys, you see. The wind created updraughts, strong updraughts that sent the flames so high into the air I thought they must burn you too and bring you down to join us. The flames leapt across buildings, onto those that were undamaged by bombs and set those ablaze too, and as the conflagration grew, fire sucked oxygen in on itself, drawing air in from the suburbs in a great howling gale and the firestorm took hold and within half an hour four square miles were a boiling mass of flame and within an hour my poor city had been consumed. In the cellars and the air-raid shelters my people cowered beneath the blasts that shook the walls of their underground hell and the firestorm above sucked the oxygen from the cellars and raised the temperature to roasting point, and thousands sat and asphyxiated or baked below ground. Those that could, hurried up cellar stairs and out into the street, but they were met there by the roar of a hellish organ, the booming resonant howl of the firestorm, beating out rhythms like the clashing of metallic drums as it whipped up hurricane winds and tornados of flame tore down the streets and across the squares and parks, ripping up trees and flinging burning human bodies high in the air and across the tops of the houses where the roofs had been. Eyes were liquefied by the heat, Tommy, jelly-like tears running down cheeks in streams, the windows in the cars and the trams began to melt and run and the fuel in bus engines exploded and bags of sugar and jars of jam and honey in grocery stores boiled and then burst – I saw all this myself – and the asphalt on the streets began to soften and then bubble beneath the feet of the fleeing people and their feet sank into the melting street and became stuck and the people collapsed into the surface of the road as their bodies lit up orange and red and blue. I saw that too. And those that made it to the water of the ponds in the park and the port docks and threw themselves in to douse the burning found that the phosphorous that burned their skin could not be extinguished by water. Tricky of you, Tommy, it continued to burn as they tried to wipe it away, smearing it across themselves, and it ate at their flesh as your flames ate their way across my city. The firestorm held this intensity for three hours and in the morning the streets were strewn with charred corpses, thousands of them, still licked by pale blue tongues of flame, those of adults shrunk to the size of infants and those of infants shrunk to very little at all. And of course many bodies simply disappeared, burnt completely away. And my wife and my son and my parents were among them, the disappeared, the house gone, all possessions gone too, no clothes, no photos, no keepsakes. Nothing at all to remember them by. Not even the street could be found, it was just rubble, everywhere rubble. I could not even find the place where we had lived, where they had died. This was your work, Tommy Bomber. Congratulations, you did it well.

And so, Tommy Bomber, what has your life been worth, what was it for? What good has come of it? No good for you now, surely, and no good for me. So remember me, Tommy, remember me please. When you look in the mirror, at that face of yours, remember me. Remember what you did – to me, to my people, to yourself – and consider for a moment the memory the world will have of you.

'He told me about that bloody letter,' said Rose. 'Used to read it every day, he said, poor lad. I never want to see the thing again.'

'Me neither,' said Norman.

He stood up and put the thing in the stove, and the fire burned it away to nothing.

MEMORIAL, 2012

Rose had always hated the smoke of cigarettes indoors, unless of course it was filtered into the room through Jacob's lungs, the lungs that nudged against his heart as he inflated them, making the smoke acceptable, something to be wished for then and longed for now, an impossibility. From any other source it was an irritation, an efficient means of stinking up the soft furnishings, and it still reminded her horribly of Ralph and the scattered ash he had always left in the wake of those dark hidden thoughts, thoughts about those days, the ones they almost had in common, a partial overlapping of experience, days and years from another lifetime lived by other people, lost young and hopeful versions of themselves. And even now the distaste was strong enough to force Rose into the garden before the thing could be lit.

It took her an age of careful descent to negotiate the two flights of stairs, a packet of Silk Cut in one hand, the other gripping the banister that the social services had installed the previous summer. She left the door on the latch and stood in the porch and struck a match. The cigarette sparked up as she stoked its fire with her inhalation. A glowing orange shape ascended a couple of miles away across the Cotswolds, slipping up into the night sky, then another, borne swiftly away on the New Year wind in the blue-white light of a bomber's moon. Rose fetched her binoculars from the front room and peered through the sights at the glowing orange lights, further away to the west now, passing high over Elm Tree Farm, their burning image shuddering upon the lens as her hands shook with age and weakness and cold. She saw the surging flames and the suggestion of dark shapes against the black-blue of the sky – hot-air balloons, bearing their occupants into the night, champagne no doubt chilling their lips as they looked down on the dim lights of the villages in these first minutes of a new year.

Rose extinguished her cigarette in the pot by the door, a midden of stubs that had failed to hasten her end. She crept back up the stairs, sat at the desk in her study, tugged back the curtain, peered across the street towards the cottage where she had first set eyes on Jacob. A light had come on in the window beneath the apex of the roof at the gable end. She peered through the binoculars and into the room behind the glass – Jacob's room, it would always be his, his childhood room, the one in which she had first seen him when she had not long since started school, the room where Jacob and Vera and William had slept before the war. They were all gone now but their ghosts hung about the place, unwilling to leave her be.

Near her desk, next to the books she had written in the decades before her eyesight began to fail, Rose kept a well-thumbed volume listing the few known facts about the nature of the incident that had initiated her demise, her long slow implosion, a steady erosion of sunlight and air, the things that had made her before fire ate her away and she filled up with smoke. 'My heart is my engine,' she had told Jacob when they were young. But her heart had combusted and burnt itself as black as a burnt-out seam of coal, starved of the oxygen his existence had given her. And the slim volume told the story, as much as was known, about what had set the fire burning, what turned her heart to coal. It was a simple black book, 224 pages of small black font, a black cover unadorned by unnecessary art or illustration, just a matter-of-fact title and a large Royal Air Force badge. *Bomber Command Losses of the Second World War, 1945*, one of a series of six volumes, 12,000 lost aircraft and 55,573 lost lives – 55,574 if she counted her own. She kept the books on a set of oak shelves, the ones Jacob had in his room when he was a boy obsessed with planes and the desire to be a pilot one day. She took the volume of losses for 1945 and turned to one of several pages concerning the night he had come down – a long list of Lancaster squadrons and serial numbers, their targets, take-off times, and whatever details were available regarding the nature of their destruction. She looked at the names of one doomed crew in particular, seven young men, small black crosses denoting the ones who had died.

***

The Bomber Command Memorial had finally received planning permission in the spring of 2010 and the necessary funds had since been raised for its completion at a site on the edge of Green Park.

The memorial had been a long time in coming and was opposed each step of the way. In 1992, the fiftieth anniversary of the first thousand-bomber raid on Cologne, a statue of Bomber Harris was unveiled by the Queen Mother outside the RAF church on the Strand. Rose and Vera stood among the crowd and they watched as the silk fell off the great bronze statue and Harris stood there with his chest stuck out as a Lancaster flew overhead, its engines drowning out the howls of the Peace Pledge Union and the others who had come to boo and jeer, the Queen Mother visibly startled at the catcalls and the shouts of 'Murderer' and 'Butcher'. The crowd eventually dispersed and when the sun rose the next day the statue had been daubed with blood-red paint. Rose and Vera had travelled back up to Chipping Norton that day on the train and Vera went to the care home where Norman spent his days now in a chair by the window, quiet as a lamb, a leg and an arm crippled by a series of strokes, and she spoke to him softly, telling him about her day in London, and he nodded occasionally and then looked at her in confusion, but with something like recognition in his eyes, and said what he had often said to her in recent months.

'I used to fly in planes, you know. I used to fly in planes with Jacob.'

'Yes, dear,' Vera said, shaking her head at the nurses in case they had overheard. 'Yes, dear, I know you did.'

'And the dog used to navigate. The dog used to bring the sheep home. Beautiful dog she was, Beauty they called her, Beauty, you know.'

'I know, dear,' Vera said again, and she patted the big strong hands that he clasped together in his lap, and she thought again of the sparrow-brown gloves she had knitted him all those years before, and her eyes remained dry but she was crying inside.

A year later both were gone, Norman buried next to Vera in the churchyard down the road, returned to the soil from which he had come, on which he had built his life since the day John Bainbridge first strapped him to an Edwardian plough in a brown-clod northern field.

***

And so, in 2012, Rose made the journey to London alone this time, taking a cab all the way from her door-step to the capital, the kind of extravagance for which she now had the money but insufficient time left in which to spend it. The cab left her at the door of the place by the river where she had stayed with Jacob on an occasion when their leave had coincided and they had spent a night among the city lights, not the streetlights and the headlamps of hurtling cars that she looked out on now, but the searchlights that had waved above the Docklands as the Heinkels roared overhead and the bombs fell away in the distance and Jacob held her in his arms, held her tight to him and whispered words of love in her ear that drowned out the noise of the bombs not with their volume but with the immensity of their meaning, words that could wipe away all the bad in the world, wrapping her in a cocoon of love that no bombs could penetrate, nor years of absence erode.

She woke early the next morning and had the receptionist call her a taxi. She murmured vague replies to the driver as he went on and on about Nicolas Sarkozy and the European Union, something he had seen in the paper that morning, and she knew that he took her murmurings as a sign of senility rather than a total lack of interest in what he was saying.

Rose paid him and struggled out onto the pavement beside the Bomber Command Memorial. The great blocks of Portland stone stood pale in the watery morning light, marked with chiselled scars, words of stone in eulogy to the squadrons of men who had given their lives. In the centre of the memorial, among the Doric columns, stood a bronze statue of the seven men of a Lancaster crew, the air around them lit by the searchlight beam of a spotlight embedded in stone at their feet. A respectful crowd gathered around the monument and then high overhead flew the last Lancaster bomber in England, releasing a torrent of poppies into the blue summer sky, and the plane's engines would have wiped out the noise of any protesters who stood out of sight, booing and hissing and calling out 'Murderers' and 'Butchers' and 'Remember Dresden', and the group of Bomber Command veterans who were seated at the front did indeed remember Dresden – and Hamburg and Essen, Berlin and Dortmund, and all the bloody others – and as they walked away at the end of the day they passed by the place where a column of smoke had earlier been, past a small group of men who had set a Union flag burning while chanting their condemnation of the wars in Iraq and Afghanistan.

That night Rose dreamed that she returned to the memorial at dawn, approaching it through a mist so thick that she did not see until the last few yards the vulgarity of the words that had been sprayed upon it overnight and the blood-red paint that was splattered across the bronze of the seven-man crew. She gently reached out and felt the paint still wet beneath her fingertips, and she took a handkerchief from her pocket and stretched as if to wipe the paint from the young men's eyes, but they were out of reach, high above her now, so she wiped the red mess from their boots instead. When she looked up there was an old man standing at her shoulder, dressed in a dark blue blazer and a beret, a medal upon his chest. Rose saw in his red-rimmed rheumy eyes the moist suggestion of memories or tears as he gazed at the crew, and then the man shook his head, turned his back on the crew, walked into the mist and was gone.

The dream dissuaded Rose from returning to the memorial the following day as she had planned, lest the fears she had dreamed be proved true. Instead she took a taxi home to Chipping Norton and in her study she took out the school exercise book that Elizabeth Arbuckle had given her as a keepsake after Jacob had been reported missing, the book in which Jacob had written as a schoolboy his stories of the future and how he would be a pilot one day. She flicked through the pages and read the fading words, admired the flowing neatness of the writing and the almost turquoise ink and the careful consideration of the phrasing for one so young. She stopped at an entry dated 1937, when Jacob was fourteen, still only a child but already just a few short years before he died. The question the teacher had set was written at the top of the page, 'What are your ambitions for the future?' and Jacob's answer was written neatly underneath. Rose mouthed the words silently as she read, remaking his words as they departed her mouth:

'My ambition is to live a good life. By this I mean an exciting life and a worthwhile one. For some people, this would mean being a doctor or a teacher or a priest – but I can't imagine myself as a priest, even though I want to live a good life and be a good person and do good things. Because I can't really be a priest if I don't believe in God, even though I know that I have to spell His name with a capital letter out of respect or similar feelings. My father does not believe in God – he says that he is my father and I do not need another one to look after me in the sky – and I believe what my father tells me, because I am a good son, and so I don't believe in God. But I do think it would be useful to have somebody in the sky who will look after me in the future, because my ambition is to be a pilot and to have adventures in airplanes and to fly around the world. Nobody believes me when I tell them this, but I shall probably manage it if I set my mind to it and try my best. And when I have seen the world, I will return to Chipping Norton and I will meet my 'one true love' (I have read about people like this in books, but I don't think I've met one yet) and we will live in a house with a fishpond and a vegetable patch and we will have some children – I don't know exactly how many yet, but I suspect quite a few – and we'll all be quite happy together.'

Rose closed the exercise book and lit herself a cigarette. She was too tired now to bother about going downstairs and into the garden and instead she opened the window, drawing in the smoke as she did so. Then she opened the drawer of her desk and took out the last piece of him she had left, the fuel that had fed his lungs with the strength to carry on through all those years in the war. The silver cigarette case had dulled with age, engraved with his name and etched by life's thousand tiny scars. She opened it and gently removed the cigarette, brown and dry, a dead little chrysalis in the palm of her hand, and she saw again the face of the broken man – the fire-starter – who had lit the thing and desperately sucked it down to a stub more than half a century before, and she wondered once more about the butterfly that might have emerged.

Then she snapped the lid shut on the stub-end of her memories and she took the other thing from the drawer, the page on which Jacob had written to her late on in the war, a man then, hanging on to the edge of the cliff of death. She unfolded the fading page, the edges dissolving with the years, the cracks along the folds letting light back in from beyond, from the time when Jacob had written down his feelings and given them to her in a poem. She read it again silently now.

The Circle of Love

The rooks are wheeling now, my love
Where night-owls used to be
The tree-tops spindly, black and bare
Against the growing rays of day

And far above, the circle of love
Packs itself away, and waits
To show its face again
Beyond the sun-burnt day

And though the sun burns off the night
The moon's still there, unseen
Until the circle turns again
And darkness sets her free

And when the night comes in again
And the sun is washed away
The moon lights up our life again
Lights up the vaulted sky

The circle turns, I turn to you
The rooks have gone away
The owl comes out on silent wings
And joins us in the sky

And then the moon, for me and you
Redraws its circle, waxes new
She's always there, even if unseen
The circle of love, for eternity

Rose lifted her gaze and looked across the street again to Jacob's window. The room behind the glass was dark now. Someone had turned out the light.

***

Later that year Rose was gone too, found by the postman beneath a cold December sky as the snow sheeted down, layering her in white as she sat on the bench in front of the house as if asleep, not waking now from a dream she had been having for more than sixty years. With no family left to speak of, her things were taken away and sold at a local auction house. The frames that held her photos of Jacob in his RAF uniform were bought as part of a jumbled job-lot in a cardboard box.

Their new owner took out the photos and dropped them in the bin, and he sold the frames for a fiver apiece at a car-boot sale on a grey Sunday morning in the rain.